**Praise for *The Man in the Photograph*:
by Linda Style, winner of the 2002
Daphne du Maurier award.**

"A tale of striking intensity...a compelling romance."
"From California to Chicago, and through the jungles of Costa Rica, author Linda Style leads the reader through a tale of striking intensity in *The Man in the Photograph*. Style has a gift for creating intriguing settings and characterizations that allow the reader to escape to a world of danger, intrigue and passion."
—*Midwest Book Review*

"Ms. Style has written a riveting tale...."
"You will be hard-pressed to put this story down. While billed as a romance, it also has a powerful element that keeps you captivated as the characters search for the truth about *The Man in the Photograph*."
—*Writers Unlimited*

"An exhilarating romantic suspense."
"Linda Style provides an exhilarating romantic suspense novel that keeps readers wondering until the end. The story line is action packed...."
—*TheBestReviews*

"An exciting, heart-stopping reading experience..."
"Ms. Style writes highly original stories that include characters with great depth. This book is no exception."
—*Old Book Barn Gazette*

Dear Reader,

I love to write stories set in my home state of Arizona because, even though I know it so well, I'm still awed by the beauty and diversity of the landscape—from the rugged snow-capped mountains to the amazing windswept sand dunes in the desert near Yuma. In this book Los Rios, Arizona, is a fictional town, but the setting is real.

A traumatic experience caused Madeline Inglewood to withdraw from life, but now she's determined to change all that, and Tripplehorne Ranch is the place she's chosen to do it. For J. D. Rivera, the ranch is just another way station. Fate has taken away everything he ever held dear. His parents, his best friend, his fiancée, his career and his future. Just getting through each day is a supreme challenge.

Can two wounded people help each other? That's exactly what happens in this story. One woman's determination to change her life ends up changing the lives of many others. It's a story about dreams and courage. I hope you enjoy it.

Wishing you the best,

Linda Style

P.S. I always enjoy hearing from my readers. You can reach me at LindaStyle@LindaStyle.com, through my Web site at www.LindaStyle.com, or write me at P.O. Box 2293, Mesa, AZ 85214.

What Madeline Wants

Linda Style

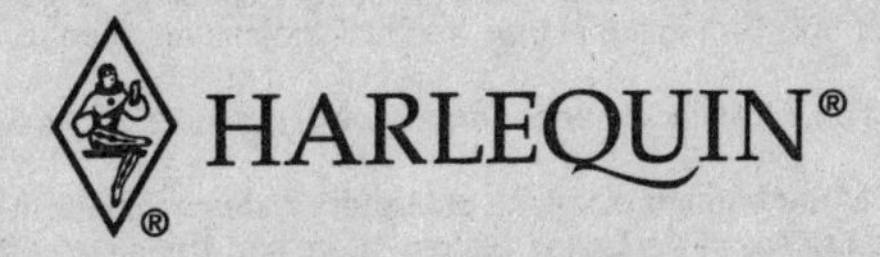

TORONTO • NEW YORK • LONDON
AMSTERDAM • PARIS • SYDNEY • HAMBURG
STOCKHOLM • ATHENS • TOKYO • MILAN • MADRID
PRAGUE • WARSAW • BUDAPEST • AUCKLAND

ISBN 0-373-71155-7

WHAT MADELINE WANTS

This edition published by arrangement with Harlequin Books S.A.

Visit us at www.eHarlequin.com

Printed in U.S.A.

To my wonderful family, my friends and colleagues
for making a difficult year much easier.

To Connie Flynn, Judy Bowden, Sharyn Liberatore,
Susan Vaughan, Ann Voss Peterson, Virginia Vail,
Sheila Seabrook, Claire Cavenaugh, Ilene Style
and Geri Style. Thank you for your love,
support and encouragement—and for listening.

To Linda Barrett and Colleen Endres
for sharing your experience and wisdom.

And especially for Jay, who's always there for me.

Acknowledgments:

Many thanks to those who contributed to the research
for this book. Elizabeth Jennings for her information on
Simultaneous Interpreting; the U.S. Immigration and
Naturalization Service; the United States Border Patrol;
Arizona State University; Distance Education for Mexican
American Farmworkers; the Chief Economist's Office;
United States Department of Agriculture; Agriculture Labor
Affairs; The National Institute of Mental Health for
information regarding cynophobia, post-traumatic stress
and anxiety/panic disorders.

Since this is a work of fiction,
I have taken some liberties. Any errors are mine.

PROLOGUE

"HEY, REB. You're up next."

J. D. Rivera, aka Rebel, watched the F-14 fall away in front of him. "Nice vapes," he said on the flyby. High speed and low altitude created dramatic vapor trails—a visual display he'd never tire of watching.

His turn. He banked left taking the Tomcat into a dive between two other F-14s, his execution flawless. The cloudless blue sky was perfect for the air show. And after one more pass, they'd be on their way home.

In plenty of time for the wedding rehearsal.

"Time to spare," he told Eric, his radar intercept operator and about-to-be best man.

Eric, aka Zeus, hadn't wanted to do the show, but J.D. had insisted. Hell, he had to do something to take his mind off the fact that in twenty-four hours he'd be walking down the aisle. Something he thought he'd never do.

"What's he doing! Watch your twelve o'clock! Zeus shouted.

The F-16 came out of nowhere, swooped up in front of them, pulling their Tomcat into its jet wash. In the turbulence, the blast distorted the airflow to his right engine and *Boom!*—in less than a second, the engine flamed out. The tail swung around in a yaw. He shoved the stick to correct, but he couldn't bring the nose up. Now they were spinning and dropping altitude fast.

"Punch out!" J.D. shouted.

"We're too low!"

"Eject! Now!" J.D. grabbed the loud handle. The canopy exploded and shot upward, and he blasted out of the cockpit on a tornado of wind, debris spraying like buckshot. Something crashed against his leg, and at the same time he heard a sickening crunch.

Through his screaming pain, J.D. felt the pilot seat fall away. His chute ballooned open, snapping him upward. He squinted, searching for Eric's chute, but saw only the black contrails of the F-14 as it crashed into the ground in a ball of flames.

J.D. bolted awake drenched in sweat.

Dr. Chastain, his physician at the V.A. Hospital, walked into the room. "How're you doing? Ready to go home?"

Home. Where the hell was that? For seventeen years, the navy had been his home. His life.

"I can't walk. How the hell am I supposed to go anywhere?"

"You've made excellent progress in the three months you've been here. It'll take a while for the surgery on your leg to heal completely, but with physical therapy you should be able to get around just fine with a cane."

"Yeah, between my cane and my disability checks every month, what more could I want?"

The doctor frowned. "You're alive. You've still got your leg, and I've got ten other patients a lot worse off than you, Rivera, so stop feeling so sorry for yourself. I made a recommendation for you to see Dr. Lange. The rest is up to you.''

A freaking shrink. What was a shrink going to do? Could he bring Eric back?

The pain of losing his career didn't even come close to the grief J.D. felt over Eric's death.

''You're going to be discharged tomorrow morning, sometime before noon. Do you have a ride?''

''Yeah. I've got transportation.'' The Yellow Cab Company. Because his fiancée—his *former fiancée*—was in Hawaii on the honeymoon they were to have taken together. Jenna had postponed the wedding as he'd expected. He hadn't expected her to dump the relationship. But why not? What good was he to anyone now?

The doctor moved toward the door.

''Doc.''

The white-haired man turned to look at J.D.

''Sorry I was such a crappy patient. I appreciate all you've done.''

Yeah. Eric was dead and he was going to walk away. They should've let him bleed to death.

CHAPTER ONE

HE KILLED A MAN.

The words—spoken in low hushed tones behind his back at the general store yesterday—echoed in J. D. Rivera's head.

Only two weeks since he'd returned to Los Rios, Arizona, and the locals were already talking. He should have stayed away. Stayed in the flea-ridden motel where he'd spent the past six months.

Twenty years away from this town hadn't changed a thing.

Bam! Bam! Bam! Three loud thuds sounded outside, the perfect accompaniment for the killer headache about to split open his skull. He burrowed under the pillow and wrapped both arms over the top. If he died right now, it wouldn't be too soon.

Probably what the two guys who'd ambushed him on the road last night had in mind. He touched the baseball-size lump on the back of his head.

The banging noise sounded again, from the front of the house somewhere. He groaned and rolled his battered body to the side of the bed, shoved both legs over the edge and sat up, vaguely aware of the cool adobe tile under his bare feet. After a few shaky starts, he made it upright, but just as he did, a lightning bolt of pain shot up his leg. His knee buckled, and he swayed to the side.

Groping wildly for something to hold on to, he crashed into the nightstand and spiraled down, knocking over the lamp and a half-empty can of Michelob before he hit the floor on his knees. Stabbing shards of pain launched him forward—flat on his face in a puddle of stale beer.

He closed his eyes, the smell of alcohol a potent reminder of all the nameless hole-in-the-wall bars where he'd spent the last year and a half.

Waiting for the pain to pass, the sting of inadequacy and his own helplessness burned in his gut.

But lying there wasn't going to get the work done. He braced himself on an elbow, sat for a second, then grasped the rumpled sheets and struggled to his feet again.

Gently, he put pressure on his leg, testing it a couple of times. Yeah. That's it... Okay. He was ready... He hoped.

As he flipped open the blinds, bright white sunlight flooded the room, the glare so intense it hurt his eyes. He braced himself against the wall. Damn. It was late. And probably blast-furnace hot outside.

Had it been this hot before? In September? He didn't think so, but then...he'd been an angry fifteen-year-old and the weather had been the last thing he'd noticed.

Since then, he'd been back to Los Rios only once on his way from Miramar Naval Air Station in California to Fallon near Reno. He wasn't used to living in an inferno.

Yeah...well, your life is shot to hell, anyway, so you might as well be living here.

Images he'd shoved into the darkest part of his brain crawled from the blackness. For eighteen months now, wherever he went, the images followed—from the Nevada mountains to the salt marshes of Maryland and finally to the sleazy Las Vegas hotel where his crazy aunt's attorney had found him four weeks ago to tell him he'd inherited the run-down ranch near Los Rios.

Like a horror movie on perpetual rerun.

Work. He needed to get to work. Ignoring the fire in his knee, he pushed off the wall and staggered into the bathroom. At the sink, he tossed down painkillers and caught his reflection in the mirror.

Man, oh, man. He looked as if he'd gone ten rounds with Rocky Balboa.

No big deal. Those creeps might have laid him out last night, but not before he'd gotten off some of his best shots. He'd bet his wings they looked worse than he did.

The battered face in the mirror mocked him. *If you had wings, buddy boy. You're finished. Done. Kaput!*

Bitterness rose like bile in his throat. Anger burned in his belly. Hands clenched, he swung out, slashing at the shelfful of pills above the sink. Bottles flew. Plastic containers bounced on the floor, spewing their contents in multicolored profusion around his bare feet.

Spent, he slumped against the old cast-iron pedestal sink, palms flat, head bowed as he tried to drag oxygen into his lungs—tried to find a reason to make it through another day.

More banging outside sent another round of cymbals clanging in his head. ''Dammit, quit making all that racket, willya.''

"Hello-o," a faint, high-pitched voice trilled from outside.

Crap. Probably some town do-gooder come to save his soul. Where the hell had they been when he could've used their concern? No one in this poor excuse for a town had ever done him any favors, and it wasn't likely they'd start now.

"Go away!"

The banging continued. He glanced down at his naked body, at the angry crimson scar that jagged along the side of his right leg—a permanent reminder that he was responsible for Eric's death. A reminder that he'd been the one who'd convinced Eric to do the air show…

He hauled in another deep breath. He should probably put on his pants.

Or…maybe not.

He grinned as his perverse side urged him to go to the door as he was. Shock the hell out of the church lady, and she'd be outta there faster than Mach 1.

But he couldn't do that in his grandmother's house; she'd lecture him from her grave.

He snatched a pair of dirty jeans from the top of the hamper and shoved one leg in and then the other. On his way through the living room, he could see a woman's form outside the front window. As he got closer, he noticed that she was young, passably pretty and severely uptight in her buttoned-to-the-neck shirt and beauty-shop hairdo that didn't move.

Prim and proper was stamped all over her. *Soul saver.*

Perfect. She'd soon find out he had no soul to save.

RIVERS OF PERSPIRATION ran down Madeline Inglewood's face and neck and between her breasts as she squinted against the blaze of the noonday sun, looking for some sign of activity. The ranch seemed deserted and her hope of finding someone at home plummeted. Down the gravel road a quarter of a mile, steam hissed from under the hood of her rental car.

Good Lord. How had she gone from her nice Midwestern girl's existence in Epiphany, Iowa, to having the life leeched from her body on a desert road in the middle of Nowhere, Arizona?

She knocked on the dilapidated door again, this time even harder. Glancing around as she waited, she saw stunted trees, thorny cacti and a dead rattlesnake draped over a rusty barbed-wire fence. A mud-brown lizard scurried past her foot—the only movement in a landscape that defied life in any form.

But she was too hot and too tired to react.

According to the directions, this was the place she'd been trying to find. But obviously it couldn't be. The map had to be wrong.

However, if no one lived here—and it certainly seemed as if no one did—she was going to die in the desert, her bones picked clean by buzzards.

So, Mr. Michael Bruchetti, number-one guru of self-help, what would you advise now? She wiped her sweaty forehead with a tissue. This was all his fault.

Then again…if she hadn't been trying to make

her best friend, Kayla, feel better when no one had come to her garage sale, Maddy wouldn't have bought the book, and if she hadn't done that, she wouldn't have decided she needed to take control of her life. And if she hadn't decided *that,* she wouldn't be here now.

But what was the alternative? Stay in Epiphany for the rest of her life?

Madeline turned to knock again, forcing herself to remain positive and in control as the book said. Just then the door opened with a jerk, and a man appeared in front of her. One eye was swollen shut, the other one was blood red and his bottom lip was split and puffy.

"Oh," she gasped, and pulled back so far she nearly tripped over her own feet. Besides his facial problems, the man wore nothing but a pair of dirty, bleached-out jeans, unbuttoned at the top, and with holes in the knees so wide, one pull on a thread and he'd be wearing shorts.

"Yeah?" he said, shoving an unlit cigarette between his lips. "What d'ya want?"

His rudeness eclipsed her relief at finding someone at home.

"I'm sorry. I knocked for such a long time I didn't think anyone was here, and...well, you startled me." She cleared her throat. "Is this the Triplehorne Ranch?"

He crossed hard-muscled arms over his bare chest, tanned and slick with sweat. The scent of stale alcohol offended her nostrils.

"Who wants to know?" His gaze drifted over her, his manner rude. Insolent.

Any empathy she might have had for the man's

condition faded. Clutching the map in her hand, she raised it and pointed to the spot she'd circled. "I'm looking for this place."

The sun beat mercilessly on her back as she waited for his response. She drew in a long breath, only it felt as if she'd pulled fire into her lungs instead of air.

With a cursory glance toward the map, the man plucked the unlit cigarette from his lips and said, "Well, you found it."

She looked around nervously. The house was falling apart. The whole ranch was falling apart. This couldn't possibly be where she was going to work for the next six weeks...could it?

For one thing, it wasn't anything like a dude ranch. She'd imagined a place like the one in that old movie where Billy Crystal went out West with his buddies and herded cattle with Jack Palance.

But...he'd said this was it. She shuddered, drew in another breath and smiled. "That's great. For a while I thought I might be lost, and my car—well, that doesn't matter right now. Is Ethel Devereaux here?"

He shifted his weight to one leg, muscles taut, his expression even more surly than when he'd first answered the door.

A man with a grudge against the world.

"I said you found *it,* lady. *It,* meaning the ranch. But whatever brand of mumbo jumbo you're selling, we don't need any."

Oh, for goodness' sake. He thought she was a salesperson.

While she was formulating an answer, he waved a hand in front of her face. "You hear me?"

"Yes," she said, the hair on the back of her neck bristling at his sharp tone. "Yes, I did, but I'm not selling anything. I'm here because I—"

He groaned suddenly, then grimaced as if in extreme pain and lifted both hands to his temples. His knuckles were raw and crusted with blood, and near his hairline was a huge lump and more dried blood. *Good Lord.* "Are you all right?"

"Do I look all right?" he retorted.

Maddy pursed her lips. "No. No, you don't." And given his attitude, he wasn't getting any sympathy from her. All she wanted to do was meet with her new employer and start working. Whatever problems this man had, they weren't hers.

Focus on the goal.

"Ms. Devereaux is expecting me. I'd appreciate it very much if you'd tell her Madeline Inglewood is here."

He scowled.

Though reluctant to give out any more information than necessary to a total stranger, she started to add, "She hired me to—"

"Okay, okay." He stopped her with a raised hand and nodded as if he'd just remembered something. He stepped closer, so close she could feel his body heat, and then he bent down a little, his face aligned with hers. "I guess you'd be the teacher, then."

"Yes. Yes, I am." She smiled, relieved that he'd heard about her arrival. Maybe he worked for the woman, too, though she couldn't imagine what kind of job would allow him to traipse around half-naked and stinking of alcohol in the middle of the day.

He wasn't the woman's husband because the lady

who'd hired her wasn't married, and was at least forty years older than this guy. It was hard to judge his age, but Madeline guessed mid to late thirties.

He took a half step back. ''Well, Teach. You're too late.''

''Oh, no. Today is the date Ms. Devereaux and I agreed on.''

''That's not what I meant. I think you better come inside for this.''

His manner seemed a little less hostile as he motioned her in, but still, she looked beyond him to see if anyone else was there. Not that she had a choice; her car was dead, her cell phone needed recharging and this was the place she'd been looking for.

Prodding herself forward, Madeline stepped over the threshold and into a dimly lit but expansive entry. It took a few seconds for her eyes to adjust to the low light inside and little more than that for an unsettling awareness to lodge inside her.

She was alone with a bloody, half-naked man—who could be a serial killer for all she knew.

Lord. She'd prepared for many eventualities, but not for anything like this.

Think it. Feel it. Believe it, she recited her new mantra, thank you, Mr. Michael Bruchetti. Or was it her former therapist who'd given her that bit of advice?

The man gestured to the left toward an archway leading into another room, an old-fashioned parlor. As she entered, he motioned for her to sit.

Her choices were a brown threadbare couch and a rickety-looking wooden chair. ''Thank you,'' she said, choosing the chair because it was closer to the door.

She assumed he would summon her employer while she waited, but instead, he propped himself against the archway wall, his navel at eye level.

Unnerving as that was, she noticed he seemed remarkably fit. He was tall and tightly muscled and might even be handsome if his face wasn't such a mess—and if his attitude wasn't so…awful.

He had a tattoo on his right arm, but she couldn't make out what it was, and there was a trace of another on his left arm, too. Military, maybe. Or gang member.

And you're staring, Madeline. She redirected her attention to her tote bag, which she'd stocked with emergency supplies, just in case. She drew the bag to her lap, pulled out a Wet-Wipe and dabbed at the moisture traveling down her neck.

"So," she said, focusing on his face. "Will Ms. Devereaux be along soon?"

"No. My dear aunt is dead."

Madeline's hand froze at her throat. Her voice did the same. Finally she managed to say, "I—I'm so sorry." For more reasons than one—she needed the job. Desperately.

But here she was thinking of herself when he must be grieving. She felt awful that she'd jumped to the conclusion he was being rude when he was really distraught.

"I didn't know," she said softly. "If I'd known, I—I could've made other arrangements. This has to be a terribly difficult time for you. I'm so sorry."

"No need to be. The old lady and me, we weren't exactly buddies," he said flatly. "But since

I'm the owner of Tripplehorne now, your business is with me.''

Oh-kay. So he *wasn't* broken up over his aunt's death, and he really *was* a rude, obnoxious man. A man who looked like he'd been in a fight—a struggle maybe? Something that had to do with his aunt's death?

''It's my understanding that you're gonna teach Juana and Carlos some English. Right?''

''I was hired to teach basic English to Ms. Devereaux's cook and gardener, but—'' she flung out a hand and glanced around ''—there must be some mistake.'' *Obviously.* The Tripplehorne Ranch didn't look as if it could support anyone, much less a cook and gardener.

''No mistake. Juana and Carlos are both here.''

''But—'' She glanced around again.

''Juana is the cook and Carlos is the gardener,'' he said, his tone impatient. He gazed at her critically. ''If you don't think you can handle the work, I won't hold you to the contract.''

Her nerves went taut. She could handle the job just fine. The bigger question was, would she have to contend with him to do it? *That,* she might have some difficulty with.

''I'm not a teacher per se, but I've studied teaching English as a second language. I speak four languages, Spanish, French, German and English, and I can teach the basics in any one of them.'' The last part was perhaps a slight overstatement.

He continued assessing her—probably thinking she was out of her element. She couldn't really blame him for that; somewhere between Tucson and the turnoff at Ajo, she'd come to the same conclusion herself. And after trudging down the gravel road in this god-awful heat, her silk blouse was ringed under her arms with sweat, her once-crisp, linen pants hung like potato sacks around her knees and her new shoes were scuffed and coated with brown dirt.

Despite all that, she couldn't possibly look as awful as he did.

As if she hadn't uttered a syllable, he added, "Things being the way they are, my aunt's death and all, I'll understand if you don't want to stay." The words, while sympathetic, belied his tone and expression. He seemed almost eager to get rid of her.

Favoring his right leg, he crossed to the couch opposite her, and after settling himself on the arm, he opened a drawer in the old oak library table next to him and pulled out a piece of paper.

"This is the contract you signed." He stared at her. "You want to leave, just repay the retainer and I'll tear it up."

Maddy's spine ground into the back of the wooden chair. She'd like nothing more than to tear up that contract and tell him to stuff it. She wanted to go back to her comfortable, safe home. But she couldn't do it. Because then she'd prove everyone right. Again.

Madeline Inglewood, daughter of Senator Randall Inglewood and his socialite wife, granddaughter of George Epiphany III, the mayor of Epiphany until he died, had been given everything she'd ever wanted. But now she was thirty years old, profoundly single, her career nonexistent and her family was trying to consume her life.

She needed help. Desperately.

Oddly, that help had come from a tattered book she'd bought at Kayla's garage sale. After reading *Take Control of Your Destiny*—written by the internationally known king of self-help books, seminars, audio and video tapes, all of which she'd subsequently purchased—she was excited, and more than ready to take control of her life.

"I hope I didn't give you the wrong impression, Mr.... Devereaux, is it?"

"Rivera. J. D. Rivera."

"Well, Mr. Rivera, I came here to do a job, and it's my intention to do that."

He was silent for a moment. Then he said, "I just thought under the circumstances, you might want to leave." He held out the paper. "Your choice."

Her choice. Hardly. She had no place to go, and no money to get there. She'd used the retainer to pay the deposit on her new apartment in Manhattan, and the rest of her salary was slated for her move to New York. If she left now, she wouldn't be able to afford the move plus she'd lose the deposit.

But, of all the reasons for her to stay, the most compelling was to prove to herself—and everyone in Epiphany—that she could do it.

She scanned the room. Old beat-up furniture, scuffed and splintered wood floor, wallpaper that was faded and peeling and, God only knew what the rest of the house was like. Not exactly the excitement and adventure she'd dreamed of. Not even close.

But she'd have all of that soon enough. In the meantime, she *had to* do this. If she couldn't do six measly weeks in Arizona, how could she handle a far more difficult job in one of the most exciting cities in the world?

"You know about the stipulation in the contract, don't you?" she asked.

"Stipulation?"

She nodded. "It says if the job I'm waiting on comes through before the contract period ends, I can leave without penalty."

He studied the paper in his hand.

"It's all there."

He looked up. "So it is."

"And you're okay with that?"

His eyes narrowed. "No. If it'd been up to me, I wouldn't have hired you in the first place. But, according to my aunt's will, I'm obligated to honor all the contracts she had in place."

Maddy didn't believe it was possible for her to get any hotter, but she felt as if someone had cranked up the furnace. Contract or not, she didn't like the man. He was rude and uncouth, and his confrontational attitude made it hard for her to think—and even harder for her to breathe.

Her mother's words played in her head. *What will you do if something unexpected happens and we're not there to help?*

No doubt this was the kind of thing her family expected she wouldn't be able to handle. She couldn't have set up a more perfect challenge if she'd tried; this was her crucible.

"May I ask why you wouldn't have hired me?"

He pushed to his feet, sauntered over and stopped at her side. "You can ask anything you want, Petunia."

Petunia?

"Doesn't mean you'll get an answer."

The tops of her ears burned. She wanted to melt into the faded wallpaper behind her. She wanted to leave. *Focus on the goal,* she reminded herself, otherwise all the positive steps she'd taken so far would be for naught.

Her resolve strengthened, she forced herself to say, "I'm sorry. It's really none of my business. I shouldn't have put you on the spot like that."

He scratched the stubble on his chin, then hooked both thumbs into the front pockets of his jeans.

She was ready to say something else when he reached out, touched the collar on her blouse and rubbed the silky fabric between his long, tanned fingers. After a moment he stopped and lifted up her right hand, turning it over, front to back. He flicked the tip of one freshly manicured fingernail and gave a snort.

"You ever do any *real* work?"

She yanked her hand away. "Mr. Rivera—"

"J.D."

"J.D." Her blood pounded in her veins as her irritation soared. "Since my job is to teach, I don't think whether I've scrubbed floors on my hands and knees or laundered my clothes on a rock at the river makes any difference. I've performed well in the positions I've held, even those not in my field of expertise. The job references I sent your aunt will verify all that."

"What kind of jobs?" His tone was dubious.

Apparently J. D. Rivera thought he knew everything about her from the way she looked. And if he thought that, he was not only wrong, he was stupid.

Furthermore, if looks were a gauge of character, the man was indictable.

"The most recent position, for the past two years, was as an administrative assistant, and before that, while in school, I worked at a video store."

He moved back to lean against the archway again. "You learn all those languages from watching foreign flicks at the video store?"

She wanted to smack him. But that was hardly an option if she was going to work for him.

"It helped," she said, raising her chin. "It also helped that I majored in language at Iowa State, and later received a graduate degree from Georgetown University."

"Ah, Iowa. The Corn Husker State," he said, completely ignoring her qualifications. "Or is that the Cheese Heads?"

"Iowa is the Hawkeye State," she said, happy to correct him. "Nebraska is the Corn Husker State. But I really don't understand the logic in that because Nebraska isn't the biggest corn producer. *Iowa* is."

He did a double take, as if she were an alien or had two heads or something. Then he gave a dry snort of a laugh. "You're actually serious, aren't you?"

"Of course. Iowa really *is* the national leader in corn production." She gave him the wide smile she'd practiced for weeks after Dr. Cravatz removed her mouthful of braces. "And the Cheese Heads, I believe, are located in Wisconsin—America's Dairyland."

He smirked. "You're just chock-full of information, aren't you?"

She felt her nose twitch, which it often did when she got angry or upset. Trouble was, she couldn't afford to be angry or upset. Her future hinged on making this job work.

Unfortunately, everything this man said infuriated her, and—unless she could control her temper—whatever came out of her mouth next would likely get her fired before she even started. She forced a smile. "Useless trivia, my family tells me. But for some reason weird facts stick in my head."

He crossed his arms over his chest, eyes narrowed, as if assessing her.

He was going to ask her to leave. She was sure of it.

"You think you can handle it?"

She thought she'd misheard, but realizing she hadn't, she answered, "If you mean teaching your employees English—absolutely. I'm ready right now."

She would most definitely *handle it.* She had to. This was her one chance to get out of Epiphany.

"Well, I'm not convinced, but you're here, so you might give it a try as well."

She didn't react to the dig. It didn't matter if he was convinced or not—as long as she had the job. "I'll be more than happy to do that. Just give me my instructions and I'll start right away."

"Tomorrow is soon enough. C'mon. I'll show you to your room."

"My luggage is in the car, stalled down the road." She waved an arm in that direction. "So I guess I'll need to call the rental place, too."

"What's wrong with the car?"

"Steam was coming from under the hood, and it

was leaking all over the road. Maybe one of the hoses.''

He rolled his eyes. ''There's a phone in the living room if you want to call. I'll wait here.''

She hurried back to where she'd come in, made the call and was told someone would retrieve the car the next day. By the time she returned to where her employer was propped against the wall waiting, her nerves were shot.

''I'll get your suitcase and have Juana bring it to you later.''

Juana was the cook, she remembered, so the woman must be around somewhere. Which meant it should be safe to stay.

Still, following him down the long, dim hallway with its yellowed, peeling wallpaper and musty scent, her mind conjured one dark scenario after another.

CHAPTER TWO

DON'T. DON'T EVEN THINK *like that,* she reprimanded herself as they continued down the hall. Her overactive imagination could wreak havoc if given free rein, and was the reason she'd spent too many years playing it safe. Finally, three months ago, she'd made the decision to change her life—and now she was on the road to doing exactly that. No matter what.

"So, why are you here?" Rivera asked, stopping near a door halfway down the long hallway.

She glanced up at him. He was at least a foot taller than her five-three. "I needed a temporary job until the permanent position I've applied for comes through."

He raised one dark eyebrow. "And what's your other reason?"

"Excuse me?"

"No one comes to a place like this because they want to. You running from something?"

Was she that transparent? She shook her head and shrugged. "Sorry to disappoint you. I'm just waiting to hear about another job and want to keep busy."

The look in his eyes said he didn't believe her, but then he gave a careless shrug, as if it didn't matter. "What's the other job?"

"Interpreting. Simultaneous interpreting. At the UN." Her fantasy job. Travel, adventure and excitement, everything she'd ever dreamed of.

"But it won't come through till late October because they're required to interview a specific number of applicants before hiring." She didn't add that she felt confident about getting the job. The human resources director had been very impressed with Maddy's qualifications.

She took another breath. "And as I said, I wanted to do something in the interim."

She *had* to do something in the interim. When she'd told her parents about her decision to move to New York, they'd gone on the defensive—just as they'd done every other time she'd tried to make a move from Epiphany. If she'd stayed at home while she waited for the other job to materialize, her family would simply have had more time to convince her they knew what was best for her.

And she knew herself well enough to know she just might cave. She was indebted to them. After all, she wouldn't have made it through her program at Georgetown if her parents hadn't been there for her after the assault...after she'd been forced to watch that monster violate her roommate and...

Oh, God! She stopped the horrible thought before she relived it again. She was grateful for her parents' support. She owed them. Which made it that much harder to leave.

"No jobs in Iowa?"

"Not in my field. Epiphany is a very small town."

"And how did you meet my aunt?" He leaned against the door.

"Oh, I didn't. But we spoke on the phone. My best friend's father is an attorney in Manhattan, and he told me that one of the firm's clients, your aunt, had a temporary job available that might be perfect for me for a couple of months. And since it was in Arizona—somewhere I'd never been—I was intrigued."

Elated in fact. Los Rios was fifteen hundred miles from Epiphany. There'd be no watchful eye on her here.

Towering over her, he let his eyes catch hers and for just the briefest flicker of a second, she saw something unexpected. A flash of empathy?

Whatever it was lasted only a microsecond. "Yeah, well, tell me in a couple days how intriguing it is," he said.

Was that what his contentious attitude was all about? He hated being here himself. "If you find it so...so unpleasant, why are *you* here then?"

A muscle twitched near his eye. "If you're looking for excitement, you won't find it in Los Rios."

He'd totally ignored her question, which told her more about him than if he'd given some flip answer. "Well, I guess I'll know soon enough, won't I?" She smiled. "What's that old saying? One man's trash is another man's treasure."

Fact was, what she thought of him or the place really *didn't* matter. Yes, she'd looked forward to seeing the West and being on a ranch, but since that wasn't really why she was here, it was a moot point.

All she had to concentrate on was making this situation work. "I wish I'd known about your aunt's death, though. Was she sick for long?"

"No. She had an accident." He motioned to a door across the hallway, then stepped forward and reached around her to turn the knob, his arm brushing against her as he did. "Your quarters. Dinner will be somewhere between six and seven." He pointed to his right. "Thataway."

With that, he turned and walked away, muttering something about discussing her job at dinner. Watching him disappear down the shadowy hallway, she forced herself to sound cheerful. "Thank you, Mr. Rivera. I'll see you at dinner then."

Jerk.

Cool air enveloped Maddy the second she stepped inside. Looking around, she was pleasantly surprised to see that the room was spacious and well-appointed, as if it'd been recently redecorated.

Feeling better, she kicked off her shoes and walked around to see where everything was. Queen-size bed, two chairs, a dresser and a large walk-in closet connected to the bathroom on her left. Another door, French doors, led to a small patio outside. The room was absolutely delightful.

After splashing her face with water that was more hot than cold, even though that's what the faucet indicated, she stripped to her underwear and sponged herself with a damp washcloth. Then she flopped across the lodgepole bed on top of a spread designed like a Mexican serape.

The two plump brown leather chairs with matching ottomans squatted like soft boulders in front of the window. The Southwestern-style Tiffany floor lamp between the chairs was a nice touch, too. Must've been Ms. Devereaux's doing. J. D. Rivera hardly seemed the type to be interested in interior decorating.

Even so, who in the world would willingly live in such a remote, isolated place? She rolled to her back and stared at the rough-sawn beams above. Her new boss, that was who. It was the perfect place for someone like him to hide from the rest of the world.

So what had happened to him? An accident? A fight? With his attitude, that was easy to envision. It was also easy to envision that he'd had something to do with his aunt's death. But she wasn't going to let herself dwell on that possibility. Whatever Rivera was about, he was not her problem.

A renewed sense of determination filled her. Despite a few minor glitches, she'd made it this far—and she was still here! A small success, but for her, it was huge.

If she could stay focused, keep her thoughts on her goal, she'd be fine. All she had to do was take things moment to moment. Take control of her life—and her destiny.

The way she had today.

Even so—an angry man could mean trouble.

She just hoped to hell he wasn't dangerous.

AFTER GETTING the teacher settled, J.D. climbed into his old Ford pickup and rumbled down the narrow gravel road toward Los Rios. Damn woman. He'd planned on her leaving and giving back some money in the process.

New York, she'd said. The city would eat her alive. She wouldn't last long in Los Rios, either.

On the outskirts of town, he pulled into Grady's Star gas station, killed the engine and got out.

Grady was standing at the pumps. "Hey, James. Man, you're a mess. You look worse than you did last night."

They shook hands, and J.D. gave Grady a friendly shot on the arm. Grady and J.D.'s teachers were the only people who'd called him by his given name. *James Devereaux Rivera,* a name that brought more ill than good in Los Rios. The Rivera part, anyway.

"I don't feel so hot, either." He rubbed his chin. Last night he'd managed to make his way back to Grady's after he'd been attacked. Grady's wife had tended his injuries. "How's Annie?"

"Except for paying homage at the porcelain altar every morning, she's fine. Doc says the nausea should ease up in about a month or so." Another car pulled up to the pump on the other side, and Grady motioned to J.D. that he'd be right back.

Grady was a stand-up guy, solid, honest and loyal—the best kind of friend to have. J.D. had been pleasantly surprised to find that Grady's wife, Annie, had no objections to the friendship. He'd expected her to disapprove of him—like everyone else in town did.

J.D. had been branded a troublemaker the second he'd set foot on Los Rios soil at five years old. And the perception had stuck.

A knot formed in his stomach. The day he'd come to live with his grandparents was burned into his brain. Devastated over his parents' deaths and all alone, he'd arrived via a rickety old bus from Mexico. His grandmother had come to pick him up, and she'd had him wait outside the general store while she shopped for a few things.

Chewing his nails, he'd searched for a friendly face. A bunch of men and women stood on the sidewalk talking among themselves. One man pointed at J.D., another man nodded and gave him a squinty-eyed look. J.D. turned away, only to see a giant of a man with thick red hair and a mean look in his eyes barreling toward him. He wore a badge.

Reaching J.D., the man leaned down, poked a hard finger in J.D.'s chest and hissed through thin lips, "I'll be watching you, kid. Just like I did your old man."

J.D. stared at the shiny star on the man's chest, his five-year-old heart pounding so hard he thought it would burst. Tears rolled down his cheeks and he peed his pants, right there in front of everyone.

And not one person came to his aid....

Now he grabbed a cloth from the gas pump and swiped at the side mirrors on his truck, his stomach churning at the memory. Even back then, the righteous enclave had let him know he was as unwelcome as his father had been.

He might've wanted acceptance at first, but it wasn't long before he didn't give a damn. The feeling hadn't changed. He didn't give a damn now, either. If his return to Los Rios meant he was a thorn in the town's collective side, so be it. That was their problem, not his.

Finished with the other car, Grady returned, giving a thumbs-up to the Buick as it drove off. "Gladys Hackert, remember her?"

"Like a bad boil," J.D. joked. How could he

forget the teacher who'd bounced him from her sixth-grade class more times than he could count. By sixth grade, he was living up to the town's worst expectations.

"Sheriff's been askin' on you," Grady said, leaning against the front fender of the rusty green pickup. "He heard you were hurt. Said he was concerned and thought the guys who waylaid you were probably border jumpers needing money."

Border jumpers, undocumented aliens, UDAs, illegal immigrants and a host of other names were used for those who crossed the Mexican border into the U.S. without papers. Border jumpers were common in the area because Los Rios was so close to Mexico. Nearly four hundred thousand illegals crossed the Arizona border each year.

In the old days, before J.D. had come to live at the ranch, his grandparents had apparently been sympathetic to the plight of those crossing over, giving them water and helping them on their way. But J.D. later learned that his mother's sister, his aunt Ethel, and some other people in town had had a problem with that. Sheriff Collier had been particularly incensed since he prided himself on the number of illegals he caught and sent back every year.

J.D. would have thought the old guy would've retired by now. But since no one else ran for the job, the sheriff just kept getting reelected. "That right? Hell, last I heard, the good sheriff was still trying to find out if I killed my aunt for her property."

Grady snorted a laugh, then stopped abruptly.

"Sorry you had to come back like this. Her dying and all."

"I hadn't seen the woman in years." Not since he was fifteen, and she'd taken over the ranch after his grandparents died. And even then, not for long. Since she was his only living relative she'd become his guardian and had immediately sent him packing to military school in Maryland. "So, you can save the sympathy."

His friend seemed uncomfortable and changed the subject. "Sheriff asked if you could identify the men who jumped you."

J.D. didn't believe for a second that the two guys who'd stopped him on the road pretending to have car trouble were UDAs. He'd lived in Los Rios long enough to know that most who crossed over illegally *didn't* want to draw attention to themselves. And after seventeen years in the military, he was savvy enough to know a setup when he saw one.

"Yeah? Funny he didn't come out or call to ask me about it." After last night, his feeling was that someone didn't like the fact that J.D. was back in town and was asking questions about the fire that had happened some thirty-five years ago. The fire his father was supposed to have started and that had killed two men.

Grady gave him a sheepish look. "That's probably my fault. I told the sheriff you couldn't identify anyone because it was too dark. Guess he figured you'd come in and file a report or something."

Grady had always taken people at their word, always given a guy the benefit of the doubt. He believed the sheriff was an honest man doing an honest job. Hell, the whole town thought that.

But J.D. knew better. Still, there was no reason to involve Grady in old problems that weren't his. In fact, he, J.D., had decided when he first came back that *he* wasn't going to deal with the past either. He was going to do what he needed to do to get the ranch in shape and keep to himself. The fewer people he had to deal with, the better.

But things changed last night. Someone was obviously worried about J.D.'s presence in Los Rios, and he wanted to know why. What were they afraid of?

"Right. In fact, I'm headed to the sheriff's office now."

Grady's shoulders relaxed. "Good. Collier will get to the bottom of the attack. He's good at that." He cracked a wide smile. "Hey, I'm glad you're okay, buddy. And I'm glad you're back."

J.D. clapped Grady on the shoulder, pleased that their friendship was still strong after all his years away. But he couldn't say he was glad to be back. If he never set foot in the town again, it would be too soon.

He took a step to leave and, as if on cue, a stab of pain shot up his leg. A reminder that it didn't matter how he felt about being here. He had nowhere else to go.

"Thanks. It's great seeing you, too. Gotta get back to work, though."

Ten minutes later, J.D. drove into the heart of Los Rios, still amazed at how little the town had changed in the years since his grandparents had passed on.

Los Rios, population 999, was one long main street with a combo beer joint–pool hall, a defunct bowling alley, a bank, a barbershop with the ubiquitous candy-cane pole outside, the Sunflower Café, the John Deere dealership that carried both tractors and cars, new and used, and Masterson's General Store and Lumberyard.

The mayor's office and the jail consisted of three rooms in the back of Charlie Masterson's store, and the town was run by the Big Three—Mayor Sikes, the sheriff and old man Masterson. A trio that had made J.D.'s youth a living hell.

After leaving Los Rios, he'd put all that out of his mind and made a new life for himself in the navy—top gun. He'd had a career. The navy had been his life. His family.

But all that was gone, and coming back to Los Rios was like opening an old wound with a dull butter knife.

Like returning to hell.

His knuckles tightened on the wheel as he pulled into one of the angled parking spaces in front of Masterson's. He had to let the past go. None of it mattered anymore. Getting through one day at a time was hard enough.

Next to the general store, Fred Billings, the barber, was sitting on a bench outside his shop, along with two other men J.D. didn't recognize. He climbed from the truck and nodded to the men as he walked by. Fred nodded back, but didn't say so much as a howdy.

"Yo, Masterson," J.D. called once inside the store. The dusty dry scent of grain and flour caught in the back of his throat. Muslin feed and flour sacks lined one entire wall, just as they had twenty years ago.

Clyde, standing behind the counter, was the grandson of old Charlie. Clyde's father was dead and Clyde stood to inherit all the Masterson money and property.

"Rivera," the man answered with a nod. "You look real bad."

J.D. leaned across the oak counter, so worn with age that it was slightly indented in the place where goods were passed back and forth. Clyde probably knew why J.D. looked so bad, because word got around in Los Rios faster than the speed of light.

"Yeah, but I feel great. I'll feel even better if the supplies I ordered a week and a half ago are here."

A tall, lean man with a narrow pointy face and haystack hair, Clyde shook his head. "Haven't heard a thing."

J.D. waited a second, his nerves bunching. He controlled his temper, then said calmly, "Last I heard, supplies usually get here in four to five days. Any chance you might be calling someone to find out why they haven't arrived?"

"Maybe," Clyde drawled. "Maybe I'll call tomorrow if they don't come."

Just then, Sheriff Collier appeared at the back of the store, his hair still as red as Orphan Annie's. Seeing J.D., the sheriff swaggered toward him, his chin jutting a little higher with each step. All the old guy needed was a ten-gallon hat and he'd be John Wayne.

When the sheriff reached J.D., both men stood in silence, each assessing the other. If anyone else in town had been jumped and assaulted, the sheriff would've been all over it.

"I don't suppose you want to file a complaint,"

Sheriff Collier said, his voice indicating he wasn't posing a question.

J.D.'s muscles coiled. "Should I, Tom? Think it would do any good? Those border jumpers are probably long gone by now."

The man's rheumy eyes narrowed and his barrel chest puffed up even more. J.D. knew the man hated when people called him Tom instead of Sheriff.

"Just askin' in case something comes up again. You and that pretty new girlfriend of yours are kind of isolated way out there, who knows what might happen?"

Two hours since the teacher arrived, and old Tom knew about it already. "She works for me. But then I guess you know that, too, don't you, considering what great friends you and Aunt Ethel were. She probably told you all about it before she passed on so suddenly."

The sheriff's shoulders went stiff. It was no secret that Tom Collier had been in love with Ethel Devereaux. No secret that she'd ditched him for another guy and made a fool of him.

"And if something does come up," J.D. added, "you'll be the first to know. I guarantee it."

"Good," the sheriff said, glaring at J.D. "This is a nice quiet town. People mind their own business and no one bothers anyone." His eyes darkened dangerously. "We want to keep it that way, boy."

CHAPTER THREE

A STRANGE SCRATCHING sound awakened Maddy with a start. She sat up slowly and gradually realized where she was.

Instead of feeling well-rested after her nap, her nerves were stretched tight and she had a hard time drawing a full breath. Her gaze shifted around the darkened room. Nothing amiss, but her pulse raced anyway. A thin film of perspiration covered her skin.

Scratch, scratch. The noise sounded as if it came from outside the door, which she noticed was open a crack. Odd. She was sure she'd shut it before she went to sleep.

As she watched the door, it slowly creaked open a few more inches and at the bottom of the opening a pair of yellow eyes blazed back at her. In the next instant, a furry thing shot across the room and leaped onto the bed like a flying squirrel.

A terror-filled scream ripped from her throat. Visions of sharp teeth and dripping blood flashed in her head. She flailed wildly, striking out, shoving the animal away before she pulled up the blanket and curled into a ball underneath, her arms protecting her head and face. Seconds later, she felt movement, and then the weight on the bed beside her was gone.

A deep male voice said, ''She won't bite. She's harmless.''

Maddy's heart thundered, and gasping for breath, she slowly peered from under the covers. Rivera was standing a few feet away from her, clutching a wiry-haired mongrel in his arms.

Oh, dear God! Her heart pummeled her ribs. She gulped air. He'd never said he had a dog. Ms. Devereaux hadn't mentioned... She'd never imagined...

Rivera's expression hardened. ''What the hell were you screaming about?''

The words penetrated Maddy's horror-stricken brain. She pulled to a sitting position again, and realizing she was wearing only her underwear, yanked up the spread for cover. ''I—I was asleep and I guess it...your d-dog startled me.'' Yes, that was it. She'd just been surprised. That's all.

That had to be all, because if it wasn't, all her therapy had been for naught. She bit her bottom lip, willing herself to calm down.

The look in Rivera's eyes went from angry to dubious. ''I hope that's all, because this dog is easily traumatized. And if she's traumatized, she won't eat.''

Maddy's mouth dropped open. She'd been scared spitless, and he was worried the dog might not eat?

''I—I didn't know you had a dog. I didn't see her before.''

''She was outside in her house. I brought her in a while ago.'' Still holding the wiry-haired mutt, he plopped down on the edge of the bed next to her.

The acrid tang of fear burned in the back of her throat. Rivera's mouth was moving and he was saying something, but all she heard was her pulse drumming in her ears.

She swallowed and her ears cleared.

''Yeah,'' he said, looking directly at Maddy. ''She might forgive you scaring her if you show her you like her. Just scratch a little right here.''

Pure white terror shot through Maddy. Unable to move, she quickly invoked her therapist's words. *You can do it. You can do anything—if you want it enough.*

She wanted it. Desperately. And if she did as he asked, he wouldn't even know she had a problem.

She glanced at her fingers. What was the worst that could happen? What was one little finger compared to the rest of her life?

Steeling herself, she reached out, hoping Rivera didn't notice her hand was trembling.

The dog's pink tongue snaked out and slurped at her fingers. She yanked her hand back, a reflex action she had no control over. The animal's tail swished from side to side.

''Hey, how about that?'' J.D. sounded genuinely surprised. ''Zelda doesn't like too many people, but she seems to like you. That's amazing.''

Maddy gave a wan smile, trying her best to hide her qualms. He didn't know anything about her problems, and she didn't want him to. This was her chance to start fresh among people who didn't know her. ''Amazing,'' she whispered.

''Right here,'' he said. ''She likes to be scratched right behind the ear. Try it.'' He took Maddy's hand and drew it closer.

''Wait—'' She pushed her heels against the mattress, scooting back against the headboard. ''I—I feel a bit sick, and—'' She flapped a hand in front of her face. Lord, she might actually puke. ''And, well, the dog startled me when I wasn't fully awake.''

Her voice sounded wobbly, and no wonder, she was about to spew the peanut-butter crackers she'd eaten earlier into her new employer's lap.

''Yeah. I can see that.''

She fanned herself with one hand. ''Probably just a reaction to the sun. I was outside for quite a while and I'm really not used to this heat. I'll be fine. No need for you to worry.''

Frowning, and still cradling the dog, he stood up. He didn't look as if he believed her at all. ''You might want to make it cooler in here.'' He pointed to the air conditioner in the window.

Just then, Maddy saw a dark-haired woman peering around the doorway. Rivera motioned for her to enter.

''This is Juana. Juana Macario. Juana, Madeline Ing—''

''Inglewood. Maddy Inglewood.''

The woman rattled off something under her breath in Spanish and, with hands flying, shoved Rivera out of the room.

''What can I do?'' Juana asked Maddy in broken English. She walked over to the window, reached up and fiddled with the knobs on the cooler.

Maddy shook her head and answered in Spanish. ''Nothing, thank you. I'm okay. Really.''

The woman's eyes lit up, so Maddy continued speaking in the woman's language. ''I was feeling a little queasy, probably from the heat. And then

Mr. Rivera's dog startled me. I'm afraid I overreacted.''

Juana nodded her understanding. ''I'm going to get you something to help you relax. Then I'll bring in your luggage.''

In less than minute, the woman had swooped in and out, and Maddy was grateful for that. Only she'd forgotten to close the door, and Maddy's chest constricted just thinking the dog could charge back into her room at any time.

She bolted from the bed and shut the door, jiggling the knob to make sure the latch had caught. If she'd done that earlier, this incident would never have happened. If she'd known the dog was here, she could've dealt with it. She'd simply been caught off guard, and all she needed was a little time to get her head in the right place again.

Standing with her back flat against the door, she reached up, her fingertips kneading the tiny scar near her ear. Plastic surgery had removed the visible evidence of the dog's teeth, but not the memory. Not the fear.

She'd only been four at the time, and everyone had said she wouldn't remember any of it. But she did. As if it was yesterday.

She went into the bathroom and dressed in her dirty clothes again. Crossing the room to open the blinds, she could only imagine what Rivera thought of her reaction to his pet.

But she couldn't take it back, no matter how embarrassed or how badly she felt about it. And she wasn't going to explain either. He already wondered if she was capable of handling the job. Any more information would simply validate his already negative opinion of her.

A light knock at the door brought her to attention again. "It's open."

Juana floated in wielding a copper tray that held a small blue teapot, a matching cup and a plate of cookies covered with powdered sugar. A soothing herbal scent followed in the woman's wake. "My special recipe," she said in Spanish. "You'll feel much better after you drink the tea."

"Gracias," Maddy said, also reverting to Spanish. "But please don't feel you have to wait on me."

Juana set the tray on the table next to the chair. "If I do something it's because I want to, or because it's my job." The outer corners of the older woman's ebony eyes crinkled when she smiled. "I want to do this."

"Well then, I thank you even more." A stocky, robust lady, Juana carried herself with confidence. Maddy liked her immediately.

"No need to thank me," Juana said on her way out of the room. She returned with Maddy's luggage, and then walked to the door.

"Please wait." Maddy stopped her. "I have a few questions."

Juana nodded and took a step back.

"Can you tell me about Ms. Devereaux? I hadn't heard she'd passed on before I came, and the news was a big shock. Mr. Rivera said she'd had an accident, but that's all he said."

The woman's eyes widened. "You didn't know?"

Maddy shook her head.

Juana's surprise quickly shifted to uncertainty. After a long pause, she said, "You better talk to Mr. Rivera about that. I don't know any more."

What was the big secret? Maddy's imagination shifted into overdrive. The woman's nephew had inherited the ranch, and he looked as if he'd been in a fight—a struggle, perhaps?

But only the old Maddy would imagine the worst and obsess about those kinds of things. The new Maddy put things in perspective and didn't look for zebras when horses were galloping by.

"Okay. Can you at least tell me where the accident happened and when?" All the arrangements for the job had been done through Ms. Devereaux's attorney, Harold Martin, Maddy's best friend's father. Why hadn't *he* told her about the woman dying?

Juana clamped her mouth shut.

"Did the accident happen here on the ranch?"

"I'm sorry. Mr. Rivera asked me not to talk to anyone about it. You should ask him," she repeated.

Obviously Juana was a loyal employee, and if she'd been told not to talk about the mishap, she wouldn't. Maddy respected that. "Okay. I will. I didn't ask him before because I could see he wasn't feeling well. Was he in an accident or something?"

Juana nodded. "Before he came back to Los Rios, he was in an accident that injured his leg. Then last night, when he was on his way home from town, someone tried to rob him. They fought and he got hurt."

"How terrible. Did they catch who did it?"

"No. Some people say it was Mexicans. Coyotes, maybe. But Mr. Rivera said he didn't believe it was them."

"Coyotes?"

"People smugglers. The coyotes take money from Mexicans to bring them into the U.S. illegally. They take the money and leave the people in the desert."

"They could die out there. It's awful."

"Yes. Many have died. Others get caught and are sent back to Mexico. It happens all the time."

"And what happens to the men who brought them into the country? The coyotes... Wouldn't they be held responsible if someone died?"

The older woman shrugged. "The coyotes don't get caught, because they bring people over the border and then disappear. The people who get deported don't tell who they are because they want to come back again and will need the coyotes' help to do it."

Maddy knew about the problems with illegal immigration—that it took a long time to get clearance and passports and work permits. Many Mexicans weren't even eligible if they had no skills or were illiterate. Most of the unskilled worked in the fields as *pizcadores. Pickers. Field workers.*

She wanted to ask more about Ms. Devereaux, but Juana kept glancing at her watch and edging out the door, obviously uncomfortable with the conversation and anxious to leave.

"I'm sorry for keeping you. Thanks for filling me in. It's good to have a little background information." She smiled warmly at Juana. "Maybe when you have more time, we can talk again."

Juana looked relieved and left the room, saying

that dinner would be ready in twenty minutes. Maddy jumped to make sure the door was closed tightly. Then she locked it.

She stood immobile for a moment, feeling suddenly overwhelmed with information—and so out of place, she might as well have been on another planet. A sudden ache of longing filled her, a longing for the warmth and safety of home, a place where she knew what life held for her.

In Epiphany, people didn't get assaulted and robbed. People didn't get left in the desert to die. Living in Epiphany meant living in comfort with people who loved and cared about her. Why was she giving all of that up?

So what if her parents were a little overzealous in their love, a little controlling. That was normal, wasn't it? And wasn't it her own fault if she let other people direct her life? There were worse things than being loved too much, weren't there?

Worse things—like living in a place where the owner had died and no one would tell you how or why.

She still couldn't understand why Mr. Martin hadn't told her about the woman's demise before she came all the way out here. The more she thought about it, the more annoyed she got. She should've been informed.

She checked the time. Damn. It was three hours later in New York, and it wasn't likely Mr. Martin would be at his office at 9:00 p.m. Well, she'd call Kayla then…maybe *she* could call her dad at home and get the information Maddy wanted.

Maddy looked for a phone. There wasn't one. Fine. She'd just have to call from the living room.

She went to the door and peered out. No dog, thank heaven. Taking a deep breath, she slipped out and hurried down the hall, her mind racing for solutions on what to do if Cujo pounced on her again.

Fortunately, all was quiet when she reached the living room. Relieved, she picked up the phone on the table next to the couch, punched in her calling-card number and then Kayla's number.

She'd feel much better about everything if she simply knew what happened to Ms. Devereaux.

And if the news isn't good? What then? She heaved a sigh. She'd get the hell out of here, that was what.

All she'd have to do was figure out how to do it without a car.

J.D. PULLED A BOTTLE of ice water from the fridge and guzzled half of it while walking to the old oak table. He put down the water, unrolled a set of blueprints and placed a small plate on each corner to anchor the sheets.

But even as he tried to concentrate on the layout, his thoughts drifted to the woman in the bedroom. Her screams had been like something out of a horror movie.

"It's okay," she'd said in her soft cultured voice. "I'm fine. No need for you to worry."

No need for *him* to worry? She was the one who'd been screaming. The last thing he needed was a hysterical woman on his hands—a half-naked woman at that.

She hadn't looked too bad that way, either. In fact, he'd had an urge to rip off the blanket and find out what the rest of her was like without all those expensive clothes.

Yeah, good move that would've been. Taking care of his aunt's employees was one of the stipulations in the will, but he was pretty sure that didn't include sex. On the other hand, if he'd followed his instincts, he might've shocked the little petunia enough that she'd be gone by now.

And J.D. wouldn't have violated the conditions of the will, which stated that any employees was free to leave of his or her own accord. In fact, if Miss Manners had left and paid back the retainer as the contract stipulated, he would've had extra money to work with until the trust money came through. If she left before she started the job, he wouldn't have to pay her the rest of the contract money, either.

But she hadn't taken the bait. And *he'd* underestimated her. The designer clothes and Jackie Kennedy demeanor had fooled him. He'd seen a wariness in her big eyes—and something that resembled fear. But she'd decided to persevere.

So he was stuck with her. And that meant more time away from his work to get her settled, more time giving instructions on what she was supposed to do, more time answering questions about things that were none of her business. He didn't need any of it.

He brought his attention back to the blueprints. The house—seven bedrooms, four baths, a parlor, living room, kitchen and what would now be called a family room—and the three bunkhouses, a storage shed and a barn, all needed to be renovated by the deadline. Six short months away.

How his aunt had arrived at that date was a mystery. How he'd get the place fixed up by then was even more of a mystery. But if he failed to make the deadline, everything would be sold and the money given to his aunt's favorite dog shelter.

Why the hell hadn't the crazy broad just done that in the first place? Why had she left him anything? Even more bizarre, why leave the ranch to him if she was going to set him up for failure?

Well, whatever game the woman was playing from her grave, he'd be damned if he was going to let her win. The thought had stuck in his craw from day one, and getting the place restored had become a challenge he was determined to meet.

Bottom line was that he had a helluva lot to do in a short time, not enough help or supplies to do it, and now he had the teacher to contend with. She'd better be smart enough to stay out of his way.

He scoffed, remembering what she'd said. *Too much sun.* The woman didn't look as if she'd ever seen the sun. She was ghostly pale, her skin was like his grandmother's fine china, the kind you can see through when you hold it to the light. She wasn't the type of woman that usually appealed to him, but seeing her half-naked in bed had gotten his blood pumping.

Starting down the hall, he heard a voice. As he got closer to the living room, he heard her talking to someone on the phone.

"Please, Kayla. See what you can find out. Your dad was her attorney. I just need to know what's going on. Something is really weird here."

Lady, you have no idea. J.D. smiled to himself

as he made his way to the kitchen and out the back door.

He stood on the weathered cedar-and-stone veranda that encircled the house and assessed the task ahead of him, just as he had every night since he'd arrived two weeks ago.

It was a huge job, one that would take all his strength. Though the lumps on his head would disappear, the leg injury from the plane crash would never heal completely. He'd always be in pain. Always be a gimp.

As his gaze fell on the dog compound, a monument to his crazy aunt's eccentricity, the floor squeaked behind him. A fresh female scent wafted past him. He didn't have to turn around to know it was her. His blood surged.

He gripped the splintered railing, annoyed that he was so aware of her. Glad that she didn't open the screen door and come out. Relieved when he thought he heard her leave.

Freaking crazy. What was it about this uptight, high-maintenance slip of a woman that had him coming alive again? Hadn't he learned anything? After his injury, Jenna couldn't even make love with him. She'd looked at him in disgust and then called off the wedding. He had no job and no future, she'd said. What were they supposed to do, live on his disability checks? That wasn't the life Jenna had in mind.

And she was right. It wasn't the life he'd had in mind either. After that, he swore off women and let booze and painkillers deaden *all* his senses.

Pills and booze. The only way he could forget that he was alive and Eric was dead. His throat closed in anguish and he bit back the tears that suddenly brimmed.

Since his aunt's attorney had found him and sobered him up, there was no forgetting.

If you think it's so unpleasant, why are you here? the teacher had asked. Good question.

If he didn't give a rat's ass if the place rotted back into the earth, why *was* he here?

He surveyed the property, his gaze stopping on the old bunkhouses that had once bustled with activity. Tripplehorne Ranch had been in the Devereaux family for more than a century, belonging first to his great-grandparents, and then his maternal grandparents. They'd loved him and made him feel he wasn't all alone in the world after his parents died. When he'd been with them on the ranch, he'd been happy.

That was it, he realized. That was the reason he was here. Despite his hatred of Los Rios, despite his doubts about staying, he was here because of his grandparents—he owed them enough to try and save the home they'd loved.

And that meant no fantasizing about soft warm skin and a petite woman who'd somehow managed to make him interested in sex again.

After his earlier conversation with his new employee, he'd pulled out her résumé. All it contained were details of her education and previous employment—working for her father, a senator no less. She'd lived in the same place all her life, with the exception of college and grad school, and after that, her address was listed as the same as her parents'. She'd lived the good life, that was apparent.

He wondered why instead of getting a job in her

field after finishing her education, she'd gone home to work for her father as an administrative assistant and stayed for four years. The free ride must've been too hard to give up, he decided.

He stuck an unlit cigarette between his lips. Well, the teacher wasn't his problem. The only thing he needed to worry about was getting his job done.

The screen door squeaked open and then snapped shut behind him. She was back, and he felt her coming to stand next to him. His pulse quickened, his physical reaction to her at odds with his good sense.

CHAPTER FOUR

MADDY STARED at a miniature replica of the White House, right down to the immaculate green lawn and azaleas surrounding it. It was just about the most bizarre thing she'd ever seen. "What on earth is that?" she asked.

"It's Zelda's house," J.D. said with a touch of sarcasm.

"Are you serious? Your dog really lives in that…that house?" The structure was a mini-estate with lights and bushes and topiary trees, a small wading pool and a long covered runway with a misting system that hissed a fine spray of water from little hoses at the top of the fence.

Looking over at J.D., she noted that his eye and lower lip weren't quite as puffy as before, though a dark purple shiner was rapidly developing. The blood on his head had been washed off and his hair was clean now, a rich dark whiskey color with golden highlights, lighter than she'd thought.

"Yep. That's where Zelda lives."

Her gaze circled, taking in other things she hadn't seen when she'd arrived. There were several dilapidated shedlike buildings, a barn in the same poor condition and a circular fenced-off area that appeared to be an arena of some kind.

She turned to J.D., a zillion questions racing

through her head. Just as she opened her mouth, he raised both hands.

"Don't even ask! None of this was my doing."

Maddy's gaze passed from the doghouse to J.D. "It's..." she searched for words. "It's quite spectacular."

"It's crazy. Just like my aunt."

Maddy blew out a breath and leaned forward, her hands on the railing next to his. "I guess she really loved your dog."

"Aunt Ethel loved control. She had her own way of doing things."

Obviously there was no love lost between J.D. and his aunt, but if that was the case, why had the woman left him the ranch and made such an elaborate place for Zelda? "I guess we all have reasons for what we do, don't we?"

He focused straight ahead.

"You trying to quit?" she asked, nodding at the unlit cigarette he rolled between his fingers.

"Yeah. Three weeks now."

"So what did you do before you came here?"

At her question, his hand clenched, the cigarette broke in half and he flicked both pieces across the yard. He took a breath, then said, "Nothing. I did absolutely nothing."

"Really? You didn't have a job?"

A long silence ensued. Finally he said gruffly, "There aren't too many jobs for a cripple."

"But you're not—I mean it doesn't look like—" She stopped. Lord. Everything that came out of her mouth sounded worse.

"I know my limitations." His mouth was tight

and grim and the next thing she knew, the screen door slammed shut behind him.

She felt awful. He was obviously very self-conscious about his injury. But an injury didn't give him carte blanche to be rude.

Just then, she saw something move. As she turned, Zelda popped out the little door in front of her house and pranced down the runway as if she were royalty. Maddy's palms went clammy, but she quickly reminded herself the dog was on the other side of the fence.

Still, her breath stalled. Then another movement caught her attention. A man wearing a baseball cap was standing inside the compound clipping away at a tiny hedge. She expelled a breath. This whole scenario was like something from a sci-fi movie.

She shook her head in disbelief and quickly followed Rivera into the house. Perhaps she should apologize? And if not that, at least say something to smooth things over. After exploring a couple of hallways in search of her employer, Maddy realized the sprawling house was much larger than it had appeared from the front.

Down each hallway were a half-dozen doors and in the center hall was a dark walnut staircase, at least five feet wide, with a window bench on a landing halfway up. The stairs were splintered and didn't look safe enough to climb.

She found Rivera in the kitchen, a huge room with a vintage stove. He was nursing a beer at a large rectangular wooden table near a long bank of windows, through which Maddy could see a mountain range in the distance.

Not knowing what was expected of her, she felt

awkward. But gritting her teeth, she walked over to the table.

Without looking up, he said, "We should talk."

"Great." She pulled up a chair across from him. "I saw a man out there doing some hedge clipping."

"Carlos."

"One of my students?" She smiled at the thought. "The gardener, right?"

J.D. nodded. "Zelda belonged to my aunt, and dear Aunt Ethel wanted to make sure her dog was comfortable, so she hired a gardener to make sure the grounds were kept up." He sighed. "Aunt Ethel liked animals more than she liked people. Apparently she'd had several dogs and a few other animals, but got sick about a year ago and couldn't take care of them. Zelda was the only one she kept."

While it was reassuring to know that Zelda had her own quarters and wouldn't be surprising Maddy at every turn, she was bothered by the thought of the little dog being caged up all the time. "Doesn't she get lonely?"

"She's a loner. Like me."

"Really? You sure had me fooled," she said.

He gave her a hard look. "That a problem for you?"

"Sorry, I was attempting to make a joke. Like I said, maybe I've been in the sun too long."

His mouth tilted, more in a grimace than a grin.

Juana sashayed into the kitchen then, her long, gauzy red skirt swishing around her bare ankles. She wore black rubber flip-flops, a yellow sleeveless tank top and was carrying a large insulated bag, the kind used for pizza delivery.

The older woman looked so cool in her breezy skirt and top that Maddy wished she'd brought different clothing. After getting her luggage, she'd changed into a white rayon blouse and another pair of linen slacks, figuring the outfit would be cooler than anything else she'd brought along. But she was still hot.

"La cená está aquí," Juana said, telling them the dinner had arrived. As she opened the bag, a delicious spicy aroma filled the room, making Maddy's mouth water.

It had been a long day, what with flying from Iowa to Tucson and then renting a car and driving another hundred-plus miles. She was famished.

"Juana makes the food at her place and brings it over," Rivera said. "Once the kitchen is finished, she'll do the cooking here."

"So you're renovating, then?"

"Yes," he said, glancing out the window. "This used to be a guest ranch when my grandparents ran the place. And one of my aunt's express desires was to restore the homestead to its former elegance."

So maybe he did care about his aunt after all? "How nice of you to carry out her wishes."

He gave a dry laugh. "It's one of the stipulations in the will."

Oh, now she got it. His disenchantment could be because he didn't want to have to do things as his aunt required.

"So I guess your aunt was living here and having the renovations done herself when…when she had the accident?"

"Something like that."

Which meant change the subject before he got

all grouchy again. But her mouth never managed to be in sync with her brain. "So, what exactly happened to her?"

He waited a moment, then said, "I don't know *exactly* and frankly I don't care. Now let's talk about your job."

"Fine." At least she'd gotten an answer.

"As you know, Juana and Carlos will be your students. They both speak a little English, but not much."

"Do they live here on the ranch, too?"

He shook his head. "They live in the *colonias* on the other side of town."

She knew the word, but listened to his explanation.

"That's the name given to the unimproved farmland the migrant workers use for housing."

When she'd taken the job and envisioned working on a ranch, she'd thought of horses and cattle and wide-open spaces. Not agriculture. But she'd seen a lot of farmland while driving here. Desert that had been irrigated so it was lush and green.

"What crops are grown around here?"

"Within a hundred-mile radius, you'll find lettuce, cotton, hay, melons, onions and other vegetables. Grapes and citrus."

"Are Carlos and Juana migrant workers?"

"Not anymore."

The man's answers were short and to the point. She wondered how many questions she could get away with before he told her to shut up. "So what exactly does one do on a guest ranch?"

"Same thing as on any ranch, except people pay to stay here and do the work along with us."

She smiled. "Like in the movie *City Slickers*?"

"Yeah." He said, grinning a little. "Like that. But you'll be long gone before then."

He sounded happy about that. She picked up a newspaper from the bench behind her and fanned herself with it.

"The swamp cooler's out again," he said.

When she gave him a blank stare, he added, "Water circulates through a big fan unit that sits on the roof and cools the air as it's blown out. Unfortunately, our unit is so old it doesn't work half the time."

"I guess I should be glad there's a separate cooler in my bedroom."

"Yeah. Aunt Ethel always took care of herself first."

Maddy gulped. "I'm staying in her room?"

"Well, she never actually had the opportunity to stay in it."

Relieved to hear she wasn't sleeping in a dead woman's bed, Maddy fanned herself again with the paper.

"Most people get used to the heat," J.D. went on. "But not Ethel. From what I hear, she lived in New York, stayed in Tucson occasionally and only drove out here to see how the renovations were going."

"But she must've planned to stay here at some point, what with building Zelda's house and all."

He shrugged. "Don't know."

Apparently, he really didn't know a whole lot about his aunt. Maybe he was being truthful when he said he didn't know what had happened to her.

She was distracted by Juana's clatter in the

kitchen. "Can I do something to help?" Maddy asked.

"No. It's all done." She brought over two place mats, plates, napkins and utensils. She went back for a steaming platter of green corn tamales, refried beans, rice, shredded lettuce, tomatoes and a crock of hot tortillas.

"Mmm. Everything looks delicious, Juana," she said. "Are these homemade tortillas?"

"Everything is homemade." The older woman smiled proudly.

"I'm impressed. Maybe you can teach me a little about Mexican cooking. I'd love to learn and be able to—"

J.D. cleared his throat, cutting off her conversation with Juana. "You can start teaching tomorrow and it's best if you use one of the buildings out back. I'll be busy in the house, so it'll probably be too noisy to conduct any kind of class there. Since Juana and Carlos have work to do during the day, you'll need to confine the sessions to evenings, five days a week." He looked up at her. *"Comprende?"*

Despite the fact that he'd seemed to soften a little in the past few hours, he was still a rude man. "Of course. I'll do the job however you want me to."

But how the heck was she going to spend the rest of her time? "Is there something else I can do during the day? I'd be more than happy to help out wherever yo—"

"No."

No? The place was in shambles, why not take all the assistance he could get? Then remembering how he'd scrutinized her when she first arrived, she decided that he didn't trust her to do a good job.

She cast about for something she could offer to do. A massive stone fireplace covered one whole wall, but it was so dirty she couldn't tell what type of stone it was. The floor was Mexican tile, some pieces missing, others gouged, chipped and darkened with age, the cupboards were dingy with doors askew or ripped off altogether. The refrigerator, however, was new.

"I can clean."

"Not necessary."

"Really. This room certainly could use a little elbow grease."

"I'm going to tear it all out."

"But until then, why not clean the room up a little and use it? That way, Juana could prepare the food here and not have to carry things back and forth. It would save time for her."

Hearing her name, Juana turned to them, so Maddy told her what she'd said.

Rivera kept eating.

Maddy concentrated on her own plate. She polished off her tamale and sat back. "Well, the offer stands if you change your mind. I'd really like to have something to fill the time when I'm not teaching."

The man's focus stayed on his dinner. Then after a sip of beer, he leaned back in his chair, his look thoughtful. Then he smiled. "Well, there *is* Zelda. She seems to like you."

"Zelda?" She choked out the dog's name.

"Yeah. Feed her, give her water, take care of her general maintenance, other stuff like that. Until now, she hasn't taken to anyone but me, and keeping up with all the stuff my aunt prescribed for the dog takes up time I could be using to work on the place.''

''What kind of stuff?''

''Make sure she's bathed and groomed, regular brushing and...well, it's all on a list.''

Oh, my. Could she do that? She didn't know. But taking care of a dog seemed such a simple thing. And what would he think of her if she refused?

What would she think of herself? This whole situation—being at the ranch—was about proving she could handle whatever came up. But this...this went right to the heart of her deepest fear.

Only he didn't know that. He didn't know anything about her. And she didn't want him to.

On a gush of air, expelled from the bottom of her lungs, she said, ''Okay. Give me the list.''

Rocking on the back legs of the chair, he angled his chin in her direction, eyebrows bunched in the middle. ''You sure about that?''

''Absolutely,'' she said, forcing an extra bit of certainty into her voice. ''It'll be good to have something else to do.''

J.D. finished his meal and shoved the plate back.

The teacher might be sure, but he wasn't. Not after her panic act earlier. He'd wanted to see her reaction, thought she might refuse, maybe even freak out and leave, but she'd actually agreed to help look after Zelda. He felt like a creep for suggesting it.

Well, he wasn't her baby-sitter. Either she'd do the job or she wouldn't.

He'd been working 24-7 on the place and was still behind. If she took over Zelda's care, he would have one less thing to worry about. So far, the teacher was the only person Zelda had taken a fancy to and he might as well take advantage of it.

He got up and carried his plate to the sink. Halfway there, Juana took the dish from him and collected Maddy's, too.

"You can set up your teaching schedule with Juana and Carlos."

He glanced at Juana then at Maddy. "I'll get you Zelda's routine later. Feel free to help yourself to what's in the refrigerator. I head into Los Rios once or twice a week for supplies, so if you need anything, or notice that something needs replacing, let me know."

"Do you have peanut butter?"

He sauntered over to the cupboard and pulled out a jar of Skippy, then walked back to the table and set it down in front of her. "Anything else you want to know?"

She tapped the cap on the jar and smiled. "No. You've made everything perfectly clear."

AWAKE AT DAWN the next morning, J.D. rolled out of bed feeling as if someone had beaten him up during the night. He was stiff and sore and felt worse than he had the day before. In the bathroom, he checked his face in the mirror. Not quite as ugly as yesterday, but no wonder Ms. Perfect Goody Two-shoes had looked at him as if he were Ghengis Khan.

About to turn on the shower, he heard a faint knocking outside. Who the hell would be here this early? Besides Juana and Carlos, who would be here at all?

He quickly brushed his teeth and pulled on a pair

of cargo pants, but by the time he got to the entry, the knocking had stopped.

He opened the door to face an entirely different view of his new employee. With her backside to him, she was folded in half and touching her toes with her fingers. She stood up then, put a foot on the railing in front of her, and stretching out one leg, she bent to touch her knee with her chin. She switched legs and did the same with the other.

Wearing a pair of skimpy jogging shorts and some kind of stretchy top that exposed her stomach, her figure was better than he'd imagined. Though she was petite, her legs were shapely and solid. Her skin was smooth and covered with a light sheen of sweat. He took a step out the door, when pain stabbed in his knee. "Damn. Son of a—"

Maddy swung around. "Good morning to you, too."

"What are you doing out here?"

"I woke early and decided to get some exercise while it was still cool. I couldn't get back in without a key." She smiled cheerily. Would you like me to make some coffee?" she asked almost in the same breath.

Rivera grunted a response, then limped off toward the kitchen.

"I guess that means 'no," Maddy said to his back, not willing to let him ruin her good mood. "So, I'll just hie myself off to wash up, then."

In her room, she slipped off her shoes and socks, then turned on the shower, anxious to get some cool water on her sticky skin. Just as she grabbed the bottom of her shirt to pull it up over her head, she heard a crash, loud cursing, then a *thump, thump,*

thump and a heavy thud. She dropped the shirt and dashed toward the kitchen.

Rivera had looked a little peaked when he'd answered the door. Maybe he'd passed out or something? Hurrying around the corner, she skidded into the kitchen, felt something wet underfoot and lost her balance. Tumbling headfirst into the room, she landed with a splat on the floor—in a puddle of—she lifted her head. Coffee grounds and eggshells. Rivera was sprawled out on the floor next to her, facedown, and he was as still as a corpse.

Seeing only the back of his head, she reached around and placed her fingertips close to his mouth. Hot breath. Good. He wasn't dead.

Quickly, she leaned over his back to see if he was unconscious, but as she did, he rolled toward her, bringing them face-to-face, nose-to-nose, close enough to give mouth-to-mouth resuscitation. Or a kiss.

"Are you all right?" she asked, suddenly a little breathless.

He glared at her.

She pushed off his chest and sat up. "I'm going to assume that means, 'Yes, I'm fine, thanks for asking.'"

No response. But he sat up next to her.

Instinctively, Maddy got to her feet and extended a hand. "Here, let me help."

A muscle twitched high in his cheek, and if looks were bullets, she'd be dead.

"I don't *need* help."

She retracted her hand. "Everyone needs help once in a while. Whether they want it or not is another thing." She brushed the coffee grounds from her thighs and reached for the roll of paper towels on the counter, trying not to watch as Rivera struggled to his feet.

His physical condition bothered him, *that* was obvious. But something more seemed to be going on inside him, something insidious that affected a lot more than just his body.

She knew what that was like. Her own fears had sapped the life right out of her, filled her with self-doubt and rendered her helpless.

After the assault at Georgetown she couldn't stay alone, she couldn't even go outside. Her parents had come to be with her so she could finish her program, and then she'd returned with them to Epiphany. After that, every time she started feeling that life was getting back to normal, something would set her back.

The outside door slammed, and within a few seconds Juana barreled in. Seeing the mess, she let out a string of Spanish phrases, ending with, "*Qué pasa? Madre de Dios!*" which, loosely translated, meant Holy-Mary-Mother-of-God! What has happened here?

"I slipped and fell," Maddy said. Juana snatched the towels from Maddy's fingers and started cleaning. She hoped Juana wouldn't ask for details, because it was obvious by the way J.D. held on to the door frame that he was in pain—and he wasn't about to admit it.

"It's a mess, I know. Here—" Maddy bent down to pick up the coffeepot. "I'll clean up the mess," she said to Juana. "No reason you should do it."

Juana shot Maddy a look that could've wilted an Iowa cornfield. She plucked the coffeepot from

Maddy's hands and shooed both her and J.D. out of the kitchen.

"*I'll* make more coffee," Juana said with authority.

J.D. left first and Maddy followed. He was waiting in the hallway for her when she came out, his eyes flashing. When she reached his side, he said in a low controlled growl, "Don't ever do that again."

Maddy felt as if she were a child standing in front of her father during one of his ruthless scoldings. But she was no longer that insecure little girl.

Confrontation wasn't her best suit, but she raised her chin, anyway. "Don't do what? I told her I fell, and that was the truth." *Think it. Feel it. Believe it.*

Hands clenched at his sides, Rivera's lips thinned, his anger coming at her in waves. "Don't patronize me."

She took a deep breath. "I was offering to help."

"When I need your help, I'll ask for it."

"No you won't. You'd die first."

He showed a brief flash of surprise at the comment, and then just as quickly he turned and hobbled down the hall.

She didn't know what demons warred within this man, but her heart went out to him. He hated himself. But for what, she didn't know.

What she did know was that whether the reason was real or imagined, the pain was the same.

And she knew right then that she was going to do whatever she could to help him.

CHAPTER FIVE

LATER, after a silent breakfast, Rivera handed Maddy a long piece of paper.

The dog list.

Her breakfast literally flipped over in her stomach. Dammit. She'd thought she'd resolved her qualms while she was out running. She'd gone through all the sessions with her therapist in her head, reassuring herself that the only way to conquer her fear was to face it.

The approach had sounded logical and possible in her mind. But the reality was—she still felt queasy.

"Thanks. I'll take care of it," she managed to say.

He frowned, the look on his face saying he'd reserve opinion on that. "Good," he said. "If you have any questions, I'll be outside."

Maddy couldn't move.

When he was gone, Juana said, "He has troubles."

She let out a long breath. "No kidding." She stared at the list. *And so do I.*

"It'll be easy," Juana said. "Just make sure the water tank is full, because it automatically flows into the bowl to keep it fresh and at a certain level.

The food is kept in the cooler, so you only need to fill the dish once a day.''

She could do that. Nothing to it, really. She took a breath.

''Oh, and you need to check later at night to make sure she ate her food. She's a finicky eater.''

There was a lot more on the list than just feeding the dog. Bathing, brushing, giving her vitamins, clipping her nails... But right now, she only had to feed Zelda, no reason to think about the rest. *Focus on the goal.*

After dawdling over her coffee for as long as she possibly could, Maddy went to the back door and peered out.

The doghouse loomed. Somehow it looked large and forbidding.

As Maddy watched the house, Zelda came prancing out, haughty, head held high. She stopped, turned and stared right at Maddy.

And then suddenly the dog seemed to grow. Maddy blinked, but the animal kept getting larger and larger in her eyes until it looked like one of those giant floats in the Macy's Thanksgiving Day parade.

Zelda barked.

Maddy's heart skipped a beat. Her lips felt numb and she couldn't move.

Zelda barked again, and like the snap of a hypnotist's fingers, brought Maddy around. She blinked again and Zelda was her normal size, her mop of a tail motoring back and forth.

A friendly sign—right? With fear in her heart, and feet that felt like battleships, Maddy took a huge breath, then forced herself to move forward.

She descended the stairs like an automaton, and every step she took toward the kennel boomed like thunder in her ears.

Think it. You can do this, Maddy. Yes, you can.

Feel it. She filled her lungs with air, squared her shoulders and kept walking.

Believe it. She still wasn't sure about that part. How could she believe she could do it when she knew she was falling to pieces inside?

Fake it. She'd done that more times than she could remember. And if she faked it long enough, maybe she could believe it.

Clearing her head, Maddy focused on the topiary tree at the other end of the compound. Once she reached the fence, she leaned to unlatch the gate and then, with sweat streaming from every pore and cold stark terror crawling up her spine, she slipped inside.

Carlos appeared from nowhere, and Maddy jumped like a toad. Though he'd scared the bejeebies out of her, he wasn't close enough to see her fear. She forced a smile. How much confidence would he have in a teacher who was afraid of a tiny dog?

Trying her best to look casual, she took a few steps toward the small shed where Juana had said they kept the dog's food.

"Close the gate, Señorita Inglewood," Carlos called to her in spanish. "You don't want the dog to run away."

She stopped abruptly, whirled around and saw the dog heading toward freedom. Oh God. She lurched forward, but her body seemed to move in slow motion. She'd never make it before the dog got out. J.D. would be furious, but even worse, he'd know she was a failure.

Carlos whistled and called the dog, Zelda stopped and looked at the gardener, who was waving a dog biscuit in the air. Come on, Zelda, Maddy urged silently. Choose food over freedom. When the dog circled around and sped toward Carlos, Maddy gave a long sigh of relief and hurried to close the gate.

Then she directed her focus to the water dish—because she absolutely couldn't allow herself to think about the dog who was at this moment prancing toward her. Zombielike, Maddy moved forward, acutely aware that the animal was now hovering somewhere in the vicinity of her ankles. At the tank, she inspected the lever to make sure it was working and that there was water in the bowl, then went to the cooler and dumped food into the dog's china dish.

Sweat rolled down her face and arms and from every pore in her body. Grinding her teeth, she started to walk back toward the gate, safety was within reach—until the dog scurried around and sat in front of her.

Maddy froze.

"She likes you," Carlos called out.

His voice sounded far away.

"She doesn't like very many people."

Oh, lucky me. Still unable to move, Maddy gave Carlos a wan smile, and then stole a look at the dog. "Nice doggy," she whispered. "Now go eat. Chomp, chomp, chomp."

Zelda's right ear perked up.

"Chomp, chomp," Maddy repeated and waved a hand toward the food.

Almost as if she understood, Zelda scurried to her bowl. Maddy practically flew out the gate, up the stairs and back into the house—right into Rivera.

"Oh, jeez. I'm sorry," she sputtered. Damn. She'd probably stepped on his foot or smacked his injured leg. "I...just realized I had to make a phone call," she lied and glanced at her watch. "And I was in a hurry, but gosh, I hope I didn't hurt anything or—"

He smiled. "It'd take a lot more than a bump from someone your size to do me in." Then, as if he might've been too friendly, he frowned. "I'm fine. Go make your call."

Later that morning, still amazed that her boss had actually been civil to her, and exceedingly proud of her small accomplishment with Zelda, Maddy stood in the middle of the old bunkhouse surveying the large rectangular room.

Sepia-toned sunlight filtered in through thin spaces between the weathered slats of wood, creating an eerie, almost romantic feel about the place.

A dozen or so rusty bedsprings were propped on their sides against one wall, empty boxes, old boards, screens and other debris lay in piles about the room. Yes, this room—once it was cleaned up, of course—might work. With only two students, Maddy didn't need a whole lot of room, just space enough to set up a table or two and some chairs. Electricity, or light of some type, would be nice, as would an easel or a chalkboard.

Rivera had said he had neither the time nor the

inclination to do anything for her, so she'd have to improvise with whatever resources she could find. Ms. Devereaux had given her the go-ahead on the supplies and had authorized Harold Martin to add that amount to Maddy's advance. So, before she'd left Iowa, she'd purchased the necessary materials and had brought them along. And now she had her classroom.

Even though she'd secured this job through Mr. Martin, she'd sought it out on her own, and it was the first real job that she'd gotten without her father's assistance. Even Fred Johnson, who ran the video store in Epiphany, had only hired her because her father owned the building he rented. Like everyone else in the small town, Fred sucked up to her father every chance he could.

She heard a noise behind her and turned. Carlos had come in. "What time will we start the lessons?" His eagerness was evident in his tone and the sparkle in his dark eyes.

"Tonight at seven o'clock," Maddy answered in Spanish. She'd asked Juana if they could eat at a regular time each night, 5:30 p.m. "We really don't need to do much, just create a work space and get some light."

Carlos nodded and smiled. Both her students were about the same age, Maddy guessed, mid-forties perhaps, and both, she'd learned, were unmarried.

Maddy wondered how they'd secured their jobs in the first place, but didn't ask. Juana had already gone home to prepare dinner, and Carlos also had work to do.

There would be time to get better acquainted

once she got the classes set up and they settled into a routine.

While she knew little about her new students, she knew even less about her employer. Juana had told her that Rivera had come from Reno, Nevada, and that he'd lived on the ranch as a child. She knew about his crazy aunt who'd willed him the ranch, that he'd had an injury that caused him to leave his job, and that he'd been robbed and beaten up a few nights ago. She wanted to know more about him, but the man wasn't talking. He was a mystery—an intriguing one.

"Carlos, do you know when Mr. Rivera will be back?" she asked, wiping a dusty hand across her shorts. The jogging shorts and top were the only clothes she had that she wouldn't swelter in.

"Soon," Carlos said. "He should be back at any time. I hope they received the supplies he ordered."

She wished she'd known J.D. was going into town because she'd have gone along and bought other clothes to wear. "Did he order something exotic that they might not have?" Maddy conversed in Carlos's native language—and would continue to do so with both her students until they learned some English.

"Just building supplies. But nothing has come in yet. I'm going to ask if I can help him," Carlos added proudly. "I'd like to learn carpentry work."

"Great." But from the response she'd received, Rivera didn't have time for anyone. She spun around. "Is Mr. Rivera a carpenter?"

Carlos nodded. "*Sí.* He's very good."

"Where did he learn that?"

The man shrugged. "He didn't say."

"Well, I hope you're as excited about learning English." She smiled at him, feeling a sense of excitement herself.

"Yes. Very much. If I learn English, I'll be able to get an even better job."

Her mind back on fixing up her classroom, she asked, "Carlos, do you know if there's an electrical connection for this building?"

The main electricity, she'd learned earlier, was provided from the town, which, like California, got its power supply from the Colorado River. But Tripplehorne also had a generator. Carlos had said most of the ranchers in the area had one in case a storm or high winds took out the city power.

She'd also learned that dust storms—with hurricane-like winds—and heavy rain, were typical during the monsoon, which was usually in August.

"I can fix it," Carlos said. "There's also a water supply for the main house and for the dog, so it would be easy to make a connection come off that and bring it here, too."

Maddy stood in the center of the room, surveying what to do first. "Wonderful. But first things first. We need light of some kind and tables and chairs. If we have those, we can get started."

He pointed to a closet in the corner. "Lots of junk is piled up in there," he said. "Chairs, too. Should I look for you?"

"No, I'll do it, thank you."

"Then," he said, "I'll go finish my work."

"Oh, right. I'm sorry I kept you away for so long. You go, and I'll see you later tonight."

After Carlos left, Maddy clicked on the portable CD player she'd brought along, and listening to *The*

Ring Sessions, her favorite Celtic music, she started clearing out a space in one corner of the room.

Above the bedsprings lined against the east wall, some photos, yellowed with age, had been tacked up, and on the shelves were old newspapers, a rusty straight-edged razor and a few other personal items, apparently left by the people who must've worked at the ranch at one time. She read a couple of news clippings and tried to imagine what it had been like to live here fifty years ago.

Before Maddy knew it, an hour had passed, and one whole section of the room was ready for use. She'd even pulled out the weeds that had grown right through the cracks in the concrete floor. Dust lodged in her nose, causing her to sneeze several times. She was hot, sweaty and covered with dirt—but she felt absolutely wonderful.

She couldn't remember the last time she'd been so energized.

As she stood in the middle of the room, she decided to look for the chairs Carlos had mentioned. A rusty lock held the door to the closet shut, but it fell to the floor when she touched it.

She gave the door a yank and stared at the pile of rubbish inside. What a mess.

After pulling out an old harness, some ranch equipment she didn't recognize and a metal tractor seat, she freed up what appeared to be a chair and pulled it out. She saw another and pulled it out, too.

Brushing off the dust with her fingers, she smiled with delight. The chairs were a lovely Eastlake style, just like some of her mother's antiques.

She went into the closet again, hoping for another big find—maybe a table. Peering through the maze, she saw the corner of a trunk covered in cobwebs. She grabbed an old rake that stood against the wall and took a well-placed swipe at it, shuddering as she did.

Just the thought of spiders made her cringe. Especially those indigenous to Arizona—black widows and tarantulas and scorpions, though she didn't know if a scorpion was technically a spider or not. She'd read about the local flora and fauna before she'd come, and she'd done all she could do to keep her imagination from running wild.

But again, that was the old Maddy—not the new warrior woman, fearless and getting more so by the day. She'd made more progress in the past two days than she had in the last year at home.

Feeling the power of her small successes, she made a decision, grabbed the leather handle and pulled out the trunk. She stood for a moment studying it, trying to decide whether she could use it as a table or something.

Using the rake handle, Maddy lifted the cover and let it drop open. The trunk was full and on the top was something wrapped in opaque blue tissue paper. She edged closer, then gently lifted the paper. Inside was a white satin dress. Fascinated, she plucked the garment and shook it out. The dress was ankle length, bias cut with thin spaghetti straps—like something from an old Jean Harlow movie. An evening dress out here in the wilds? A wedding dress, maybe?

She pressed it against her chest, swaying to the music on her CD. Transported to another time, Maddy swirled around and around until, in the middle of a swirl, she stopped abruptly, startled by a long shadow thrown from behind her.

She spun and came face-to-face with the scowling countenance of J. D. Rivera.

"Hi," Maddy said, feeling her cheeks redden, "I was just trying to clean up, to make the place more...uh, conducive to learning. Carlos told me I could find some chairs in there and I found this old trunk—"

Rivera snatched the dress from her, the white fragile satin like neon against his bronze hands. He slowly folded the garment, and the care with which he did so conflicted sharply with the anger she saw in his face.

Then he placed the dress inside the trunk and slammed the lid.

"I thought the trunk could be used as a table, and I wanted to make sure it wasn't full of spiders or...whatever."

He said nothing, then after a moment he pushed the trunk back into the closet, pulled out two more chairs and dropped them next to the others. Hands on his hips, he said, "Anything else you need?"

She bit her lower lip, unsure if she should press her luck. But what the hell? He'd asked—and she might not get the opportunity again.

"Well, now that you mention it, I could use a table—and an easel and a light of some kind. If we're working in the evening, it'll get dark in here."

"Anything else?"

"I could use a car."

He did a double take. "A car? You want me to get you a car?"

"Well, I do need some way to get around."

When he just stood there, she added, "I need to go into Los Rios to buy some clothes." She pointed to her shorts. "This is all I have because everything else is...well, not suitable. And since your aunt told me I could use her car, I thought that would still apply."

"Well, she's not here and neither is her car."

"Oh." The woman had had one, Maddy knew, or she wouldn't have offered it to her. What had Rivera done with it? "Maybe you could rent one for me?"

"Sure. No problem. I'll just take the money out of your salary?"

She laughed. "There wouldn't be much left after that, would there?" Ms. D. had been wealthy, that much Maddy knew. And if she'd left Rivera the ranch, she must've left him money as well.

"Okay, if that's not an option, maybe I could use yours—or you could take me with you the next time you go into town."

"Lady, I can guarantee that you're not going to find what you want in Los Rios."

"They don't sell clothes in Los Rios?"

His gaze scrutinized her. "Not the kind you wear."

He was doing it again—making judgments about her with no information whatsoever. Hands on her hips, she faced him. "It's not like I need an evening gown to teach in a shed. It doesn't *have* to be Versace, but I do need something cooler to wear than what I have."

She saw a flicker of amusement in his eyes.

"Well, you'll just have to improvise." He turned and left.

"Ohhhh," she said through gritted teeth when he was out of earshot. She'd improvise all right. And she wasn't going to worry over what he might think about it, either.

Still, the man puzzled her. How could someone so concerned about an old dress be so obtuse about everything else. And why *had* he reacted so strongly over her touching the dress? It wasn't as if she'd been using it to mop the floor.

Well, the last thing she needed was to get involved in J. D. Rivera's problems. She had enough of her own to deal with; taking care of Zelda, teaching for the first time—and getting through the next few weeks without committing an act of homicide.

When she finished cleaning up and was about to leave, she was surprised to see Rivera and Carlos heading her way with a long table between them. She stepped aside as they came in and placed it in the space she'd cleared.

"Carlos will bring a Coleman lamp for tonight," Rivera said. "The electricity will be connected tomorrow."

"That's wonderful," she exuded, unable to contain her excitement. "Thank you so much," she said to Rivera, then turned to Carlos. *"Gracias."*

"De nada." Carlos smiled and motioned to Rivera. "He asked me to help bring the table."

"Really?" Maddy said, smiling at her boss. Maybe he wasn't such a curmudgeon after all.

As if he knew they were talking about him, Rivera frowned at Carlos and Maddy. On his way out, he motioned to Carlos. "C'mon. There's work to do."

Maddy spent the rest of the afternoon going over her lesson plans. She was confident in her language skills, but she wanted to be sure that her teaching methods would work with Carlos and Juana.

First, she had to assess her students' level of understanding in both English and Spanish. Both knew a scattered assortment of English words and even some short phrases. But what they understood was probably more than they could speak. She also didn't know where they fell on the literacy scale. How knowledgeable were they in their own language? From what she'd seen so far, it looked as if she'd be teaching little more than survival English.

When it was nearly time for dinner, she went back to the house and made a quick call to Kayla, only to hear that Mr. Martin had gone to Europe on business and wouldn't be back for two weeks. She made Kayla promise to ask her father to call Maddy the next time she spoke with him.

After her conversation with her friend, Maddy went out to check Zelda's water and to make sure the dog had eaten. She remembered Rivera saying the animal wouldn't eat if she was traumatized. He hadn't, however, explained how a dog could get traumatized or what one would do in that situation.

After a five minute lecture to boost her courage, Maddy was standing at the gate to the dog compound again, staring at the bowl near the back fence. The water was full and the food bowl was empty. Clearly, it was only Rivera who had been upset by her outburst the other day—not the dog.

Gathering her courage hadn't even been necessary since she didn't need to go inside the kennel.

Zelda pranced over to the fence where Maddy stood. On reflex, Maddy took a step back. Silly, she realized. There was a fence between them. Besides, how would she ever get over her cynophobia if she kept putting off the inevitable? How would she ever get through the list of duties?

But talking to herself didn't seem to help either. Within seconds, she felt clammy and sweaty and her pulse rate launched into rocket speed.

Zelda didn't seem to notice and bounced up and down in front of Maddy, her tail swishing from side to side. Then the dog sat on her haunches, her big brown eyes gazing up at Maddy, begging for a morsel of attention. Even through her fear, Maddy's heart melted. It must be horrible to be cooped up in a pen all day long, no matter how nice the surroundings—sort of like living in Epiphany all her life.

Looking at the dog's appealing face, Maddy was reminded of a small dog on an old television show. Zelda had the same shaggy hair, the same soft soulful eyes, the same black button nose and pink tongue. Her heart told her she should pet the little animal, but her insides quaked at the thought.

If you want something badly enough…

She did. She wanted desperately to live a normal life without trembling every time she encountered a dog. That was the reason she'd started seeing a therapist in the first place, and after a few months, they'd both been pleased with her progress.

So what was the big deal now? Was it the fact that she had to do this alone? Had she only been okay when Dr. Sheridan had been there to hold her hand?

Maddy inhaled, inched forward a step, then knelt to the dog's level. With one hand splayed against the fence for support, she poked a couple of fingers through to pet the top of Zelda's head. No sooner had she touched the surprisingly silky hair, than she yanked her hand back.

Still, a feeling of accomplishment grew in her. That brief touch on her own was enough to give her confidence to try again. On another day.

Rising, she gave Zelda a wave and then left to go back into the house. On her way, she saw movement at the window in the kitchen. Juana, maybe? She hoped it was Juana and not Rivera.

Entering the kitchen, the distinct aroma of Mexican food made her mouth water. Juana was standing at the counter taking containers from the insulated case, and Rivera was standing next to the fridge. "Want something to drink?" he asked.

"Sure," she said with a smile. "What are you selling today?"

"Beer, soda, diet or regular, iced tea and water."

"Wow, one of everything. "Any caffeine-free diet soda?"

He scoffed. "That's like drinking nothing."

"Iced tea is fine." Maddy faced Juana and asked if she was set for the class tonight.

The woman's dark eyes lit up. "Yes, and so is Carlos. Seven o'clock."

Juana's long black hair, pulled back with a barrette at her nape, shone like a sheet of black satin. She wore another long gauzy skirt, this time in a pink floral pattern, and another sleeveless top, also in pink. "I like your skirts, Juana. Very pretty."

And very different from Maddy's makeshift outfit. Late this afternoon after her second shower of the day, she'd hacked off a pair of Donna Karan pants and rolled up the frayed cuffs to make shorts. Then she'd cut the sleeves from one of her blouses and tied the front tails at her midriff. The only flat shoes she had were her jogging sneakers, so she'd put them on without socks.

Her hair hadn't been doing anything wonderful in this heat, either, so she'd tried flipping out the ends with her curling iron, but she now looked as if she'd taken an eggbeater to her head. And Rivera was eyeing her strangely, as if he'd just noticed what a mess she was.

"I feel much cooler this way," she explained before he had the chance to speak.

He shrugged. "I didn't say a word."

But now he was staring at her legs. "However, if you plan to go outside like that, you'd better put on some sunscreen."

He handed her a glass of tea, took out a Dos Equis and a slice of lime, rubbed the rind around the mouth of the bottle and then shoved the whole peel inside. He went to sit at the table where Juana had made two place settings. Maddy followed, sliding into the chair on his left.

"Sunscreen is a good idea—and I could get some in Los Rios if I had a way to get there." She smiled sweetly.

He took a swig of his beer. "I've got work to do."

"So, I guess I'll have to stay inside then."

He glanced at her from the corner of an eye. The swelling on his face had gone down, the whites of his eyes were clear, his irises a dark amber with gold flecks, almost the same tawny color as his hair.

Except for the pale yellow bruises near one eye and a small cut where the lump had been, he looked fairly normal. For the first time, she realized how utterly handsome he was.

His hair, long and reaching beyond his collar, was thick and shiny and a little wild. Realizing she was staring again, she averted her eyes. "Unless you have some sunscreen I can use?"

He placed his arm directly next to hers on the table. "Don't you think it's a little late for me?"

Next to his forearm, hers appeared slight and fragile—and anemic. "It couldn't hurt. I've heard ultraviolet rays aren't good for the skin no matter what the skin tone."

Their arms weren't touching but she felt his heat all the same.

"You probably heard a lot of stuff I don't even think about."

His tone was matter-of-fact, his words almost perfunctory, as if he didn't care about much of anything. But she knew differently. She'd seen how much he'd cared about the dress in the trunk.

So what was he afraid of? Did he believe letting people see he cared would make him seem weak? Or was he afraid that if he cared, he might get hurt?

Maybe if she could get him to talk…

"Well, maybe you *should* think about a lot of things that you don't."

His head snapped up. "All I care about is getting this place done by March first."

Whoa. He'd actually revealed something almost personal. "And if you don't?" she asked, hoping to draw him out.

"If I don't finish by then, I lose the ranch."

"Lose the ranch? I...I don't understand. How can you lose something that's yours?"

He gave a long sigh. "Believe me, if it's not done by then, I'm outta here. Aunt Ethel wanted the place renovated and one of the stipulations was that it be done by March first."

"Why would she do that? That seems an odd requirement."

"Your guess is as good as mine. She was one eccentric lady."

No wonder he was upset about not getting his supplies. Every delay would put him further behind.

"Time to eat," Juana said in Spanish as she brought over their dinner. Rice and refried beans and green-corn tamales. "I don't always make Mexican food," she said. "But this week, that's what's on the menu. If you like it hot, use that salsa." She pointed out a red sauce. "And if you like it not so hot, use that one." She pointed to a green liquid in another bowl.

Not wanting to end her talk with Rivera, Maddy thanked Juana and turned back to her boss, "But you couldn't just leave, could you? What about Zelda and Juana and Carlos? They depend on you."

He picked up a fork. "They got along fine before I came, they'll get along fine when I'm gone." He started to eat. "Better stick to the mild salsa," he said, dumping spoonfuls of the hotter sauce on his own.

"I'm going home," Juana told Maddy. "But I'll

come back in time to clean up and start the lessons.''

Maddy relayed the message to Rivera who simply nodded. After that, they ate in silence until the jingle of a telephone broke the quiet. Rivera fished a small cell phone from the back pocket of his jeans.

''Yeah,'' he said, then listened. ''Great, tomorrow morning between eight and noon. That'll work out just fine.'' He clicked off, pocketed the phone again and then went back to eating.

She wanted to know what was happening tomorrow morning between eight and noon but didn't ask. It wasn't any of her business. Rivera wasn't her business either, but she found herself wondering more and more about him—what secrets lay behind that stoic facade. What had happened to make him so self-contained—so afraid to show his feelings.

Out of the blue, he said, ''That was the Tucson lumberyard. They'll be here in the morning with my supplies.''

''I thought you'd ordered from the store in Los Rios?''

''I canceled that order.'' Frowning, he asked, ''You know how to drive a stick shift?''

''Why?''

''Well, if you do, you can take my truck into Los Rios in the morning to get your sunscreen, and some other stuff I need.''

Dumbstruck, she felt her nerves tingle with excitement.

''So can you drive a manual transmission?''

''Sure. I might be a little rusty, though. It's been a while.'' More than rusty. Her father had taught her when she was sixteen. If she could remember which way the shift went…

“Okay, that’s settled,” he said, glancing at his watch. “And you’ve got a class to give.”

“You’re right. It wouldn’t be good if the teacher was late on the very first day.”

Hurrying, she went to her room for her books and papers and then headed toward the bunkhouse. Anticipation mixed with trepidation; she wanted to do this right—to show everyone that she could do the job. To prove it to herself.

That Rivera trusted her enough to let her drive his car warmed her insides. That he’d made sure she had the table and other things she needed, surprised her—adding another dimension to an already complicated man.

But she needed to remember that just because he’d been accommodating a couple of times didn’t mean he’d turned into Mr. Nice Guy. It didn’t mean he thought differently about her. He might be the most handsome man she’d ever met, but that didn’t change his personality.

When she reached the door, she was glad it was still light enough to see inside. She’d have to keep the Coleman lantern near the door if the electricity wasn’t connected by tomorrow.

Crossing to the table, she saw a large white rectangle on the wall in front of the table. A white board with several washable felt-tip pens on the ledge. Who…? Had Rivera done this? She’d only mentioned her needs to him once, and she hadn’t really expected anything to come of it.

Damn, he was a hard guy to figure. Swinging

around to straighten her papers, she heard voices at the door across the room.

Juana came inside with Carlos close behind.

"Good evening," Maddy said cheerily, then went to the board and wrote in English, Welcome. Today is Wednesday, September 15.

CHAPTER SIX

THE LAST THING J.D. had planned to do was give the petunia the keys to his vehicle, and it grated that he'd had to do it.

But like it or not, he couldn't be in two places at once. It was more important to make sure the delivery from Tucson was complete, and he was the only one who could do that. Besides, surely she couldn't screw up too much, driving a few miles to pick up what he needed in town.

He hoped.

He kicked off the sheet and glowered at the red digital numbers on his clock: 1:00 a.m.—and he was still thinking about the woman in the other room.

After watching her last encounter with the dog, his earlier assessment had been verified. Her screams the other day had been filled with pure terror. But then she'd gone on to act as if her reaction was nothing. She'd even agreed to feed Zelda.

Her determination was admirable, and he'd been surprised by it. What surprised him even more was that he thought about her at all. Since the accident, he hadn't given any woman more than a passing glance.

So why couldn't he get Madeline Inglewood out of his head? Hell, he wasn't even attracted to her.

Short, mousy-blond hair, an average face, average shape, everything about her was average...except...maybe her eyes. Yeah. There was something about her eyes. Not their color—he wasn't even sure what color they were—but their size. Big lost-soul eyes.

Now that he thought about it, her mouth was one of her better features, too. Full lips. Sexy lips.

He scoffed, shook the image of her from his head, rolled over and punched the pillow. *You're losing it, buddy boy.*

A dull thud sounded outside. He sat upright, an instant flashback to the ambush the other night racing through his head. He grabbed a pair of cutoff sweats from the bottom of the bed, pulled them on and slipped quietly across the room to his grandfather's gun cabinet.

He said a quick thank-you to his crazy aunt Ethel for not getting rid of his grandparents' possessions, and then pulled out the 12-gauge, checking to make sure the safety was on. He took a couple shells from the drawer below, loaded the gun and stole toward the bedroom door.

He crept down the long hallway to the back door. The outside light, which he always left on, glowed through the window. Not bright enough to let him see more than a few feet around the steps. If someone was lurking out there, he had good cover.

At the door, J.D. stood to the side and peered through the window. Nothing seemed out of the ordinary. He grabbed a flashlight from the shelf, stuck it under his arm and quietly slipped outside. He waited a moment while his vision adjusted. Then he noticed a light on in the bunkhouse.

The teacher had probably forgotten to turn off the Coleman after her class and more than likely it had attracted some animal. Grumbling, he went down the steps. If an animal tipped over the lamp, the place could go up in flames.

He opened the bunkhouse door with caution. The Coleman was centered on the long table that he'd brought from the house earlier. He smiled, remembering how the teacher's eyes had lit up when she'd seen it. He scanned the room quickly, then walked over to the table.

He set down his gun and flashlight and lowered himself into a chair, leaned back and stretched out his legs. His gaze traveled to the board where the teacher had printed some words in Spanish and then in English. Below was a sentence, written in both languages, using the words she'd written above.

Cleaned up, the place felt warm and inviting, almost the way it had been when he was a kid and the ranch had bustled with life.

Once, when he was seven, he'd helped his grandfather round up stock, and as a treat the old man let J.D. sleep in the bunkhouse with the guys who worked for him. For the first time since his parents had died, he'd felt a part of something important. A sense of belonging.

But all his good feelings were severed when his grandparents passed on and his aunt sent him away. He'd known then what it was like to be truly alone in the world. It wasn't until he joined the navy that he finally felt as if he belonged somewhere. He had a family again.

He rubbed his eyes. Ancient history. His life would never be the same. He had no family—and no future. But it was no more than he deserved. *He* should have died in the crash…not Eric.

Something clattered behind him, and he jerked around. He grabbed his gun in one hand and the flashlight in the other, shining it into the pile of furniture and junk in the small room off to his right.

Shining the light around, a white piece of fabric caught his eye.

He got up, picked up the Coleman and walked toward the storage closet. Getting closer, he saw a small hand and then…big black, scared-to-death eyes staring back at him.

"Benito? What the blazes are you doing in there."

NARROW SLITS of sunlight filtered through the blinds, waking Maddy. She stretched out on the bed, feeling warm and comfortable and satisfied with the way her class had gone last night.

The evening had been extremely productive and she'd felt exhilarated. It'd been difficult getting to sleep after that. In fact, everything was going so well, it was hard to keep her perspective.

She was only going to be here for a short time and then she'd be off to New York. But, while that was exciting, she found she wasn't thinking about the prospect nearly as much as before. Her life on the ranch took up all her thoughts.

Despite Rivera's scowling face and occasional outburst, she'd managed to face one of her greatest fears without running away as she'd done in the past. Her success made her spirits soar.

This morning, she hoped, would bring more of the same. The fact that Rivera had enough confidence in her to let her use his truck filled her with even more good feelings.

She stretched out again and feeling her muscles resist, decided to forgo her morning jog. It was early, and there was plenty of time to feed the dog and have breakfast before she left for town.

A loud banging roused her from the bed. She went to the window and peered out, but couldn't see anything. After a quick shower, she dressed and went outside to the dog compound, reminding herself that she had to brush Zelda and give her vitamins at some point today.

Zelda was huddled near the door of her house with her head on her front paws. That's odd, Maddy thought. Every time she'd seen Zelda, the dog had been bouncing all over the place. But it was early, maybe Zelda liked to sleep in.

Maddy took a few steps closer and as usual her palms became clammy and her heart rate soared. All her rationalizations couldn't stop her body from reacting to the fear deep inside her.

Still, she kept on walking. As she got closer, the dog's tail raised, and then made one listless thump.

Maddy checked the water level in both the bowl and the cooler, filled the other bowl with food and went to kneel in front of Zelda. "What's the matter, pup?"

Maddy slowly inched out a shaky hand, willing herself to stay calm as she touched the dog and then rubbed behind her ear. Zelda, still lying on her belly, pawed closer, her big soulful eyes looking up at Maddy, almost as if she knew how hard it was for Maddy. As if she understood the effort Maddy was making. Her heart melted. So far she'd only done what was necessary for the dog—maybe Zelda just needed a little more attention.

She took a big gulp of air and rubbed behind Zelda's ear one more time before she drew her hand back and stood up on legs that felt like spaghetti.

That was good, Madeline. Good enough for now. She closed the gate behind her and headed toward the house. Her heart was still racing when she saw Juana walking toward her.

"*Hola,*" she said as casually as she could manage. "*Cómo está usted?*"

"I'm fine," Juana replied with a smile and handed Maddy a brown paper sack. "Something for you."

"Really?" Maddy peeked inside the bag and saw a piece of purple fabric.

"It's a skirt like mine," Juana said. "Only smaller to fit you."

"Oh, I love your skirts, Juana. How nice of you to pick one up for me." She pulled out the pale lavender skirt and held it against herself. The fabric was gauzy and crinkled just like the garments Juana wore. Inside the bag was a matching tank top and a fringed shawl in varying shades of purple. "The skirt looks like the perfect size. How much was it? I'll pay you before I go into town."

Juana scowled and shook her head. "It's a gift. My sister made it for you. She likes to sew. It's a way for her to make extra money. She's a widow and has five children to feed."

"Then I insist on paying her."

Juana shook her head. "I do many things for her. So she made it for me to give to you. It didn't cost anything."

From what Juana had said previously, Maddy knew the woman's resources were limited and that she sent most of her money to relatives in Mexico. Maddy couldn't possibly take the skirt as a gift if Juana had spent her hard-earned wages on it. But she'd said she hadn't, and if Maddy insisted on paying, she might offend her.

She reached out and gave Juana a hug. "Well, then, I thank you. What an absolutely sweet thing for you to do."

At that, Juana left and Maddy took the outfit to her room, delighted at the woman's generous and thoughtful gesture. She couldn't remember the last time someone had surprised her with a gift for no reason at all.

A few minutes later, she headed back toward the kitchen. As she got closer, she heard Rivera and Juana talking, but apparently Rivera didn't understand because Juana kept repeating herself.

"Can I interpret?" Maddy asked as she came into the room.

J.D. was sitting at the table, wearing a pair of faded jeans and a white T-shirt, looking sexier than any man she'd ever known. Juana was at the old stove, and next to her on the counter were some eggs, chiles, onions and cheese.

"Mr. Rivera doesn't understand a word I'm saying," Juana lamented as she poured Maddy a cup of coffee and handed it to her.

Maddy laughed. "Well, soon that won't be a problem, will it?"

Maddy sat next to J.D., who kept his gaze focused out the window. Following his line of vision, she saw Carlos standing by one of the outbuildings pulling nails and stripping off some rotted boards. ''What's he doing?''

J.D. made a dismissing gesture. ''Working.''

''Mr. Rivera is teaching Carlos to work with wood,'' Juana added, apparently understanding more English than she'd let on.

''Really,'' Maddy said and smiled at J.D. ''Is that true?''

''Is what true?''

''That you're teaching Carlos to do carpentry.''

''I need a good worker, he needs more money.'' He shrugged and took a swig of his coffee.

And he'd never admit to doing something nice. She'd been wrong about him, and was pleasantly surprised.

''Is that what you did before you came here?''

He shook his head. ''Summer jobs during high school. Are you ready to go into town? I've got a list of things I need.''

''Sure. I'm ready anytime. Just point me to the truck, tell me what you need, and I'll be on the road.'' Elbows on the table, she leaned toward him, smiled and added, ''After breakfast.''

He gave her a funny look, as if he couldn't figure her out. But he wasn't nearly as snarly as when she'd first arrived.

A half hour later she was sitting in the driver's seat of an old green truck, so full of rust it looked as if it might disintegrate on the first big bump in the road. She listened as Rivera gave instructions on the vehicle's idiosyncracies. Holding the driver's door open, he leaned inside, his head next to hers. His hair, still wet from his shower, was combed straight back, but one little loop hung over his forehead.

"Gun the engine when you start it, but not enough to flood it, put the emergency brake on when you stop, and—"

He was still talking, but his instructions blended into a mishmash of words and sentences that she wouldn't remember anyway. All she could think of was how delicious he smelled, clean and fresh like soap and shampoo, and he was so close that if she turned, her mouth would be right next to his.

He leaned across her and shoved the key into the ignition. "Remember those few things and you should be fine." He stepped back.

She took a breath, twisted the key, and when the engine started right off, she felt an immense surge of relief. Last night she'd gone over everything she could remember from her brother's lessons. The H formation, bottom left was first, up, across and up again was second, and straight down was third. Piece of cake.

"Okay?"

When she nodded, he closed the door and stood back. She grabbed the shift and shoved it into what she hoped was first gear, then put pressure on the accelerator. The truck lurched forward, stopped, then lurched forward again. After a few embarrassing minutes bouncing down the road, she jerked toward the highway and out of Rivera's sight.

Nearing the outskirts of town, she cruised by a gas station where a man came out, waving his arms at her as if he wanted her to stop. But she didn't. She couldn't.

First of all, she wasn't sure she'd get the truck

started again if she stopped now. And second, the attack on Rivera the other night was reason enough for her to be cautious. She just hoped there wasn't some kind of emergency.

Driving on, she passed some verdant farmland, and a big sign on the fields that said, La Mancha Ranches. She'd thought Arizona nothing but desert, but she'd been dead wrong. She'd seen miles of citrus groves while flying over Phoenix, and dairy farms and now irrigated fields.

Some parts, like the area between Tucson and Los Rios, the part that stretched into Mexico, was bleak, and she wondered if it had always been that way.

A few miles later, she was driving into Los Rios, and, according to the sign, the town was even smaller than Epiphany.

She spied Masterson's General Store, where Rivera wanted her to go, and maneuvered the truck into one of the diagonal parking spaces, right next to a police car.

A few stores away, four men outside a barbershop stopped their conversation to watch her climb from the truck. They probably recognized the vehicle as Rivera's.

She wondered how well they knew him and if he was as crabby with them as he was with her. She grabbed her tote bag and the list and walked into the store.

The place was a relic of the past. A big room with long tables in the center full of clothing and tools and gadgets of all kinds. On the side where she'd entered were several bins full of penny candy and a checkout counter with no one behind it. Some kind of flour or feed sacks lined another wall. Two large paddle fans hung from the ceiling, both with strips of flypaper dangling from their chains.

It was so quiet, all she heard was the whir of the fans stirring the air. "Hello," she called. "Anyone here?"

"Can I help you?" A man's deep voice came from the back of the room. A ruddy-faced, red-haired man who appeared to be in his mid-sixties swaggered toward her down the center aisle. Like her father, he oozed authority. Except for the bib tucked into his shirt at the neck. Early lunchtime, she guessed.

"Yes. Do you work here?"

"You could say that." His eyes shifted from her face to the big picture window in front where she'd parked Rivera's truck.

"Good. I need several items, and perhaps you can point me in the right direction."

He laughed.

Taken aback, she said, "I'm sorry. Did I say something wrong?"

"I'm the sheriff. Tom Collier's my name." He pulled off the bib, revealing a badge underneath. "My office is in back, but workin' at the store, that's Clyde's job." He nodded toward the entry just as she heard a bell jingle.

She swung around. A tall lanky man came in, one of the guys who'd been standing in front of the barbershop. Apparently business wasn't exactly hopping in Los Rios.

"And who might you be, young lady?" the sheriff asked.

"Madeline Inglewood." She offered her hand. "I work at the Tripplehorne Ranch."

The other man ambled inside and went around the counter. "Can I help you, ma'am?"

"Young lady here is stayin' at the Tripplehorne," the sheriff said. "She probably came for those supplies, Clyde."

"Not likely. Rivera canceled on me. How's that for gratitude?"

Maddy glanced from one to the other. "Actually, I'm interested in some clothing."

"You don't say."

The sheriff's patronizing tone irked her, but she decided to ignore it. "I didn't anticipate the climate very well and brought the wrong kind of clothes."

Collier gave her another once-over. "Uh-huh. The wrong kind you say. What exactly are you doing out there?"

She didn't like the innuendo. "I'm doing exactly what I came to do." She turned to Clyde. "Do you have any clothing in a size four?"

Clyde laughed, snorting several times in the process. "We're a general store, ma'am. Not one of those fancy bo-tiques. We don't have much in the way of clothes and what we do have comes in small, medium and large." He gave the sheriff a covert look and chuckled. "Oh, we also have extra large and jumbo size."

"You're not going to find what you want in Los Rios," the sheriff said.

She squared her shoulders, an uneasy feeling settling in her bones. She forced a smile. "You may be right, but I'd like to see for myself."

"Sure. Help yourself." Clyde opened his arms

in an expansive gesture. ''What we have is right on that table, except the overalls are hanging near Sheriff Collier's door in the back.''

She walked to the table he'd indicated and began sifting through the piles. T-shirts, underwear, hats and a few blouses were all lumped together. Most of the T-shirts had some cutesy saying on the front and the rest were so ugly it was hard to believe anyone had actually purchased them to sell. Happily, on one table she found a pair of black rubber flip-flops and slipped one on her foot. It fit perfectly.

After that she found a couple of T-shirts in size small, one pink with a roadrunner on the front and one army green with the American flag and some kind of gun emblem espousing the right to bear arms. Not exactly what she'd hoped for, but right now she couldn't be choosy. She also picked up two pairs of boxer shorts and a man's white undershirt, the kind without sleeves. She decided it would work as a tank top and grabbed three of them before she went to the back where the bib overalls were hanging.

''You're not staying long, are you?'' The sheriff suddenly appeared beside her. He leaned against the wall, his manner disturbingly aggressive. *Power trip.*

''Just the time specified in my contract,'' she answered casually, wanting him to know she wasn't easily intimidated. She continued thumbing through the overalls, looking at tags for the size.

''Might be wise not to stay too long. Considering.''

Annoyed at the sheriff's obvious bullying, she faced him directly. "Considering what?"

"That employer of yours. Bad temper. Unpredictable. He was a troublemaker when he lived here before, and I don't see that he's changed much. Got kicked out of the military after he killed a man."

Oh, God. She couldn't suppress her shock, and from the sheriff's satisfied expression, that was exactly the response he'd wanted.

"Couldn't prosecute him for it because no one knew what actually happened. But since you're new here, I figure you ought to know what you're getting yourself into. Might want to be extra careful while you're staying out there."

The military? Yes, she could've guessed that from the precise way Rivera dealt with things, his no-nonsense way of getting things done. His pride.

She pulled the items she wanted and laid them over one arm, taking her time going to the counter. "I know exactly what I'm doing, Sheriff, so no need to worry." She turned to Clyde. "My employer needs a few other things, too." She pulled out Rivera's list and handed it to him.

Clyde shoved it back at her. "Sorry, ma'am. We're outta all that."

The hair on the back of Maddy's neck bristled. She pointed to the shelf behind him. "Then I'll have that box right there."

"That one's reserved," Clyde said without even glancing behind him. "I sure feel awful about this, ma'am. Your boss probably won't like it much either."

Her annoyance mushroomed into anger, but she held herself in check as she paid for the clothing.

When Clyde put the change into her hand, she said sweetly, ''No problem at all. I'm sure Mr. Rivera will get the items elsewhere, just as he did his lumber. I'll tell him about your concern, though.''

Bag in hand, she sauntered toward the door, and as she did, she heard the sheriff say, ''If I were you, I'd be careful out there, ma'am. I'd be very careful.''

Though she wanted to get away as fast as possible, Maddy made herself stroll to the truck. Earlier, she'd planned to do a little sight-seeing, investigate the town, perhaps even stop for a coffee and meet a few of the locals. But after her experience at the general store, she didn't feel much like socializing.

Climbing into the truck, she saw Clyde and the sheriff standing in the doorway. Two men walked over from the barbershop to stand with them, and they all watched her fumble with the keys.

The engine started immediately, and thank God, the truck didn't jerk when she put it into gear.

Driving down the narrow highway, she fought the urge to believe the worst. She didn't like either of those men, but she didn't know Rivera all that well either. According to the sheriff, J.D. was a hothead, prone to violence and not to be trusted.

In the little time she'd spent with Rivera, she knew he was carrying a heavy burden. Had he really killed a man?

What reason would the sheriff have for lying or for wanting her to distrust J.D.? Why wouldn't Clyde sell her the supplies? Why would Ms. Devereaux bequeath the ranch to her nephew with such strange stipulations? Questions and more questions. All without answers.

Passing the same gas station as before, she saw the man who'd been waving at her, but this time he was pumping gas in someone's car.

She couldn't just drive on by without finding out if something had been wrong, so she pulled into the stall next to him, rolled down her window and waited. When he finished what he was doing, he came over.

"Hello," she said. "I saw you waving at me when I drove by earlier. I'm sorry I couldn't stop just then."

He gave her a curious look and a big white smile. "I saw the truck and thought you were my friend James. Now I'm wondering what a beautiful woman is doing with his truck."

"James? Oh, do you mean J.D.?"

"James Devereaux Rivera. One and the same."

"You're friends?"

"Since we were kids." He leaned an elbow against the truck door. "Didn't see much of him between then and now, not till he moved back a few weeks ago." He was looking at her with open curiosity. "You must be the teacher."

She nodded. "Yes. I'm Madeline Inglewood." She reached out to shake his hand. "People call me Maddy."

"Grady Holt, gas station owner and father to be."

Maddy smiled. "Congratulations." It was a relief to meet a nice friendly man. Especially compared to the two she'd just left.

"Maybe you can help me. Do you know if

there's another store nearby where I might be able to get some items for my boss?''

''Well, that depends on what he needs.''

She pulled out the list and showed it to him.

Two deep lines creased his forehead. ''Clyde didn't have any of these?''

She shook her head. ''No. Not any he was willing to part with.''

Grady chewed on his bottom lip, then snatched the list from her fingers. ''Can you mind the station for a few minutes?''

''Me? I wouldn't know what to do.''

''Just sit over there and look pretty. If anyone comes, you tell them to do it themselves, or come back in a half hour when I get back. Or—'' he winked ''—you can pump gas if you want.''

''Okay,'' she agreed. She could certainly pump gas if she had to.

Grady opened the door for her and took her arm as she stepped down from the truck. He handed her a key. ''That's for the door. If you have any problems, just lock up. Anyone comes by, tell them I'm closed. Just don't let anyone get gas and leave without paying.''

She nodded, not sure how she'd stop someone if they decided to do that.

''Great.'' He winked at her again, turned and strode over to a shiny new, red pickup. ''By the way, my wife, Annie, is supposed to be here any minute. Keep her company, will you?'' He hopped inside the truck and in seconds was spitting gravel down the road toward Los Rios.

CHAPTER SEVEN

BY THE TIME she returned to the ranch, Maddy was feeling quite pleased with herself. She'd met Annie Holt, and they'd gotten along well. Eager to tell Rivera what she'd accomplished, she drove the truck around the house to the back.

Carlos was on a ladder pounding nails on the side of one of the buildings, and Juana was standing below handing him something Maddy couldn't see. J.D. was nearby, next to a pile of lumber. He was gesturing to a young Hispanic boy.

She got out of the truck, and as she did, the boy, who appeared to be about ten, stumbled over a pile of wood and let out a string of expletives in Spanish. J.D. helped the boy up and brushed him off.

"Hi," she said, walking over to them.

The boy slipped behind Rivera, who wiped the smile off his own face the moment he saw her.

"You shouldn't swear like that," Maddy said to the boy in his own language. "It's not respectful, even if the person doesn't understand you." His eyes got big. She turned to Rivera and smiled.

"How'd you do?" he asked.

"Great! It's all in the back."

He strode toward the truck, and as he did, the boy took off in the other direction toward Carlos.

"No problems?"

Maddy followed, trying to keep up with his long strides, but she remained a couple paces behind. ‘‘Yes. The man at the store, Clyde, I think his name was, wouldn’t sell me any of the items on your list.’’

J.D. kept walking. ‘‘I thought you said you got it all?’’

‘‘I did. But only because when I was driving back, I went into this gas station and talked to your friend.’’

‘‘You saw Grady?’’

‘‘Uh-huh. I didn’t know he was your friend when I stopped. He was a big help in getting your stuff.’’

She caught up to him just as she finished her sentence.

He rounded on her. ‘‘You asked Grady to help you?’’

She flinched at his harsh tone. ‘‘No. I didn’t. I told him what happened at the general store and asked if he knew where else I could go to find what you needed. Then he took it upon himself to go and get everything on the list. I thought it was very nice of him to do that.’’

Rivera slammed down the tailgate, dragged out a bag of cement, slung it over his shoulder and looked her in the eyes. ‘‘What you think doesn’t matter. I asked you to do something, not have someone else do it.’’

She stiffened. ‘‘He’s your friend and he wanted to help.’’

The scowl on his face deepened. His lips thinned. ‘‘If I need his help, I’ll ask for it.’’

She stifled a sarcastic retort and gritted her teeth.

How could anyone be so ungrateful? So rude? So…so awful.

She took a deep breath and studied the man in front of her. How deep was his hurt that he couldn't let anyone get close to him—not even someone he considered his friend?

Maddy felt his pain almost as if it were her own. She knew what being alone was like—knew how isolation could destroy a life. The need to help him grew more intense.

But no matter what she did, she couldn't seem to avoid upsetting him. Well, maybe that was okay. If expressing her opinion was the only way to get a rise out of him…so be it. An emotional reaction, even an angry one, was better than no reaction at all.

Besides that, she rather liked her new persona. It was refreshing not to play the senator's daughter all the time. She liked saying what she thought and doing what she wanted.

Smiling to herself, she grabbed a small sack from the truck and followed Rivera. Coming up behind him, she asked, "Where do you want me to put this?"

He jumped at her voice, apparently not expecting her to follow. When he turned to look at her, she thought the hardness in his eyes had softened a little. He shook his head and pointed to a shelf next to the building. "Over there."

She carried her bag to one of the shelves and set it down, then went back to fetch another load. She made a few more trips until all that was left were the heavier bags. She walked over to where Carlos was working. "Who's the little boy?"

"Benito Perez," Carlos said, continuing to pound nails. "Mr. Rivera gave him some money, and the boy didn't want to take it without doing some work."

Rivera's charity surprised her.

"He can't be more than ten. Shouldn't he be in school?"

Carlos shrugged. "His parents are in Mexico, and he's staying with relatives."

"I guess the schools in Mexico have a different schedule, huh?"

"I don't think he goes to school."

Maddy glanced at Rivera. Perhaps he wasn't aware of the boy's situation. She crossed to where he was working on one of the other outbuildings.

"What now?" he asked when she reached him.

"Did you know that little boy doesn't go to school?"

J.D. looked at Benito. "He's learning a trade."

"But he's too young for that."

"A kid's never too young to learn how to take care of himself. And if he's going to remain in the States, he'll need a trade."

"There are child labor laws."

J.D.'s shoulders visibly tightened. "Do you know anything about Benito's situation?"

"No. But I do know that a ten-year-old should be in school getting an education that just might get him a better job than pounding nails for minimum wage for the rest of his life."

J.D. banged in another nail. "He can't go to school here because he's just visiting."

True. But if what Carlos said was true, the boy didn't go to school in Mexico, either. "Maybe he could come along with Juana and Carlos in the evenings. It wouldn't be any harder for me to have another student sitting in, and it would benefit him to learn English, no matter what he does in the future. I'd be happy to talk to his guardians about it."

A long silence ensued, until finally J.D. said, "I'll ask. If he wants to do it, fine. If not, then you'll drop the idea."

"Okay, that's fair." She smiled and then added, "So what else can I do?"

He stopped his raised hammer in midair. "You never quit, do you?"

She shook her head and smiled. "Nope. So you might as well give me a job."

"You have a job."

"Something more."

"Taking care of Zelda and teaching isn't enough?"

"No. I have hours to spare." She gave him a big-eyed pleading look.

He frowned and turning away, grumbled, "If I can think of anything, I'll let you know. In the meantime, stay out of my hair."

AFTER RIVERA TOLD HER to get lost, Maddy went into the house, smiling to herself because—despite what he'd said—he'd definitely acquiesced a little.

The rest of the afternoon she busied herself, checking on the dog first, and then trying on the clothes she'd purchased at the store. She made herself a new wardrobe by cutting off the legs on one pair of bib overalls and the bottoms off all three of the men's sleeveless undershirts so they didn't hang down to her knees. After locating an ancient washer and dryer in a storage room, she washed and dried everything, including her jogging outfit. The bib overalls, though a size small, were still big and baggy, so she washed and dried them a couple of times hoping they'd shrink.

So much for being a fashion plate, but at least she'd be comfortable. When she brought her load of clothes into the kitchen to fold, she found Juana cleaning the oven.

"What are you doing?" she asked the woman. "I thought you weren't going to use the kitchen until it's renovated?"

"That was his idea," Juana said, angling her head toward the window and J.D. outside. "Not mine. I figure if I clean it, there's no reason not to use it." The woman spoke Spanish, sprinkling in the few English words she'd learned in Maddy's class.

"I agree with you," Maddy said in English. Immersion really was the best way to teach a second language.

Juana repeated what Maddy had said, then translated it into Spanish. She smiled widely.

"Great," Maddy said, going back to the language they both knew. "Can I help? If we work together, we can get it done in no time."

"No, no." Juana shook her head. "Señor Rivera wouldn't like that. He won't like me doing it, but he'll get even angrier if I let you."

"What's with him?" Maddy said hotly. "Why on earth is he so stubborn?"

"He's a proud man," Juana said. "If a man's pride is all he has, he must be careful to protect it."

"I don't understand. He already has others doing extra work, why won't he let me?"

"You'll have to ask him that. He doesn't confide in me, either." Juana smiled and shook her head.

"What do you know about Benito?" Maddy asked, pointing out the window at the little boy.

"Benito?" Juana answered. "He says he's staying with relatives. Lots of people come up from Mexico to work for a while, then go home. Or they stay and send money to their families."

"But he's a little boy! He shouldn't be working. He should be in school."

"If he has a family and he earns money, he'll send it to them. It's good for him to learn how to work hard while he has the opportunity. If he learns a trade like carpentry, it's even better. Mr. Rivera knows that."

Maddy still couldn't accept the idea that a child of ten was working anywhere, except maybe mowing lawns or taking out the trash at home.

"Have you ever been to Mexico?" Juana asked.

"No." She'd gone on vacation with her parents every summer to a cabin in northern Minnesota because her dad liked to fish.

"Sometimes," Juana continued, "it's hard to understand another culture without experiencing it."

Maddy felt her face go hot. It was true. But while she might not understand the culture, she knew without a doubt that the boy would have a better chance at almost anything if he learned some English. "Maybe I should visit Mexico while I'm so close," Maddy added. "And learn firsthand."

Juana smiled. "Puerto Peñasco is only a few hours away."

"Really? That close."

"Mexico is very different than where you come from."

To Maddy, the differences were the exciting part. But she didn't think that was what Juana meant. And though she'd love to visit Mexico, it wasn't likely she'd be going anywhere during her brief stay at the ranch. Not without a car or someone to drive her. "I probably won't get a chance to do that, though. And when this job is finished, I'm moving to New York."

"New York," Juana repeated. "You can fit many towns like Puerto Peñasco into New York City."

Maddy had barely thought about the move or the new job in the past few days, but with the reminder, a fresh shiver of excitement skittered through her.

"I've heard it's dangerous there," Juana said with concern.

Maddy's mother's harangue about that very thing echoed in Maddy's head. Life was definitely different since 9/11, but no matter what anxiety she felt about that, she agreed with those who said people's lives must go on as usual.

Besides, the UN job would be the opportunity of her life and no matter what qualms she had about making the move, if they offered her the job she was going to take it.

"Won't your family miss you when you move away?"

"Yes, of course." Maddy sighed, remembering that she needed to call her parents. A knot formed in her stomach just thinking about it; she knew exactly how the conversation would go, and then she'd hang up feeling bad about being an ungrateful daughter.

"Maybe you'll find yourself a nice man in New York, get married and have lots of children."

"Nope," Maddy replied quickly. "That's not in my game plan."

Juana gave a wave of dismissal. "You just haven't found the right man."

"There isn't a right man. Besides, I don't need a man to complete my life or be happy," she said. It wasn't that she didn't *ever* want a relationship, she just didn't want another person controlling her life. And she didn't want to put herself in a position where that might happen.

She had to make it on her own before she could even give a thought to a relationship.

On that note, she steeled her resolve and went to make the call to her parents. There was no point in avoiding it any longer.

Avoidance had been her modus operandi all her life. She was an expert on it.

But no more. Not with her mother or father.

Not with anyone.

Michael Bruchetti would be proud.

J.D. FINISHED UP the last of his work and headed for the house. Now that some of the building materials had arrived, he'd start on the interior tomorrow. Because his aunt had had the plans, the supply list and blueprints drawn up by professionals, he only needed to assess what he could do himself and what he'd have to hire other people to do—if he could find anyone who'd work for him.

He'd begun on the outside—tearing apart whatever needed replacing. He'd sold Ethel's car for immediate cash to purchase some of the supplies so he could move ahead. He'd used his own disability checks to make up the difference. Once the trust kicked in next week, he'd see what he could do about hiring some help. Carlos had mentioned he knew a few people who might be available.

But first, J.D. had to have a talk with Grady.

His friend's motives were good, but dammit, he didn't need anyone fighting his battles. Especially not a family man with a wife and a baby on the way.

If the big guns in town wanted to shut J.D. out, they would not look favorably on anyone who stuck by him. And he damn sure wasn't going to be responsible for destroying another man's life.

Going to his room to shower and change, he heard Maddy's voice in the living room, probably talking on the phone. He wanted to tell her he wouldn't be there for dinner, so he continued down the hall.

"I'm working," he heard Maddy say. "I *have* a job right here, and when it's finished I'm going to New York. The personnel director assured me I was perfect for the position, and he all but told me the job was mine."

There was a long pause, and J.D. assumed she was listening to someone talk. He hadn't planned on eavesdropping, but couldn't tear himself away.

"I'm sorry you feel that way, Mother." Another pause. "I know you want me there, but anyone could do what I was doing. Randy can do it, and it would be good for him to know Daddy needs him. He wouldn't have started refurbishing old houses if he'd had something else to do. He'd be a big help to Daddy and—''

He heard a deep sigh. ''Yes. No. That's not a problem. This place? It's…nice. Really. And my students are wonderful. For the first time I feel like I'm doing something worthwhi—'' She stopped again, as if interrupted. Then she said more softly, ''I *have* to do it, that's why. For me. I've worked hard and the job at the UN is the culmination of all I've worked for. I want it more than anything. Can't you understand that?''

He felt like slime. He shouldn't be listening. Just as he took a step to leave, she said, ''I'm sorry, I can't talk anymore, Mother.'' Her voice cracked on the last word.

A hot surge of protectiveness pulsed through him.

''I'll call you later.'' Another pause before she said even more softly, ''Yes, I promise.'' He heard the receiver clunk down and after that, total silence.

That was definitely his cue to leave. Turning, he retreated a step, but stopped when he heard a soft sob. Hell, now he had to get out of there for sure. But just then Maddy came through the doorway, and when she saw him standing there, she seemed embarrassed and quickly wiped away the moistness on her cheeks.

''I was just coming to tell you and Juana that I won't be here for dinner tonight,'' he told her.

She took a shaky breath and looked away. ''Juana's not here. Just me. I—I was on the phone.''

He shifted his weight and crossed his arms over his chest to fight the crazy urge he had to give her a sympathetic hug. ''Well, I wanted you both to know I won't be back until late, but if you need anything...you can get me on my cell phone."

She forced a smile and nodded. "Okay. I'll tell Juana. Anything else?"

Damn. She looked as if she really needed a hug. He shook his head. "No, nothing else." And this time, he managed to get out of there.

"JUANA, PLEASE GO HOME and don't worry about dinner, I can make my own." Maddy stood at the kitchen door looking out. "I can't see any reason for you to cook for one person."

Feet apart and arms akimbo, Juana's black eyes flashed. Maddy wasn't sure Juana always understood the more formal Castilian Spanish Maddy had been taught in college.

"It's my job. If you're here, I'm cooking."

It was obvious Juana did understand. It was also obvious Maddy wasn't going to get Juana to budge on the issue. "Okay, but only under one condition."

Juana's forehead furrowed. "What condition?"

"That you eat with me." Maddy saw movement outside the window. Carlos and Benito were both still working. She cleared her throat. "I mean...that you and Carlos have dinner with me."

The expression on Juana's face said she was going to say no, so Maddy quickly said, "Mr. Rivera told me I could choose where to conduct the class—and tonight, I've decided to do it in this kitchen. It'll be fun to do our lesson over dinner. That would mean you could both go home early and enjoy more of the evening with your families."

Juana thought for a moment, then finally said,

"Okay. But I don't know how Carlos will feel about it."

"I'll ask him. And since the stove is clean, why don't you cook here, and then I can watch and maybe even learn." Maddy smiled.

Juana nodded, albeit grudgingly. She obviously liked to do things her own way. "I'll go and get the food."

"I'll come with you to help."

"Thank you for offering," Juana said, "but my sister is picking me up and she'll have her children with her. The car will be full."

Juana's sister was a widow with five children, Maddy remembered.

"She drops me off in the morning so she can use my car during the day. Then she picks me up when I'm ready."

Juana's life seemed more complicated than Maddy had imagined. "Okay. I'll wait here until you return. I'd love to meet your sister, though, so I can thank her for the lovely outfit. She does beautiful work."

Juana beamed at the compliment. Maddy knew that—in addition to sending money to her family in Mexico—she helped her sister, too. Maddy liked *that* kind of family togetherness. The kind that gave without expectation. The kind that didn't suffocate a person…

"So I'll go tell Carlos the plan, and you let me know when your sister arrives, okay?"

"Okay." Juana nodded.

Carlos was pounding nails into the siding on the building next to the bunkhouse and Benito was pounding right alongside him. Maddy hadn't formally met the boy yet and was anxious to do so.

Carlos stopped hammering as soon as she reached him. "*Hola,* Carlos." As he nodded his greeting, she continued in Spanish, "I see you have an assistant today."

The boy gave her a fleeting glance, his dark eyes wary.

"This is Benito. I'm teaching him what I'm learning from Mr. Rivera."

She said hello and smiled at Benito, but the boy averted his gaze, obviously uncomfortable in her presence. Maybe she shouldn't have reprimanded him for swearing. He spoke to Carlos in a low muffled tone and then quickly retreated to the other side of the building.

"That's great, Carlos. But I still believe he's a little young to learn a trade."

"The sooner the better, *señorita.*"

She decided not to push the issue since J.D. was going to follow up with the boy's relatives about attending her class. "I guess you know best," she said, then told Carlos about the plan for a dinner class tonight. He seemed delighted.

She returned to the house just in time to meet Juana's sister. The woman was delicately pretty with soft brown eyes and shiny auburn hair pulled back from her face. She didn't seem old enough to be married, much less have five children.

"This is my sister, Mariela Ortega-Macario," Juana said proudly. Five pairs of eyes peered at Maddy from inside the car. The children ranged in age from about one year to ten or so.

"Nice to meet you, Mariela. Thank you so much

for making me the beautiful outfit. The clothes you make are lovely enough to sell in a boutique.''

Mariela thanked Maddy, and Juana added, ''I'm teaching her the English I'm learning. When she knows a little, it'll be easier for her to sell her clothes here.''

An idea suddenly occurred to Maddy. ''Why doesn't she just come with you and learn for herself?''

''She has no one to watch the babies.''

''Bring them along. Make it a family learning experience. I'd love to have you all in class.''

When the women still seemed hesitant, Maddy added, ''Well, why don't you give it a little thought, Mariela? Juana can give you all the details, and if you decide to come, I'd be very pleased.''

Later, when Juana returned at five with the ingredients to make their dinner, Maddy was in the kitchen cleaning the soot-stained fireplace.

Juana's eyes narrowed in obvious displeasure.

''What? This fireplace is beautiful under all the grime. Natural stone. Come here and look.'' Maddy motioned Juana over.

Nodding, Juana said, ''Yes, but you're doing a lot of work for nothing. Mr. Rivera plans to tear it all out.''

''Why on earth would he want to do that? With the exception of a few loose pieces, it's magnificent.''

''I don't know why, all I know is that he said it has to go. That was Ms. Devereaux's plan.'' She motioned to the long roll of papers on the counter in the corner. ''And if you want to learn how to make mole poblano, you need to stop cleaning and come over here.''

''Okay,'' Maddy said, wiping her hands on her bib overalls. ''I'll go wash up first.'' She walked to the counter. ''Wow, that's a lot of stuff. Are you making dessert, too?'' Maddy pointed to the chocolate.

''Mole poblano is made with chocolate.'' She picked up a chicken and brought it to the sink.

''Chicken and chocolate? And all those other ingredients, too?''

Juana shooed her off. ''Chicken and Mexican spiced chocolate. I make it like my grandmother did.''

''Lots of work, huh?''

''Yes. It is.'' Juana smiled then. ''Most good things are lots of work.''

As Maddy turned to go wash up, Juana said, ''My sister and her children will be coming with me to class on Monday.''

''Great.'' Smiling to herself, Maddy went down the hall to her room. What Juana had said was exactly right. Nothing at Tripplehorne Ranch seemed easy, but Maddy felt a real sense of satisfaction in what she'd achieved here so far.

Good things *were* a lot of work—but the results were worth the effort.

CHAPTER EIGHT

"HEY, BUDDY," J.D. said on his way into Grady's tiny office in one corner of the gas station.

"James D., what a surprise." Grady immediately jumped from his chair and pulled over another for J.D., scraping it noisily across the concrete floor. "I've had the pleasure of your company twice in two days. Must be a record."

"Yeah. Guess so."

"C'mon. Have a seat. It's slow tonight, and I was going to close early anyway. Thought I'd give it another fifteen minutes, but what the heck." Grady flipped over the sign on the door to Closed, then went over and dropped into a swivel chair.

But J.D. wasn't there to visit, and he didn't want his friend to think he was. Instead of sitting comfortably on the offered seat, he perched on the corner of Grady's desk.

"Uh-oh. I can see right now this isn't gonna be a nice little chitchat." Grady frowned, leaned back in his chair and crossed his arms. "What's on your mind, my friend?"

"It's about this morning."

"This morning?" Then, as if he'd just remembered, he added, "Oh, you mean when your friend Maddy came by?"

"First—she's not my friend. She's an employee,

hired by the old bat herself. And second, she's not the reason I came by."

Grady gave one of his wide boyish smiles. "Good. I'd hate to see a sweet girl like her get on your bad side," he said.

"I don't have a bad side," J.D. grumbled. It was tough to stay angry at Grady. "But if I did, you're the one who'd be on it."

Grady's eyebrows arched, then his expression grew serious. "Nothing wrong with a friend helping out a little, is there?"

"Yes, there is. I told you that right off." J.D. rose abruptly and paced the floor in front of the battered metal desk. "You've got a wife and a kid on the way. I'm going to be out of this place sooner or later, and you and your family will still be living here. No reason for you to get yourself on the wrong side of the First Family, is there?"

"Nope. No reason—except that I wouldn't respect myself much if I didn't stand by what's right. I'm your friend, James."

J.D. took a deep breath. "The last guy who stood by me is dead."

"It wasn't your fault."

J.D.'s chest suddenly felt hollow. He gave a wry laugh and his voice was hoarse. "Yeah, tell that to Eric."

Ignoring the comment, Grady got up, lumbered over to the small refrigerator and pulled out two beers. Handing one to J.D., he said, "Let's have us a toast to friendship, then."

J.D. snatched the beer from Grady's hand. "You hear anything I said?"

"Nope. So you might as well quit yammering about it."

J.D. shook his head at his buddy's stubbornness. Grady wasn't going to listen to reason. And if that was the case, J.D. would have to be very careful. He might even have to stay away from his friend or even sever their relationship.

"So," Grady said, sitting down again. He motioned for J.D. to do the same. "I want to hear more about Madeline. Annie met her when she was here and they really hit it off."

"Temporary employee. Short term. She'll do her job and in a few weeks, she'll be gone."

As the words left his mouth, a car pulled up and Annie stepped out. "I think that's my cue to leave," J.D. added.

Annie was tall, blond and wholesome. She and Grady made a perfect couple and they'd have great-looking kids and would live happily ever after—as long as Grady didn't get involved with problems that weren't his business.

The big guy flew to his feet and opened the door for his wife. Annie's eyes flicked over J.D., then to the beer in his hand. She cleared her throat. "Sorry, I didn't mean to interrupt the party."

"Hi, Annie." J.D. set his beer down. "You're not interrupting anything. We're finished here."

"Well, don't leave on my account." Annie smiled at Grady, who reached over and gave her a squeeze.

"Annie's got one of those women's parties to attend at her mother's tonight. So you might as well stick around for a while."

"It's not a women's party. It's a bridal shower

for Angela MacIntyre.'' She turned to J.D. ''Weren't you two in the same class in high school?''

''I don't remember anything from that long ago.''

Grady nudged J.D. and clicked his tongue. ''You don't remember the park? The bandstand? Man, you're really losing it.''

J.D. did remember Angela. At least he remembered her father having him arrested and the sheriff beating the crap out of him when he refused to get into the car. He remembered Angela telling him she couldn't see him anymore because her father didn't want her dating a Mexican. He plastered on a fake smile. ''I recall the important things. Guess that wasn't one of them.''

''Well, I gotta go,'' Annie said. ''Please say hello to Maddy for me, will you? And tell her I'll pick her up early on Saturday morning.''

''Saturday?'' J.D. asked. Not that he was really interested. Whatever Maddy did on her own time was her business, not his.

''Yes, Saturday—9:00 a.m.'' Then Annie kissed her husband and sashayed out the door. ''I probably won't be home till late, sweetie. You two have fun.''

Much later, after a few too many beers and far too much reminiscing about boyhood pranks, J.D. was on his way home. By the time he hit the turnoff to the ranch, it was close to midnight. Ever since the discussion with Grady about Maddy, he hadn't been able to get the woman out of his mind.

She'd grown up a senator's daughter, was used to the luxuries that came with it, and he'd expected her to be a spoiled little rich girl. But she'd surprised him.

In one afternoon she'd turned the bunkhouse into a workable classroom, and he'd been surprised at her resourcefulness. On her first night teaching, he'd been standing outside and had caught her in action. Watching her, he found that his own interest was piqued, and for the longest time he just stood there absorbing the lesson as if he were one of her students.

Either she'd woven some kind of spell over him or she was just that good. In fact, she seemed so comfortable teaching, she could've been at the job for years.

Without the beauty-shop hairdo and her fancy designer clothes, she seemed more real. But J.D. knew better than anyone, new clothes didn't change who a person was.

She was still a senator's daughter, and he was the son of a *pizcador,* a Mexican field hand. A man who'd married a woman no one considered him good enough to marry, a man who'd supposedly started a fire and killed two people in the process. How much of it was true didn't matter—not to the people of Los Rios.

Beaten and bruised, Raphael Rivera had somehow escaped from the Los Rios jail and had fled to Mexico with his wife and baby son. J.D.'s mother had never seen her parents again until she was dying.

Right or wrong, J.D. carried his father's legacy, and the powers that be in Los Rios would never let J.D. forget who he was. *He* couldn't forget it.

At first he'd wanted to succeed to prove to everyone he was better than they thought he was. But in the end, he really wanted to prove it to himself.

He cranked the steering wheel to the left, turning down the long driveway into the ranch. There was no point to thinking about his life. He didn't have a life—and he for sure didn't have a future.

He drove into the backyard, cut the ignition and climbed out of the truck, noticing that the lights were still on in the kitchen. Maybe Ms. Madeline was afraid of the dark.

He went in through the back and toward the kitchen. As he got closer, he heard music and stopped at the door. Maddy was sitting on the floor in front of the fireplace, her head and shoulders bobbing and bouncing to the beat of an old Beatles song coming from his grandmother's ancient radio. She had a scrub brush in hand and a pail of murky water on the floor next to her. Damn! The woman just didn't listen.

But oddly, he felt a sense of calm as he watched her. He couldn't help admiring her determination to do whatever the hell she wanted. Maybe she was more like him than he'd thought.

"You plan on staying up all night?"

She jumped a foot, he was sure. Eyes wide, she made a startled sound, hitting the pail with her elbow. Seeing him, she released a gush of air. "Oh, it's just you."

"You were expecting someone else?"

She quickly stuck the scrub brush behind her back and smiled sheepishly. "Uh...no."

Her hair was pulled into some kind of ponytail, with little sprigs popping out everywhere.

"Actually...I was expecting to be done before you got here."

She was honest; he had to give her that. And she had a great smile. "Done with what?" He walked toward her.

Maddy's first instinct was to keep him from seeing what she was doing. She scrambled to her feet and came around to face him, her back to the fireplace, blocking the evidence. But that was ridiculous. He must've seen what she was doing while he was standing there. "Just cleaning the fireplace." She pointed behind her.

Moving closer, he peered around her.

"I was curious about what the stones were like under all the grime," she said. "And, after cleaning a little bit, I wanted to see more, and then...well, I sort of got carried away."

He took another step forward and leaned down for a closer view. His arm brushed hers.

"Too bad you wasted your time," he said, his face in front of hers, his mouth seductively close.

"But...see how lovely the stones are."

"So?"

He was really close now, and she realized he wasn't looking at the fireplace at all, but at her and in a way he hadn't before. He smelled hot and salty, and even though the cooler was running full blast, it felt as if someone had pumped up the heat.

"So—" she moistened her lips "—good news. You don't have to tear out the fireplace. With a little cleaning, maybe some sand blasting on the difficult parts, you can restore it to its original condition." She tipped her head toward the mass of stone covering the wall behind her, but didn't move otherwise because she'd have to touch him if she did.

"You'll probably have to replace a stone or two since some are chipped," she babbled on. "And you'll need to recement those that are loose. A different mantel, maybe, but that's it."

He didn't seem to be listening, and when he shoved a finger under the strap on her bib overalls and tugged her closer, she stopped breathing. His hand was warm, his breath hot and moist on her cheek. Suddenly her mind spun with possibilities that two days ago she'd never in a million years have dreamed of.

Not with J. D. Rivera.

But his nearness was intoxicating and she felt as if she was tempting danger—and it was exhilarating.

"Are you planning on plowing the cornfields?"

It took a fraction of a second before she realized what he'd asked. Mentally shaking herself, she stepped away, bumping his arm in the process.

His dark gaze roamed over her.

"Oh, you mean these..." The white sleeveless T-shirt she wore underneath the baggy overalls had shrunk in the dryer, which she'd wanted, but she should've waited to cut off the bottom. Because now the shirt ended at her midriff and there was a wide gap of skin between her shirt and pants. She was also filthy.

Her mother would have a stroke if she saw her.

"I got these at Masterson's." She whirled, as if modeling the latest Anne Klein. "*Très* chic, don't you think?"

A low growl of laughter was his response, and

she couldn't help smiling, too. It felt good to let go and be herself. Even if he was making fun of her.

The fact that she had the ability to make him laugh at all sent a rush of warmth through her veins. She stepped closer. "Be truthful now."

He stiffened a little, then raked the hair out of his eyes with one hand. Nice hair. Smooth and silky. Great eyes, rimmed with long black lashes.

He leaned in and brought his face close to hers. "Being truthful...I think—" he said, his voice husky but firm "—you'd better stop cleaning and go to bed."

Her response was so soft and low she almost didn't recognize it as her own. "Okay. But first tell me what you think about restoring the fireplace."

His breathing visibly deepened. He placed one hand on the fireplace directly behind her head.

His eyes darkened, then his gaze shifted to her mouth. "I think it's a bad idea," he said softly.

She moistened her lips again. "I disagree."

The words were barely out when his mouth met hers. She tasted beer and mint, and his lips were unbelievably soft and warm and every bit as delicious as she'd imagined. And she *had* imagined.

He backed her up against the fireplace, and with her hands pressed against the wall of stone behind her, she parted her lips and melted against him, hungry for more. They kissed again and again, slow, wet exploring kisses. Exciting. And dangerous.

Then suddenly he went still, as if listening to something. He pulled away and raised a finger to his mouth. "Shh."

Hard to be quiet when her chest was heaving and

her heart was thudding so loudly the people in Los Rios could probably hear it. But then she heard a noise outside. And footsteps.

Neither of them moved.

"What's that?" she whispered.

He placed a finger over her mouth, still hot from his kisses, then motioned for her to stay put as he stole toward the back door. A bright light flashed outside, then cut a swath of shimmering yellow through the glass in the door and throughout the kitchen. A burglar? Fear skittered up her spine. Suddenly she was reliving the whole nightmare in Georgetown. The incident that had turned her life inside out.

J.D. grabbed a long slender rod from a drawer, for protection, she guessed, flicked on the outside light and flung open the door. A large dark form filled the frame.

"Evening, Rivera."

"Sheriff," J.D. greeted the man, but didn't stand aside. "Kinda late to be calling on your neighbors, isn't it?"

The sheriff tipped his hat to the back of his head and scratched his chin. Noticing Maddy in the background, he nodded at her. "Ma'am." Then his focus went back to J.D. "Yep. Much too late for social calls. Especially way out here. But when I've got a job to do, I do it."

J.D. glanced at his watch. "Must be real urgent then."

"Anything that involves a kid is urgent. Wouldn't you say?"

The sheriff reached to his side and yanked a pint-size boy up by his shirt. Though the kid's head was bowed and J.D. couldn't see his face, he knew the clothes.

"Benito?"

The child looked up and scowled, his eyes filled with defiance.

"Ornery little cuss. He's under sixteen and I caught him out after curfew, but he wouldn't say a word. Except he mentioned your name. I figured rather than keeping him in jail for the night, I'd ask you where he lives so I could bring him home." He paused. "Gotta be a reason he's not talking."

J.D. straightened, his nerves drawing tight, his stomach muscles knotting. He knew exactly what the sheriff was saying. He believed Benito's relatives were undocumented immigrants—in the country illegally. And J.D. had personally experienced Collier's method of dealing with UDAs.

Maddy stepped forward and took Benito's hand in hers. "I'd like to talk to him for a minute. Okay?"

Without waiting for the sheriff's response, Maddy led the boy inside. J.D. held his position at the door.

After several moments with Benito, Maddy called J.D. over. "He says he went to get a drink, saw some older kids outside his window and went to play with them. They were just hanging out near the road when the sheriff came along. He was the only child under curfew age, so the sheriff took him in."

Talking low so Collier wouldn't hear, J.D. said, "Ask him why he didn't tell the sheriff where he lived so he could take him home."

She asked, and the boy bowed his head again, mumbling his explanation.

When she'd finished listening, Maddy whispered to J.D., "He says he was scared that he'd get his aunt and uncle in trouble because they went to Mexico overnight and he was alone. He told the sheriff he was staying here till they return because he thought the sheriff might let him go." Her gaze darted to Benito, then to the sheriff and back to J.D. "So, what do we do now?"

"Stay here. I'll deal with this," J.D. said and walked to the door. "I'm afraid this is my fault, Sheriff. I was supposed to pick him up, and the time just got away from me. Guess I'm not much good in the child care department."

Collier's eyes narrowed to slits. "You telling me you're baby-sitting?"

"I guess you could call it that. Sorry if the boy was a bother for you, Sheriff."

The man's face hardened. He'd obviously had other plans for the child and his family if they didn't have papers, and he'd wanted J.D. to know it. Well, J.D. wasn't about to let anyone experience the humiliation he had as a kid.

Maddy suddenly piped up from behind them. "Thank you for bringing him home, Sheriff. Very kind of you to do so."

The sheriff coughed, a hacking chain-smoker's cough. He said, "Tell the kid he got lucky this time. I'm letting him off with a warning, but I won't do it again." He coughed again, then clomped down the stairs and swaggered away.

After the sheriff was gone, J.D. turned to Maddy.

"You lied to the sheriff," she said. "How come?"

"How come you went along with it?" He shrugged and went over to Benito.

"Because I can't imagine how his relatives could leave a child this young alone overnight. But even worse, I can't imagine what it would be like for a little boy to spend a night in jail." A second later, she said, "What you did was wonderful."

J.D. shook off the compliment. "It's called protecting my investment. He can't work if he's in jail."

Her face fell.

"Now, can you please tell him I want him to bunk here until his relatives come back?" After a second, he added, "And find out who he's staying with."

"Protecting your investment?" Maddy practically spat out. "Is that all you care about?"

"At the moment, yes."

She frowned. Her expression told him that any credit for kindness she'd attributed to him had dissolved. But she did as he asked.

After a quick exchange with Benito, she said, "He's staying with an aunt and uncle, but won't tell me their names because he's afraid he'll get them into trouble. He says they'll be back tomorrow and he can get a ride home with Carlos after work."

"Yeah?" It was a good story, but J.D. doubted it was true. Seeing the boy's wary expression, he said, "Well then, tell him to come with me and I'll show him where he'll sleep tonight."

J.D. raised his chin to Benito. "C'mon, buddy. Let's hit the sack."

MADDY WOKE AT DAWN, stretched like the old Siamese cat she'd had as a kid and tossed off the sheet, unable to think of anything except J.D. Despite what he'd said about Benito's being an investment, Rivera's actions didn't mesh with his words.

And then there was that other little issue—the kiss. Her cheeks warmed at the memory of it. She'd responded to him like a love-starved teenager, and heaven help her, she'd felt like one. His touch had sent a current of electricity to her brain, obviously frying any common sense she might've had before.

She shouldn't have kissed him back, but she'd never been kissed quite so thoroughly. And it was delicious and wonderful and she hadn't wanted to stop.

Jeez. As if his opinion of her wasn't low enough, what would he think of her now? She buried her head under the pillow. There had to be more important matters to dwell on, but she couldn't quell the wild fantasies invading her mind.

What it would be like to make love with J.D. What her life would be like if she stayed here on the ranch. What it would feel like to be loved by him.

Oh, she'd had sex before. And she'd had infatuations. But the few relationships she'd been in had never made her feel this way. Could she be falling…in love with J.D.?

Finally, she got up, dressed to go jogging and made her way to the kitchen, all the while wondering if *he* was up yet, and if so, what she should do. Avoid him or talk to him about last night?

What would she say? That she found him attractive? Sexy? She couldn't tell him that. She couldn't tell him she'd discovered that maybe J. D. Rivera wasn't as tough as he made himself out to be. She couldn't say she liked the man she saw under the facade or even that she liked his smile and wanted to see him do it more often. She couldn't say any of that, so maybe it would be better to say nothing—just wait to see if he brought the subject up.

If he didn't, she'd pretend the kiss had never happened.

In the kitchen, she decided it was too early to check on Zelda, so she'd jog first. She filled her water bottle and attached it to her waistband. Hearing a hammering noise outside, she went to the window. J.D. was on a ladder working on one of the outbuildings.

It was also too early for Juana to be here, so Maddy quickly put on a pot of coffee and when it finished percolating, she filled a thermal cup that she'd seen J.D. using before and carried it out to him.

As she neared, he glanced up and saw her, his expression softening as she came closer. ''Morning,'' he said.

Her hearing must be off because he sounded almost cheerful.

''*Buenos días.*'' She smiled and handed the drink up to him.

''*Gracias.*'' His fingers brushed hers as he took the cup from her hand.

''*De nada. Yo no supe que usted habló el español.*''

He laughed and held up a hand. ''Hold it, Petunia. *Gracias* and *Qué pasa* are the extent of my foreign-language skills.''

''Oh. I thought maybe you were holding out on me—that maybe you learned Spanish as a kid since you grew up here.''

He arched one dark eyebrow. ''Where'd you hear that?''

''From people. And I heard some other things while I was in town, too.'' She grinned. ''But I didn't believe any of the bad stuff they said.''

He laughed. ''Well, you oughta. If what you heard was bad, it's true. And if it wasn't bad, it's a lie.''

She chuckled, liking his sense of humor. Until now, she'd doubted he had one.

''Your family's been in the area a long time, didn't anyone speak Spanish?''

Pensive, he sipped the coffee, then set the cup on the ladder shelf. ''My father did. I did as a little kid, but when I came to live with my grandparents, I spoke only English. I forgot most of my Spanish. But my father would've wanted it that way, so it was okay.''

''Really? How odd. I'd think parents would want their children to be bilingual, especially here in Arizona where there's such a large Spanish-speaking population.''

''Nope. My father wanted me to be the all-American kid.''

''And were you?''

''Not by a long shot.''

''Did you *want* to be?''

He took a deep breath. ''I learned a long time

ago that what I wanted didn't matter to anyone but me.'' Bitterness edged his words.

She felt a pang of empathy. *That* she could understand. What *she* wanted had never mattered to her family. Only what they wanted for her. But at least she'd known they cared.

Surely his parents or grandparents had cared. She thought about asking, but didn't, because she was afraid he'd stop talking if she got too personal.

''And I made sure I lived up to everyone's worst expectations.''

She smiled. ''I'll bet you did.''

They shared another laugh and then she said, ''But that was a long time ago. I'm sure you've done some good in the interim. Right?''

He became quiet. A muscle flicked angrily in his jaw, his expression suddenly somber. Then, he said, his words sharp and precise, ''I killed a man in the interim.''

CHAPTER NINE

THE AIR LEFT Maddy's lungs. If he'd wanted to shock her, he'd succeeded. Even though the sheriff had told her the same thing, hearing it from J.D., hearing the hurt and anger in his voice, sent a chill through her.

"You want to know more, just ask the sheriff or anyone in town. They'll tell you all kinds of stuff about me—stuff even I don't know." The pain in his eyes conflicted with the lightness of his words.

"I prefer to draw my own conclusions about people."

He drove in another nail. "Suit yourself."

"Okay. Was it an accident?"

He turned to her, his eyes pooling with remorse. "I was responsible. It doesn't matter whether it was an accident or not."

She wasn't sure what to say. She knew all about guilt. She'd carried her own burden for so long that her life had come to a screeching halt. She'd felt enormous guilt after Georgetown. The man who'd broken into her apartment wielding a gun, had bound and gagged her, and then violated her roommate as Maddy watched in terror. Whenever Maddy closed her eyes, he'd hit her in the face with his gun. Though she'd been helpless, she couldn't stop feeling she could've done something. Anything.

When the police finally apprehended the man and she discovered who he was, guilt took over her life. She'd gone back to Epiphany, and it had taken four years and lots of therapy before she was ready for a new start.

"And you're doing penance for the rest of your life because of it," she said softly.

"What?"

He obviously hadn't expected the comment. "You feel guilty, so you're not going to cut yourself any slack."

The muscles in his jaw tightened. "What's this, the morning version of the Dr. Phil show? Psychoanalysis with coffee?"

"I know what living with guilt is like," she said.

He hauled in a deep breath, then quietly, evenly, said, "You don't know anything about how I feel." The pain in his voice was unmistakable.

She shriveled a little inside and had to look away. He'd put her in her place—and truth be told, he had a point. She didn't really know how he felt. She couldn't. "You're right, and I apologize for making that assumption. Really. I'm sorry."

He went back to pounding nails and she stood there, quiet for a bit. Finally, she said, "So, have you decided what you'd like me to do around here? I'm perfectly willing to donate my time. You wouldn't have to pay me or anything—"

He looked at her in disbelief, then laughed. "You're too much, you know that?"

"Please. I really need to keep busy." Damn. She felt like a little kid begging for candy.

Exhaling loudly, he stepped down from the ladder. "You're the most irritatingly persistent person I know."

She grinned weakly. "I know that. But you need me."

"*I* need *you?*" The amusement shone in his eyes. "Yeah. Now that you mention it, I do have some needs that aren't being met." He lifted a hand to her face and brushed his thumb against her bottom lip.

Her heart thumped in her chest. The idea of calling his bluff suddenly appealed to her. Instead of pulling away, she leaned closer. "Well, like I said, I'll be more than happy to lend a hand. Just tell me what you'd like me to do," she said softly.

A quick flash of surprise crossed his face. It was the only indication that she'd caught him off guard. In the next instant, he smiled, self-assured and confident.

"I think you should stick to what you're good at," he said. "And since you're the one who offered, why don't you tell me your other areas of expertise."

He sounded serious, as if he might reconsider. Okay. She had his ear. Exude confidence. Be convincing.

"Well, my brother buys old homes and fixes them up for resale, and I've helped him some with redecorating and refinishing. So, you could do the same in your kitchen. Instead of ripping it apart, why not work with what's there? The result would be more authentic. With a little elbow grease, the cabinets could be stripped and refinished to look like new, and the fireplace, well, you saw how great it could be with just a cleaning. Then there are the walls… I have some great ideas about those if you want to hear them. It would be faster, easier and cheaper to refinish than reconstruct. And as I said, more authentic. You wouldn't have to hire anyone and—"

"Cut." He held up one hand.

Maddy stopped, her mouth half-open, but when he didn't say anything immediately, she began again. "It's really the best way to—"

"Okay. Okay!" He glared at her, then went back to his work. "I'll think about it."

Her pulse raced. Wow. He'd actually agreed. Well, not agreed, but he was going to consider her ideas.

She felt a sudden sense of accomplishment. "Great. I'm ready whenever."

Apparently finished with the conversation, he climbed the ladder and started hammering again.

Maddy knew little about J. D. Rivera, and it struck her that she wanted to know so much more. She wanted to know all about him—what had happened to him in the years between living on the ranch as a kid and when he'd returned a few weeks ago. What made him so afraid to let his feelings show.

Her gaze swept over his backside, over faded jeans and the white V-neck T-shirt that accented hard muscles and bronzed skin tones, and a quick heat grew low in her stomach. She'd never felt this way—not even when she'd been madly in lust with Harvey Hepplewhite in high school. But mostly, she couldn't stop thinking about how wonderful she'd felt when he'd kissed her, how warm and delicious his mouth had been and how solid and hard his body had been against hers.

She leaned against the side of the building and a light breeze wafted over her. He'd been in a happy mood, and talking about his past seemed only to stir up hurtful memories and bad feelings. But she knew better than anyone that sometimes those feelings had to be recognized before a person could let them go.

"Benito still asleep?"

"Yep. Guess he had a tough night." He tapped a nail into the window frame, then with two hard swift strokes, drove it in all the way.

"What do you think of his relatives leaving him alone like that? Seems kind of strange, doesn't it?"

He drove in another nail. "No. In fact, it's probably the norm. These kids learn early on to take care of themselves."

Like you? He'd said as much when he told her no one cared about him but himself. Was that why he'd lied for Benito last night? "Well, I'm all for children learning self-sufficiency as they grow older, but there's also something to be said for protecting them and letting them be children while they can. No child should have to work full-time, especially not at such a young age. And I can't imagine his parents wanting him to do that, much less wanting him to be left alone. That's child abuse as far as I'm concerned."

"But you're not concerned. It's none of your business," he said flatly.

She squared her shoulders. "Well, I believe it is, and it should be yours, too. I don't see how you can dismiss the issue so easily."

The words had barely left her lips when she saw his back muscles tense. Now she really had said too much. Maybe even spoiled the fragile rapport they'd developed so far. But she couldn't change how she felt, and if she'd learned anything in her week at the ranch, it was that she'd never get anything by being quiet. Still, she didn't want to be pushy and possibly make things even worse.

"To each his own," she said quickly, then decided to leave.

She was only a few feet away when the hammering stopped, and in a softer tone he said, "Listen...about last night..."

She froze, then turned, ready to tell him she was okay with what had happened, that they didn't need to make a big deal out of it and he didn't owe her any explanation, when he said, "I had too much to drink and...alcohol sometimes has a negative effect on me."

The blood in her veins felt as if it had drained to her toes. Even though she'd tasted alcohol on his breath and considered briefly that he might be under the influence—she'd dismissed it. He'd seemed fine. And now...

Hell, what had she expected? That after one kiss he'd express his undying love?

Not really. But she rather liked thinking that he found her desirable, that he liked her and...and what? And nothing. Except that she'd made a complete fool of herself.

"I was out of line," he said. Final words that cut into her fragile ego like a sharp knife.

Waving a hand in dismissal, she managed to say,

''No need to apologize. I understand perfectly.'' All she wanted to do now was get out of there.

She took a half-dozen steps toward the road, when she heard him call out, ''Be careful.''

She kept on going, her humiliation burning a hole in her chest.

A couple steps later, he called out again, ''And stay on the road. The desert can be a dangerous place.''

NO KIDDING! But the only danger in her case was massive injury to her self-esteem not her health or well-being. Maddy plodded down the road, mentally whipping herself with each thud of her feet on the hard-packed sand. Stupid. How could she have been so stupid? Lord, when did she start wanting to feel desirable and attractive? When did she start thinking about romance in her life?

She'd given up on all that long ago.

She jogged a half mile or so and took a left on a smaller road, one she'd taken before, and then veered off on a smaller path that circled around and came back to the main road. The first time she'd gone down the narrow path, she'd noticed that the desert wasn't flat as she'd always thought, but was patterned with a series of hills and washes, some parts lush with plants and trees. Paloverde trees, she'd read, and mesquite. The air was crisp, clear and fresh and she was astonished at how far she could see.

One morning a long-eared rabbit had loped across the road in front of her, and birds and lizards were all around. The desert was alive. She liked it, liked the feel of nature in the raw—a place where man was truly the outsider.

She stopped in the middle of the path to rest, bending at the waist to catch her breath. Despite her stupidity, she was pleased she'd stayed to complete the contract. She felt happier than she had in years.

But she had to remember that this job was simply a way station, something to do until her real life began.

Why she'd been fantasizing about J.D. was a mystery. Romance wasn't even on her list. It was something that might or might not happen when she got the rest of her life straightened out. If and when it did, her dream man certainly wouldn't be a cynical guy like J. D. Rivera.

Rested, she touched her toes to stretch her muscles, and as she did, she noticed a footprint. A footprint that wasn't hers. She glanced around. There were several footprints and what appeared to be smudges—as if someone had tried to disguise them. Or maybe there'd been a scuffle or fight. She followed one set of footprints for a few feet but then they disappeared altogether. Odd. She made a mental note to mention it to J.D.

Twenty minutes later when she rounded the curve on the road to the ranch, she saw a big black limo in the driveway. As she got closer, she noticed a man in a uniform loitering in the shade next to the vehicle. A driver. Someone to see J.D.?

She quickly scanned the yard. J.D. was still working on the same building, and Carlos and Benito were alongside him. She started walking over to J.D., but as she got closer, he called out, "Some lady is here to see you."

"Me?" Who'd be there to see her?

"I told her to wait inside."

"Did she say what it was about?"

"Nope."

"Okay. Thanks," she said, and headed back to the house. The second she stepped inside, the familiar scent of Chanel N°5 hung heavy in the air. *Oh, God.* Her stomach knotted. Not here. She couldn't be *here.*

With dread, Maddy went into the parlor.

"Hello, Madeline," her mother said, smiling as if her being in Arizona at the Tripplehorne Ranch was nothing unusual at all.

Rachel Inglewood was sitting in the same chair Maddy had sat in when she'd first arrived. Rachel's back was rigid, her posture perfect, just like everything else about her. The woman didn't allow a hair out of place.

"Mother, what are you doing here?" Maddy puffed, still out of breath from jogging.

Her mother sobered. "Is that any way to greet your mother who's made a very long trip just to see you?"

No, it wasn't a proper greeting, but Maddy felt as if her private little world had been invaded. "I'm sorry, I'm just surprised to see you." She crossed to her mother and leaned down to give her a hug, but Rachel gestured to Maddy's sweat-soaked jogging clothes. Maddy stepped back.

"I've missed you terribly," her mother said. "We all miss you."

"I've been gone a week, Mother."

"Well, dear, it's long enough." Rachel glanced around, her lips pursed in distaste. "Your father and I have decided it's time for you come home."

"Really? You and Daddy decided that?"

"Well, yes. We've been worried, especially with your history...well, you know. And when we didn't hear from you except that one time, I had to make sure you were okay." Stopping only briefly for a quick breath, Rachel went on. "And now that I've seen the deplorable conditions—" she shook her head and made a tsk-tsk sound. "—your father would have a coronary if he knew you were living in such squalor."

Maddy's blood pressure hiked up another notch, but she recited Dr. Sheridan's words to calm herself. *You can do anything if...*

"It's not squalor, Mother. Look around. The place is being renovated. My room has been completely redone and it's very nice. Besides which, I have a job here. I can't leave on a whim."

"I'm sure they can find someone to replace you, dear."

"I signed a contract."

Rachel held up a hand to silence her. "A minor thing. Your father can take care of it. He's never let you down yet, has he?"

"No, of course not." She didn't want to hurt her mother's feelings or seem ungrateful, but she had to make her understand. "You've been wonderful. You and Dad. I couldn't ask for better parents, and I'll always be grateful for all you've done." She sighed, trying to find just the right words.

"I know you just want to help, but the thing

is...I don't want help right now. I don't want anyone to take care of anything for me.''

Suddenly she remembered J.D. saying the same thing to her. She hadn't listened to him then. But that was different. Very different.

''I have to finish this contract. I *need* to do it—for myself.''

Almost before the words left Maddy's mouth, her mother started again. ''Well, I didn't want to say anything, but your father can't get anyone to do the job as well as you did. I guess that's because no one cares as much as family.''

Maddy gulped some air, a giant knot of frustration and guilt forming in her stomach. ''Did you give Randy a chance? He can do anything I can. He only started fixing up old homes because he didn't know what else to do in Epiphany. I'm sure he'd be happy to help.'' She *was* sure of it. Her brother had always felt bad that their father came to Maddy when he wanted someone to work for him. He never asked Randy. Maddy knew why. Her dad couldn't accept that Randy had rebelled at an early age against his father's authoritarian ways. Senator Inglewood couldn't accept that his son didn't want to follow in his father's political footsteps. Maddy had always been more malleable.

The expression on her mother's face switched from determination to irritation. Then she sighed as if finally accepting Maddy's choice. But Maddy knew better. Rachel was simply gearing up to try another approach.

''Okay, dear. But your father will worry himself sick if you don't call more often. Please promise me that you'll call, and promise that if you need anything, or plan to come home sooner, you'll let us know immediately."

Her mother talked as if Maddy was going to come back for good once this job was finished. But why get into that now? All Maddy wanted was for her mother to go home and leave her to do her job. "I will. I'll call as often as I can."

"Good. I'm glad that's settled. Now, is there a room here for me to stay tonight?"

"H-here?" Maddy sputtered.

"Of course. Though I can't imagine..." Her voice trailed off as she scanned her surroundings. "But you said your room was nice, didn't you?"

"I work here, Mother, I can't be inviting guests to stay."

"Perhaps a nice hotel then, somewhere close. I can get us a suite, and then you can show me around the area. We can do lunch tomorrow and have some fun shopping, just the two of us—like we used to."

So this was Rachel's new strategy. Maddy shook her head. "I have a job to do. People to teach. I can't run off sight-seeing."

Her mother's face hardened. "Well, I'm certainly not going to have the driver take me all the way back to Tucson today. How would that look? There must be a hotel around here, and I'm sure you'll have some time when you're not teaching. You don't do that twenty-four hours a day, do you?"

If her mother stayed anywhere nearby, she'd be back tomorrow to try again. Rachel Inglewood never gave up. "I have...other things to do besides teaching. I'm helping with the renovations." It wasn't a total lie. She *was* helping. Besides her teaching, she was taking care of Zelda. "And the closest hotels are in Tucson or Yuma."

Clearly pretending she hadn't heard a word, Rachel said, "Well, why don't you ask that hired man I spoke with outside. Maybe he knows of a good hotel nearby."

As if on cue, a knock sounded behind Maddy, and J.D. sauntered into the room. She gave him a tentative smile, hoping that he hadn't overheard the conversation. But from his expression, she could tell that he had.

He walked over to stand next to her, lifted the bottom of his T-shirt and wiped the sweat from his face, revealing hard, tanned stomach muscles in the process.

Rachel's mouth fell open, obviously aghast at his bad manners. The bomb was about to detonate, Maddy was sure.

Then, as J.D. let his shirt drop, he said to Maddy, "Just wondering when you might be starting that work in the kitchen."

"Uh...today. Right now. I mean, as soon as—" she couldn't look at Rachel "—as soon as my mother leaves."

J.D. turned to look at her mother.

Rachel rose to her feet, her body rigid.

"Mad-e-line," Rachel said softly in the same firm tone she'd always used when Maddy was a child and had needed reprimanding.

"Oh, I'm sorry. Mother, this is my employer, J. D. Rivera. J.D., this is my mother, Rachel Inglewood."

Rivera nodded toward her mother. "Nice to meet you, ma'am. I'd shake hands but I'm all dirty." He wiped a grubby hand across his sweat-soaked T-shirt.

Rachel's shock couldn't be disguised. But being the well-mannered lady that she was, she pulled herself up and managed a civil "How do you do, Mr. Rivera."

"Let me know as soon as you're ready," J.D. said to Maddy, "so I can go over the plans with you." He gave Rachel another nod. "Have a nice trip home, ma'am." He gave her a two-finger salute and left the room.

Maddy didn't know whether to be excited or wary. Was he actually going to let her help? "I'll be there in a few minutes," she called after him. "Right after I take a quick shower."

CHAPTER TEN

J.D. KEPT WORKING OUTSIDE for another half hour after Madeline's mother had left, and then he headed for the kitchen. Why he'd told the teacher she could help he didn't know. Yes, he did. He hated to see anyone being manipulated. Hell, couldn't Madeline tell that her mother was doing exactly that?

And after Maddy's impassioned plea earlier, he'd given her ideas on the kitchen some serious consideration. She had a point. Why tear everything out when restoration might work? And if it saved him money, all the better. But time was the important factor. If he tried her way and it didn't work out, he'd have to start over.

"Hi," Madeline greeted him cheerily as he came into the kitchen.

She was standing next to the table studying the blueprints he'd laid out earlier. The sunlight coming through the windows formed a golden aura around her head. Her hair, still a little wet from her shower, appeared lighter than when she'd arrived. "I'm still on the fence about this," he grumbled, then walked over to her.

She smelled fresh and clean, like fruit or something, not all perfumey like some women.

A droplet of water rolled down her temple, and

he felt an overwhelming urge to lick it off. An obvious case of repressed testosterone, that was all it was. The last thing he needed to be thinking about was a woman. Especially not a rich, I'm-looking-for-excitement type. Tripplehorne was just a blip on the teacher's radar screen, a touch-and-go on her way to New York and her big-time job at the UN.

"And what's going to make you jump over that fence?"

He thought for a moment. "You tell me exactly what you have in mind, how long it will take, how much money it'll cost me, what type of expertise is required and how much manpower is involved. After you get that information for me, I'll make a decision."

Without preamble, she said, "Great! I'll put a work plan together right now. That way you can see everything on paper." Her eyes sparkled as she talked, and the timbre of her voice rose in proportion to her obvious excitement.

Blue. Her eyes were blue, he realized. Sky blue. And as clear as a cloudless day.

He didn't want to notice her eyes. He didn't want to feel anything—not even irritation. For nearly three weeks, he'd worked from sunup till he dropped into bed at night, too tired to think or feel or remember. If it got too dark to work outside, he worked inside. All he had to do was go through the motions of living.

And if he didn't make the deadline, he'd crawl back to another two-bit Vegas motel and numb his brain with more pills and alcohol. That was his backup plan.

But now, this woman had him thinking again. Feeling again. And he hated it.

EARLY THE NEXT MORNING, Saturday, Maddy stood outside on the back deck waiting for Annie to pick her up. They were going to Los Rios. She wasn't sure she should even be horning in on Annie's friends, but since she'd had no response from J.D. about the work plan she'd given him last night, she didn't have anything else to do. She'd wanted to discuss the suggestions with him right away, but he'd said he'd look at it and they could talk later.

"Going somewhere?"

Maddy turned. J.D. stood in the doorway. His arms were crossed and his tanned skin contrasted with the white T-shirt that seemed to be his work uniform. "Annie's picking me up for some kind of brunch with her friends."

"Ah, the good ladies of Los Rios," he said with no small amount of sarcasm.

"I hesitated about going, but decided since I didn't have anything else to do, I might as well. Besides, I really like Annie."

He went over to the stove and poured himself a cup of coffee. "You make this? It smells different."

She nodded. "My special blend. Vanilla hazelnut. I brought a little bit with me."

"I prefer the regular kind—black and strong."

"Oh, for goodness' sake. Quit complaining and taste it. Then you can give me your opinion." She surprised herself with her outburst, but how could he have an opinion about something he hadn't even tried?

He backed up as if she were a cat baring her claws. Then he took a sip and gave her a so-so gesture with his hand. "Not bad. Not great, but not bad, either."

"And you wouldn't admit if it was fantastic."

At that, he laughed. "Okay, you got me."

"Really? I feel better already."

"But don't test your luck."

He took another sip. Finally he said, "I like your plan. I've got some questions, though. Maybe we can talk about it when you come back."

She couldn't stop the wide smile that erupted. He liked her plan. *He* liked *her* plan! He'd said so. Amazing. "Of course."

"So how long will you be gone?"

"I don't know. A half day, maybe."

Just as he was going out the back door, Annie pulled up. Grabbing her purse, Maddy suddenly realized she'd forgotten to check on Zelda. She slipped out the door practically on J.D.'s heels. "Can you please tell Annie I'll be right there, as soon as I finish with Zelda."

J.D. looked at her askance, but said, "Sure. If she comes around back where I'm working."

As Maddy hurried to take care of Zelda, her heart raced. If she'd gone off with Annie and forgotten to feed the dog, no telling what might've happened. And then the little confidence J.D. had in her would be impaired.

But she hadn't forgotten. Even in her excitement, she'd remembered. Feeling good about that, she hurried to the compound and went in without developing a single butterfly in her stomach. She didn't have time for shaky nerves right now.

Zelda didn't seem to be around and Maddy figured she was probably still sleeping inside her fancy house. She smiled to herself. All dogs should be so lucky. Then, as she finished filling the food bowl, she noticed Zelda poke her little dark nose outside her door. The animal dropped down, head on her front paws, soft brown eyes peering up at Maddy.

"What's up, pup? You've got everything you need." Maddy motioned to the food and water cache. "So, no big eyes, okay?"

As she closed the gate, Maddy had a fleeting sense that Zelda wasn't herself. Come to think of it, she'd been listless the day before, too. There'd been no big welcome from her.

"Maddy? You coming?" Annie's voice sounded from behind.

"I'll be back later, Zelda," Maddy said and hurried out, shutting the gate behind her. Coming around the side of the house she found her new friend standing by the open door of a small white SUV. Annie waved when she saw Maddy coming.

"Good morning," Maddy said. "Sorry, I was checking on the dog."

She went to the passenger side, got in and fastened her seat belt, and as she did, she saw J.D. turn to look at them.

She pressed the button, opened the window and asked, "Do you want me to pick up anything while I'm in town?"

He shook his head.

"You sure? Last chance."

"Positive."

She turned to Annie and shrugged. Annie shifted into gear and they were off.

"He likes you," Annie said as she pulled onto the main road. "Which is really unusual since he hardly likes anyone."

Maddy gave an offhand laugh, but her insides warmed at the comment. "He has to put up with me, that's all. His aunt hired me, and he's stuck with it."

"Right. And that's why—according to Grady—his eyes light up whenever your name is mentioned."

That was news to her. "Grady's imagining things."

Annie smirked. "You can think what you want."

A half hour later, in the back room of the Sunflower Café, Maddy and Annie were chatting with eight other women, all members of the Los Rios Ladies Club. Carolyn, Abigail and Mary appeared to be somewhere in their late forties and early fifties, Annie, Jennifer and Serena, late twenties to mid-thirties, Kelsey, who looked no more than sixteen, and Gertrude who was pushing eighty if she was a day. According to Annie, the group met biweekly to work on whatever town project was on the agenda, eat sinful food and gossip about everyone. The topic at hand was the September Festival, slated for the next weekend.

"We'd love to have you join our group," the woman named Carolyn said.

"What she means is we're desperate for help," Annie interjected.

"I'll be happy to do what I can. But as far as joining the group, I'm only going to be here a few weeks."

"Just as well," Gertrude said. "Considering."

"Considering what, Gram?" Kelsey, who was carrying in coffee and tea from the restaurant, impaled the older woman with a critical gaze.

Gertrude raised her chin. "Considering she's staying out there with that Rivera man," she said to the group as a whole, then to Maddy, "You be very careful out there, dear. He killed a man, you know."

"Gram!" Kelsey dropped the tray on the table with a crash. "It was an *accident.* I read it in the newspapers. You can't condemn someone for an accident."

"It's true, Gert," one of the other women piped up. "I read it myself."

Gert sniffed. "Maybe so. But I say, like father, like son. There's bad blood in the man and nothing can change that."

Kelsey rolled her eyes and mumbled something unintelligible under her breath, and then said, "Well, if the rest of the guys around here looked like he does—"

"Kelsey!" Carolyn snapped. "Watch your mouth. As far as that man goes, we should all just mind our own business."

"Mom!" Kelsey rounded on the older woman. "That's everyone's solution to everything around here."

"We wouldn't even be having this conversation if that man hadn't come back here in the first place," Carolyn retorted.

"Ohhhh." Kelsey's face went red. "And you wonder why I can't wait to turn eighteen and leave this town?"

"This isn't the place to be airing your gripes, young lady," the girl's mother reprimanded.

To which Kelsey shrugged dramatically, "There must be someplace in this country where people are more open-minded."

Having been raised in a small town herself, Maddy had wondered the same thing many times. Then after going away to school, she'd learned that the people in Epiphany were no different than people anywhere else.

But she had to admit, Gert's comment about J.D. grated. What had the woman meant about bad blood? What had J.D.'s father done that was so bad?

"Moving away isn't necessarily a solution," Maddy said to Kelsey, hoping she might be able to smooth things over. "Prejudice is alive and well in the big cities as much as it is in small towns."

Carolyn stiffened at the comment and several other ladies exchanged quick glances. Realizing what she'd just said, Maddy fumbled to correct her faux pas. "What I meant is that attitudes are the same everywhere. People are people."

"We know what you meant, Maddy," Annie said. "No point belaboring the issue. It's time to get on with our projects. We've got a lot of work to do."

Maddy was grateful for the save.

Abigail, who'd been silent during the earlier exchange, said, "I agree. We all have different opinions, so let's put the subject to rest. On another note, we'd love to have you join us at the festival, Madeline, whether you have time to help or not."

"Thank you," Maddy said. "I'll be happy to do whatever I can."

IT WAS AFTER 1:00 p.m. when they headed back to the ranch. "What was all that about bad blood?" Maddy asked Annie as the car bumped down the road.

"Y'know, I wasn't even born when it all went down over thirty years ago, but I heard it had something to do with a fire and a couple of people dying. J.D.'s father was arrested. But some people in this town have a way of blowing things out of proportion. And that stuff about bad blood—who even thinks like that?"

"Gertrude, and apparently her daughter, Carolyn."

"Well, pay no attention to them. They don't know what they're talking about."

Maddy wasn't so sure that was true. But she didn't see any point in asking more questions, since her friend didn't have any answers. "Do you have a computer, Annie?"

"Sure. Why?"

"I need to get some information, and I thought about having my brother send my laptop out here, but J.D. doesn't have a connection at the ranch."

"You can use my computer anytime you want. I only need it to do the accounting for the business and to get recipes from the Internet once in a while."

Annie liked to cook, Maddy had learned earlier. Her dream was to open a catering business someday.

"Thanks. I may have to do that. I don't know

where else to get information around here. There's not even a library in town."

"There's one in the school. You could use that."

"Tough without transportation. I can't even get to your place without wheels."

Annie pondered that for a minute, then said, "I can look up the information for you. It might even force me get more experience on the computer." She laughed. "I'm so computer challenged."

"Gosh, I wish I had a car. I could help you with that. I was a real techno geek in school. But, yeah, I need information, and maybe you could get it for me."

Once they agreed on that, Maddy approached Annie about her other idea. "Remember the woman I told you about, Juana's sister, Mariela?"

Annie nodded. "Sure. The one who makes great clothes."

"Well, I was wondering if it would be possible to get her a booth at the festival."

"Of course. All she has to do is fill out a form and pay the money."

"That's what I figured. But she doesn't speak English, and I don't think she has much money."

Annie thought for a minute. "I might know a solution for that."

They talked it over, and finally Maddy was back at the ranch, where she waved goodbye to Annie and headed toward the house. Scanning the yard for J.D., she noticed no one seemed to be working.

Strange. J.D. and company—Carlos and Benito—practically worked round the clock, but today their hammers were mute.

She glanced at Zelda's run. Zelda was half in and

half out of her house, her head resting on her paws. Nothing unusual, so Maddy went inside.

The rest of her lunch with the ladies had gone well with no more confrontations. The women had planned the festival down to the last toothpick. Maddy had made suggestions where she could. They'd planned the decorations for two different booths, and Maddy had agreed to work in one of them for an hour or so on Saturday and do any other tasks they wanted to assign her.

Kelsey had stuck by Maddy's side the whole time, firing off questions, one after the other. What was Maddy going to do when she left Los Rios? How had she decided on a career and where she wanted to live? Did she think J.D. was hot and was he as gorgeous close up as he was from a distance?

The girl was brimming with energy and Maddy was reminded of herself at that age—before she'd changed into someone she hardly knew.

But now she was back on track, thanks in large part to the opportunity J.D. had given her. He was a strange man. On the one hand, she wasn't sure he thought she was competent, but on the other, he seemed to push her into doing things. She'd never have gone near Zelda if he hadn't nudged her. She'd never have taken such a dilapidated truck into Los Rios alone if he hadn't asked her to do it. And if she hadn't done that, she'd never have met Annie.

With each small success, she felt her self-confidence building, and her determination to make changes in her life became even stronger.

She stepped inside the house. No J.D., Juana or

Carlos. Where were they? She'd hoped to discuss the plan she'd given J.D. and maybe start working.

In her room, she changed clothes, and since she couldn't do any real work in the kitchen without first talking to J.D., she decided to read for a while. Two hours later, she awakened from an unplanned nap, got up, splashed her face and went to the kitchen again, hoping to find someone. But there wasn't a soul around.

She checked outside. She began to check everywhere and when she got to J.D.'s room, the door was ajar. She knocked. No answer. She knocked again, harder this time, and the door creaked open a little more.

With one hand on the knob, she leaned forward and peered inside. The blinds were drawn, the light was dim. "J.D. Are you in here? I'd like to talk for a minute if you have time."

Nada.

When her eyes adjusted, she saw the bed was unmade, and the door on a gun cabinet against one wall was ajar. What the— She crossed to the cabinet where several rifles stood on end, all securely locked in their slots—except one. She whirled around.

"J.D.?" The bathroom door was open, but he wasn't there, either.

Seeing some rolls of papers on the dresser, she went over. More blueprints. And next to those, two framed photographs, both yellowed with age. She picked up the one on her left. Judging from the veil and formal attire of the subjects, it was a wedding picture. Maddy peered closer. The bride's gown was just like the one Maddy had found in the trunk.

She set the photo down and picked up the picture next to it. This one was more recent. The woman was wearing the same veil and the same dress, but the hairstyle was more modern. Mid to late 1960s maybe. The young woman was tall, blond and beautiful, and the groom…looked very much like J.D.

Lost in thought, she ran her thumb over the man's face. He was every bit as handsome as J.D. except that his hair was a little darker and his eyes were darker, too.

"Looking for something?" J.D.'s deep voice came from behind her.

Maddy turned abruptly, nearly dropping the picture she held in her hands. "Oh…J.D.!" She felt her face go hot, and quickly set the photo down, making a loud thump on the dresser as she did. "I'm not…um…this isn't what you might think."

He leaned against the wall by the door with a rifle in his hand, watching her fumble for words. "No? What is it then?"

She edged away from the dresser and walked toward him, wanting to flee, but he was blocking the doorway and that left her standing in the middle of the room without anything to hold on to for support.

"Well…uh, there was no one around when I came home, and after a few hours I got a little worried. I knocked and called for you but got no answer, and the door was ajar, so I peeked in because I thought something might be wrong…that maybe you were hurt or something like befo—"

His eyes narrowed. His mouth drew into a tight line.

"And you thought you'd lend the cripple a hand." It was a statement not a question.

Her spine stiffened. Dammit. She was tired of his attitude. So what if he had a bum leg. Lots of people dealt with disabilities worse than his all the time. "That's right," she said crisply. "As a matter of fact, I really get off on that kind of thing. But hell, it's no fun unless I've got someone willing to grovel." After a second, she added, "And it's even less fun when a person isn't smart enough to want to help himself."

His eyes locked with hers, as if in combat. Then, oddly, he gave a quick laugh and shook his head. He crossed the room to the gun cabinet, placed the rifle in the empty slot and locked the glass door.

When he finished, he directed his attention to Maddy. "So, what's your point?"

It was a simple question. But now she wasn't sure what her point was. She was no authority when it came to fixing people's lives. She could barely pull her own together. "The point is that understanding when you need help and accepting it isn't a bad thing."

"So, what makes you the expert?"

"I'm no expert, but I've had some firsthand experience and my instincts are pretty good."

He studied her, his eyes seeming to warm as he did. Then he said softly, "Well, your instincts are off kilter this time, Madeline. So, please save your self-help therapy for someone who wants it." Holding her gaze, he added even more softly, "Is that clear?"

She squared her shoulders. "Crystal."

Even though he was essentially telling her to

mind her own business, she sensed a change in his attitude toward her—as if they understood each other. She wondered if he felt it, too, and wanting to continue the conversation, she asked, ''What's with the gun?''

He walked to the dresser and laid one hand on the top near the photos. ''I got a message that some people were in trouble in the desert and went to see what I could do. I took the gun for protection.''

He straightened. ''Someone hit the panic button on one of the beacons.''

''Beacon?''

''Tall towers with solar lights, strategically placed in the desert to assist anyone who might be stranded.''

''People trying to get into the country illegally?''

He nodded. ''Usually.''

''What good is a light?''

''If people are in trouble and see the beacon, they know to head toward it. Once there, all they need to do is hit the button to call for help. Instructions are printed in both English and Spanish.''

''And if they're illiterate?''

''There are simple pictures, too. But people still die in the desert.'' He closed his eyes for a second, as if remembering something.

''You mean they die because they don't want to alert the authorities?''

He nodded and let out a long breath. ''Right. Most of the time they come in groups and, while one person might want to push the panic button, others in the group resist and want to go on.''

''I see.'' But she wasn't sure she really did. ''So,

why would you go when the authorities should be taking care of it?"

"The authorities don't always make it in time. If I get there with water before the authorities, I could save a life."

"And you need the gun for protection from the people you're trying to save?"

"No. From bandits and drug dealers."

What an admirable thing for him to do, she thought. But she was sure he wouldn't want to hear that from her.

"I'd appreciate it if you'd keep this conversation between us."

She wanted to know more, but he abruptly picked up the photo on his right and said, "My parents." He set it down and picked up the other photo. "And my grandparents."

"I'm sorry, I didn't mean to pry." But she was happy that what she'd suspected all along was true. He wasn't cold and unfeeling at all. He'd been upset about her unpacking the dress in the trunk because it was a symbol of something good for him, a memory of people he'd loved.

"No big deal," he said. "My family history is an open book in this town." He leaned against the dresser, seeming more relaxed than before.

Taking his cue, she rested a hand against one of the posts on his bed.

"Do you have other family somewhere? Brothers or sisters?"

He shook his head. "No. Aunt Ethel, my mother's sister, was the last."

"Oh." Maddy couldn't imagine what it'd be like having no family at all. No wonder J.D. was such a loner. "I thought maybe she was your great-aunt because she was so much older."

"Seventeen years between my mother and Ethel. They weren't close. I never met the lady until after my grandparents died and she inherited the ranch." He paused a moment, then said, "I take that back, I was born here on the ranch and probably met her then. But we moved away when I was a baby. After Aunt Ethel inherited the place, she let it go to ruin. My grandparents would never have let it end up like this."

"But why wouldn't she just sell it?"

He shrugged. "Your guess is as good as mine. I was fifteen when my grandparents died. Aunt Ethel came back for the funeral and as my only living relative and guardian, immediately packed me off to school in Maryland. While she paid my bills, I never saw her again, never heard from her, or about her until her attorney contacted me after she died."

Kayla's father. "Harold Martin? Is he the attorney who contacted you?"

J.D. nodded and gave a curt laugh. "That's the guy. He and I spent some quality time together before I came here."

"Really." That was a surprise. So Mr. Martin *had* known a lot that he hadn't told Maddy. But then, maybe it was all confidential client-attorney stuff. "Mr. Martin's a nice man. I've known him since I was a little girl and he lived in Epiphany. He's my best friend's father and told me about this job back in June." She stopped. "I guess I mentioned all that before, didn't I?"

"If you did, I didn't make the connection."

"You weren't exactly feeling well the day I arrived."

J.D. frowned. "It's strange that he didn't tell you about my aunt's death since she died in July—two months before you came."

Maddy nodded "Yes, it is. And I've been trying to find out why ever since I arrived. But he's overseas right now and hasn't called me back."

J.D. came over and sat on the edge of the bed near her. "I have some questions of my own that need answering. I think I'll give him a call, and if he responds I'll hand him over to you when I'm done."

Maddy smiled. They'd agreed on something. Her adrenaline rushed and her pulse quickened. "Great," she said, touching his shoulder. "It's really nice of you to do that."

He glanced at her hand on his arm. Too familiar, she guessed, and took it away.

"No big deal. I have business to talk over with him."

She'd made him uncomfortable. Or maybe he felt he'd said too much. Whatever the case, they'd shared a nice moment.

He launched to his feet and started for the door. "C'mon." He motioned to her. "No one's working today, and Juana's at one of those big Mexican-wedding shindigs, so we're going to have to fend for ourselves for dinner."

They'd be alone—and she'd have another opportunity to get to know him better.

"Can you cook?"

She wrinkled her nose. "Ramen noodles in college."

He rolled his eyes.

CHAPTER ELEVEN

"HOW'S ZELDA?"

Sitting at the kitchen table with J.D. after a dinner of leftovers, Maddy's stomach dropped. She'd been so focused on discussing the renovation plans with J.D. tonight that she'd completely forgotten to check on Zelda. "I groomed her yesterday, gave her the vitamins and took her for a walk. I'm going to peek in on her again in a few minutes."

"Good." J.D. got up from the table and carried the leftovers to the refrigerator. "I'm happy with the way things have worked out with you and Zelda. It's one less thing for me to worry about."

"But you still work too much," Maddy said. "A person has to take some time off now and then to maintain a balance."

He laughed. "The only balance I need is the kind that'll keep me from falling off my ladder."

"I'm serious," she said. "Everyone needs a break once in a while." She got up, stacked the plates and brought them to the sink.

"Everyone but me. And even if I was to take a break, there's nothing to do in this one-horse town."

"*Au contraire.* There are all kinds of activities, including the festival next Saturday. I'm working a couple of the booths for an hour or so and helping out wherever I can. You should come. It's going to be fun.''

He walked to the sink, stopped by her side and placed a hand on her shoulder. ''Fun for you. Not me.''

His hand was warm and the warmth was sending messages to parts of her body that had been dormant for longer than she cared to admit.

''Oh, I'll bet you'd have a great time. There's a parade, booths with food and crafts and games, face painting for the kids and bands playing music throughout the day. There's even a dance in the evening.''

J.D. reached up and lifted a strand of hair from her eyes. She was sweet, a truly caring person, and her presence had brought some brightness into his dark life. Each day he found himself looking forward more and more to seeing her. He liked her cheery smile and bubbly laugh. Hell, he even liked when she needled him. He felt more alive than he had in months and was suddenly meeting each day with new zest.

''You could come and work the booth with me,'' she said.

She didn't know. He figured she would've heard everything from the good ladies of Los Ríos. But apparently not. Which didn't change the fact that if he showed up at the festival, there'd be a black cloud hanging over everything. If he went, Maddy would know exactly what the townspeople thought of him, and he doubted she'd have any fun at all.

''That might be your idea of excitement, but it's not mine.''

''Oh, you'd rather stay here and work?''

"I'd rather get ahead with the job."

She pursed her lips. "A few hours off won't make a big difference and everyone needs some playtime. You've heard the old adage, all work and no play makes—"

"Makes me more likely to get the place finished by the deadline."

She opened her mouth to respond, but he cut her off. "Didn't you say you needed to check on Zelda?"

Her big blues widened. "Yes, I'll do that right now." A second later, she was out the door and he felt no small amount of relief. He'd been only a millimeter away from agreeing to go with her.

Which made no sense at all. The woman was only going to be here a few weeks. Still, she'd wormed her way into his unconscious, even at night in his dreams. He'd dreamed more than once about making love to Madeline Inglewood. Yeah, that was a laugh. A woman like her with a failure like him? A rich senator's daughter with her whole future ahead of her and a cripple with no future? Who was he kidding? The only good thing about dreaming about her was that he'd had fewer nightmares about the accident.

The reminder of his partner's death twisted deep in his gut. He drew a long, hard breath. Whatever thoughts he might have about Maddy, they would remain exactly that. It didn't pay to get close to anyone.

He knew that as well as he knew his name.

Because people always leave.

One way or another.

"ZELDA. Hey, pup, where are you?" It was dusk when Maddy slipped inside Zelda's compound. This time her heart began its usual racing, her hands went clammy and her breath came short.

The only occasion she hadn't reacted was when she'd been in a hurry and thinking about something else. Maybe that was the solution. Don't think about it.

Which didn't help her right now. But she continued forward toward Zelda's house, anyway. She didn't see the dog at all.

Deciding Zelda was probably sleeping, she checked the food and water supply. Everything seemed to be in working order. No problem there.

She started to walk away when it hit her—the food and water level hadn't gone down. Which could only mean Zelda hadn't eaten all day.

Panic seized Maddy's chest. She dashed to the doghouse and bent to look inside. Zelda lay listlessly in almost the same position as this morning.

"Hey, girl. What's going on here?"

The familiar wagging tail didn't move.

"What's wrong, pup? How come you're not eating?" She remembered J.D.'s words about the dog being easily traumatized, yet didn't know of anything that had happened to make her feel that way. But then, she hadn't been there since morning. J.D. had. Maybe he'd know what was going on.

"C'mon, sweetheart," she tried again, kneeling in front of the door so Zelda could see her. "C'mon out here and let's get some dinner. Yummy, yummy. Great stuff."

Nothing. In fact, the dog actually looked away, ignoring Maddy altogether. Maddy's stomach dropped. Something was wrong. Very wrong. Zelda had responded to her from the beginning, even when Maddy was scared to death of her. It was almost as if the dog had sensed Maddy's fear and was trying to make *her* more comfortable.

Which was ridiculous. Dogs didn't think, did they? She looked at Zelda again, at her big eyes that seemed to reflect a sadness Maddy hadn't noticed before. Maybe she did have thoughts and emotions? Once again Maddy wondered whether maybe Zelda was lonely.

Whatever the case, she had to tell J.D. and find out what to do about it. Maddy's heart sank to her toes. J.D. had asked her to do one little thing and she'd screwed it up.

She closed her eyes. What should she have done differently? She hadn't spent a lot of time with Zelda, but she'd done most of what was on the list. Other than that, nothing came to mind. She wasn't a dog person and had no experience with them.

"C'mon, Zelda. Come see me." Maddy patted her thighs.

With no response, Maddy got up and headed for the house, her steps heavy with dread. As much as she was worried about Zelda, she was worried about what J.D. would think. He'd trusted her, given her a responsibility and expected her to carry it out. And she hadn't.

Inside in the kitchen, the radio was playing, and J.D. was standing on a stool removing a cabinet door. He glanced up, his eyes bright when he saw her. "Hey," he said with a big smile.

"What're you doing?"

"It'll be easier for you to strip the wood if the doors are off.

"Good thinking."

"How's Zelda?"

"Well…I'm not sure."

He stopped what he was doing. "What do you mean?"

"I mean I don't know." She shifted her feet. "I haven't been around dogs very much and I can't tell if her listlessness is because something's wrong or if that's normal sometimes."

"What about her food?"

"It's still there from this morning."

At that, he dropped his screwdriver on the counter, stepped down from the stool and strode outside.

Maddy followed on his heels, hoping the dog's lethargy was just a normal thing. But she had an ominous feeling.

When J.D. got to the doghouse, he fell to his knees and stretched both arms inside. Maddy knelt next to him. A moment later, cradling a listless Zelda in his arms, he turned to Maddy.

He blamed her. She saw it in his eyes.

"She needs a vet."

"Is she sick? How can you tell?"

A muscle twitched in his cheek. "I can't. But I think we need to find out what's wrong as soon as possible. To do that I've got to take her to Yuma to the vet." He looked off, at the setting sun, a golden glow of burnt sienna on the horizon. "I'll have to go in the morning."

"Tomorrow is Sunday. Are they open on Sunday?"

He shook his head. "I doubt it."

"Not even in an emergency? She could get worse."

"Maybe. Damn. Even if I can get someone to see her, I can't afford to lose another day's work." He rubbed Zelda behind the ears, cooing at her as he did.

Oh, God. He was going to lose a day's work and it was her fault. She should've checked on Zelda earlier, made sure she was eating.

"How far is it to Yuma?"

"A couple hours," he said offhandedly, as if his mind was elsewhere. "I'll call the vet's office and leave a message. Maybe someone will call me back."

"I'm sorry. Maybe if I hadn't gone off with Annie today...if I'd stayed here with her—"

He looked at her. "It's not your fault."

"I wish there was something I could do."

J.D. gently placed Zelda inside her house on the cushion. They both rose to their feet and stood silently just looking at the dog for a while. Then, as if he'd had an inspiration, J.D. smiled, his eyes lit and he took Maddy by both arms. "That's it."

She smiled back. "That's what?"

"You said you wished you could do something. You can and it'll save me losing a day's work."

"Great. What is it?"

"Take Zelda to the vet."

Maddy's mouth opened but no words came out. Her pulse raced. He wanted her to drive to Yuma, a hundred miles one way, with a dog. She broke out in a cold sweat just thinking about it. As much as she wanted to help him, she didn't know if she could. What if she freaked out?

"What do you think?"

"Can't someone else do it?"

He stepped back, putting distance between them, his expression puzzled. "I can't spare Carlos and I wouldn't ask Juana with all her other responsibilities. There's no one except you."

She didn't know what to say, couldn't think of a logical way to refuse his request.

After a few long moments of silence, he said, "Never mind. It was a bad idea."

THAT NIGHT IN BED, Maddy chastised herself over and over about her inability to do what J.D. had asked. She'd been so sure she was making progress, so sure her life was on track, but she hadn't changed at all. She was the same insecure, phobia-prone person she'd been when she'd lived in Epiphany. Leaving Iowa hadn't changed a thing.

J.D. wasn't the kind of man to ask favors of anyone, but he'd asked her. He trusted her with Zelda. He had faith that she could make the trip to Yuma. He wouldn't have even suggested it if he hadn't. She knew that much about him.

He'd counted on her and she'd let him down. Failed.

The story of her life. God, she felt horrible.

You can do anything if you want it badly enough. She recited the phrase over and over. If she tried to do this and failed, would she feel any worse than she did this moment?

Maybe she couldn't toss her fears aside, but she could force herself to carry on despite her feelings.

What was the worst that could happen? She might be a basket case when she returned and J.D. would see it, but was that any worse than having him think his trust in her was misplaced?

Maddy spent the rest of the night in turmoil. If she couldn't do this one small thing, what were her chances of succeeding in the rest of her life? She didn't know what was worse. Reliving the dog attack or failing the one person who seemed to have a little faith in her.

Somewhere in the wee hours, she decided it had to be the latter. Because that was the one that would hurt the most.

When she awakened in sweat-drenched sheets at 4:30 a.m., it was obvious what she had to do. J.D. would be up at five, as always, to get in as many hours of work as he could. If ever there was a determined man, it was J. D. Rivera. He might even be up already and have gone to Yuma. She leaped from the bed.

Then she heard a hammer outside and dashed to the small patio door and peeked out. He was there. Relief swept through her.

She showered quickly, dressed in her good clothes and went to the kitchen for coffee. She needed fortification to do this. After a few sips, she walked outside.

''Good morning,'' she said, crossing the yard to where J.D. was standing on a ladder pounding nails. ''Did you call the vet last night?''

He nodded, his back as stiff as the hammer in his hand.

''Did he say what the problem might be? What we should do?''

"I didn't talk to him, just his service. They'll contact the vet, get her an emergency appointment today, and will call back to give us the time."

"Okay. I'll need the information and instructions on where to go and what to do."

He stopped pounding and stared at her.

"If I leave now, I'll get a head start, and when they call back, you can let them know I'm on my way."

Stepping from his ladder, his eyes narrowed. "You sure you want to do this?"

Maddy's heart raced. Could he see her fear? Was she that transparent? She nodded. "Yes, of course. But I'd like to have someone to ride with me. Remembering what happened to my rental car, I'd hate to drive all that way alone."

Maddy saw Benito walking toward them from the road. He was up early, too. "I know Carlos and Juana are busy, but what about Benito? I bet he'd love to come along and help with Zelda. Kids love animals."

J.D. shrugged, and walking away, said, "Fine with me. Just tell him his job today is to go along with you to Yuma and that he'll get the same pay."

Maddy waved Benito over to her and told him—in Spanish since he knew little English—exactly what J.D. had said. The boy's eyes lit up. "I get paid the same for riding in a car?" he asked.

Maddy nodded. "And for helping with Zelda."

He smiled, then wiped his hands on his grubby shorts. "I'm ready."

"Great," Maddy said. "Now all I need to do is call your family to make sure it's okay with them."

Benito's face fell. "They have no phone, but it's

okay with them that I come here to work for Mr. Rivera, and if I go along, I'll be working for him.'' He shrugged and gave her another of his charming smiles.

A glint of mischief shone in his eyes. If the boy wasn't a con artist already, he was well on his way. She was uncomfortable taking his word on it, so she walked over and told J.D. what the boy had said.

J.D. didn't appear to have any qualms. ''If he's working for me, he's working for me,'' he said and tossed her the keys. ''It doesn't matter where.''

She caught the keys.

''The place is called Pet Haven and the vet's name is Kendrick,'' J.D. continued. ''I don't have the exact address, but it's in the book in the kitchen. When I hear, I'll let them know you're on the way.''

Maddy moistened her lips, her nerves as tight as a guitar string. If she survived today, she could survive anything.

Twenty minutes later, she and Benito—with Zelda on his lap—were on the road to Yuma. It was a straight run. Nothing to worry about there. So far, so good.

The truck had only the basics, no radio and no air-conditioning. But the weather seemed to be cooling and with the windows open, a nice breeze blew over them. ''Benito,'' Maddy said to break the silence. ''Are you ready to start classes tomorrow night?''

Benito kept his eyes on the road ahead and one hand on Zelda. ''I promised Mr. Rivera I'd come.

He said if I don't like it after a week, it's okay to quit.''

The hair on the back of Maddy's neck prickled. What kind of thing was that to tell a child who wasn't old enough to be making those decisions? ''Well, I'd hate it if you quit, Benito. I know it's hard to see the benefits right now, but a good education will help you in the long run. If you learn to speak and read and write in English, you'll be able to get jobs doing many different things. You could even read that comic book you've got in your back pocket.''

He touched the comic book with one hand. ''Lots of stuff is in Spanish, too.''

And from what she'd learned from Carlos, Benito was close to illiterate in his native language as well.

''True. But knowing more than one language is very special. Not many people are bilingual, not even Mr. Rivera.''

Benito sat up a little straighter. ''What's so special about it?''

''Well, take me for example. I can speak four different languages and after I'm done with my job here, I'm hoping to go to New York to work for the United Nations as a simultaneous interpreter. That's someone who listens to a person talking in one language then tells another person who can't speak that language what the other person is saying.'' An oversimplification, but an explanation he could understand.

''Do you get lots of money to do that?''

''A whole lot more than I would pounding nails. And I also get to travel and see the world.''

Benito frowned, seeming to consider the idea.

"Quitting something just because you don't like it or find it hard to do isn't always the best decision."

"Why not?"

She searched for a reason to which he could relate. "Well, take Mr. Rivera. He's working hard on the ranch to get it fixed up so people can come and enjoy the place. He works many hours each day at that job, and he probably doesn't like working all those long hours. But he does it anyway because he'll have a nice place when he's finished and people will pay to visit. All his hard work will be worth it in the end."

Benito was silent, so she added, "A person's goal, what he wants in the end, is sometimes more important than what he wants right this minute. For example, by learning to read and write well, in either English or Spanish, you could create your own comic book someday."

His eyes went wide. "I could?"

She nodded. "You could."

"Could I be a sheriff?"

"You could be anything you wanted. Even president."

Benito didn't answer after that, but Maddy thought she might've made an impression.

They sailed along and after passing some agricultural areas, the scenery changed and the highway was flanked on both sides by scrubby desert plants, cacti and lots of sand. She tried unsuccessfully to get Benito to talk about himself. She asked about his home in Mexico and his parents, about the aunt and uncle he was staying with, but the only response she got was when she asked why he was working for J.D.

"Working in the field is hard and it doesn't pay much money. Mr. Rivera pays me more."

"What's not much money?"

"Four dollars an hour."

She didn't know what minimum wage was, but she was sure it was higher than that. "Do all the workers get paid the same?"

"Some get five dollars an hour maybe. It's a lot more than anyone can make in Tacámbaro. Workers there are lucky if they make five dollars for a whole day. And there aren't enough jobs for everyone."

Something personal at last. The town he mentioned was probably where he was from, where his parents lived. Tacámbaro. She'd have to remember that and look it up on the map.

"Still, five dollars an hour isn't really a lot. That's only two hundred dollars a week. Surely not enough to pay rent and buy food for a whole family."

Benito looked up at her, his eyes suddenly wary. She wasn't sure he was going to answer, but then he said, "Many families live together and share the rent. The *colonias* are very crowded. That's why I'm lucky to work for Mr. Rivera. He pays me more and gives me food, too."

"Really. Food for you to take to your aunt and uncle?"

The boy glanced at her, as if gauging her reactions, before he nodded.

"I didn't know that. It's nice of him to help out."

Just then, Zelda lifted her head to look at Maddy.

"Hey, girl," Maddy said, hoping Zelda wouldn't

try to crawl onto her lap. Driving J.D.'s truck was all she could handle at the moment.

"She's got to go," Benito said.

"Go?"

"You know—outside."

"Oh, yes." Where was her mind? She hadn't even thought of that. She pulled off the road and into a place where other cars were parked and tall sand dunes, dotted with tufts of salt grass at the base, lined both sides of the road. Other people had stopped to walk their dogs, too, and in the distance several ATVs buzzed up and down the tall dunes like ants, the noise disrupting what would otherwise have been a serene landscape. On the map, it looked as if they were about two-thirds of the way to Yuma, and she was relieved to be close. "Keep her leash tight. Okay?"

Benito hopped out with Zelda and Maddy climbed from the truck, too. She walked a little to stretch her legs and then came back to lean against the fender. An arid breeze ruffled her hair, reminding her of the night she'd stood on the back deck with J.D. The man confused her. He professed to be a loner, but yet he went out of his way to help Benito's family. He blamed himself for his friend's death, that was obvious.

Survivor's guilt? Lord, she knew all about that. For the last four years, not a day went by that she didn't wonder if she could've done something to help her roommate. Something that might've prevented the attack.

"I think Zelda needs something to drink," Benito said, coming over to her.

Glad he'd brought her out of her reverie, Maddy pulled out a plastic bowl and a water bottle that

J.D. had put in a small cooler in the back of the truck. Zelda watched with interest, and when Maddy finished pouring, the dog lapped up the cool liquid as if she'd been without water for days. Maddy smiled. "She's drinking, Benito. That's a good sign."

WITHIN THE HOUR, Maddy, Benito and Zelda pulled into a parking spot at Pet Haven—A Care Center for Animals. Several hours later, they were finished and on their way back to Tripplehorne Ranch. Zelda had a common bacterial infection that wasn't anything serious, the vet had said, and gave Maddy a prescription for a canine antibiotic that he filled for her.

They stopped for lunch at the local fast-food Burger Palace and then, driving back, Benito slept most of the way, as did Zelda, with her head in the boy's lap. Every now and then the dog stared up at Maddy and her little tail started clicking back and forth, lifting Maddy's spirits. If Zelda had been really sick because of something Maddy had done, she would never have forgiven herself. But an infection could have come from anywhere. And the little dog seemed to be getting perkier by the moment.

Maddy smiled at Zelda, feeling more confident than she had in years. She had not allowed her fear to paralyze her. Now, while a little success didn't mean she was home free, she certainly felt stronger emotionally than she had in a long time and vowed to be more attentive to the little dog's needs in the future.

Her therapist was right; success was about a person's willingness to risk doing something difficult. No risk, no reward.

That, she decided, was going to be her motto from now on. No risk, no reward.

"Are we there yet?" Benito asked, raising his head.

"Soon. We're on the outskirts of Los Rios, close to where your aunt and uncle live."

Benito gave no response and looked away. If conditions were really as bad as he said, maybe he was embarrassed about it. Curious, Maddy turned down a side street, wanting to get a look for herself.

"No, *señorita,* you're going the wrong way."

"I just want to see the *colonias* you were telling me about, Benito."

"I didn't lie. Do you think I lied?"

"No, but I'm thinking if the conditions are as bad as you say, maybe I can do something to help."

Benito inched down in his seat. A normal response for a ten-year-old, she guessed. Her brother had done the same thing when she'd had to take him places. He'd been mortified to go anywhere with his big sister.

A couple miles down the road, the street suddenly turned to dirt, and she realized it wasn't really a street at all, but an alley that was lined with trash cans, some filled to the brim with garbage and others tipped over with gaunt dogs rummaging through them. A dozen or so tiny wooden shacks with tin roofs and windows that had no glass flanked both sides, along with several outhouses.

Depressed, Maddy quickly headed back to the main road. How could the citizens of Los Rios let people live like this?

As she drove out of the area and back onto the main road, Benito said, "You can let me off at the next crossroad."

Maddy glanced at him. ''There's nothing there but fields. How about if you go with me to the ranch, we drop off Zelda, and then I'll drive you home afterward. I'd like to talk with your aunt and uncle, anyway.''

Benito's dark brown eyes widened like two full moons. The boy suddenly looked terrified.

''It's okay. I'm not going to say anything that'll get you in trouble, Benito. I just want to tell them what a great kid you are.''

He didn't seem to hear her, but pushed forward to sit on the edge of the seat, one hand on the dash. And when she stopped at the crossroad, he opened the door, jumped out and ran like the wind. Zelda barked and in a split second, she was gone from the truck and following Benito.

Oh, God! ''Benito! Zelda!'' She pulled the truck to the side of the road and scrambled out, calling as she did. ''Benito, come back! Zelda's following you. She'll get lost.''

Benito stopped. *''Vamos.''* He waved his arms at Zelda, who barked three or four times at him.

Then Maddy watched in horror as Benito took off to the right and Zelda dashed into the field on the left. Panic grabbed her by the throat, and though she tried to call after them, all that came out was a croak.

Stop. Think it through. She drew a deep breath. *You can't go after both of them, so make a decision. One or the other.* Benito obviously knew his way around and how to get home. Zelda had never been out of the dog run except on the ranch. Maddy took off after the dog.

But it was dusky and hard to see.

And Zelda had vanished.

CHAPTER TWELVE

"CAN YOU REPEAT THAT? I think my hearing must be impaired because I thought you said you'd *lost* Zelda." J.D.'s voice rose a few decibels on the word *lost,* and his eyes rounded with disbelief.

"I'm so sorry. I searched everywhere for her, but it was getting dark and I couldn't see where she went. I figured it would be better to come back and see if you had any ideas about what to do."

He didn't acknowledge her apology but slammed a fist into the palm of his other hand. "Damn!" He crossed the room, then paced back again. "Where's Benito?"

"I don't know."

"I can't believe that between the two of you, you couldn't manage to take care of one small dog for a few hours."

"It was a whole day, and it didn't happen because we were careless."

He stopped dead in front of her, his expression incredulous. "Really. Zelda's gone because you were so conscientious?"

"She's gone because Benito jumped from the truck and left the door open."

Incredulity switched to puzzlement. "Why would he do that?"

An ironic laugh escaped her lips. "I wish to hell

I knew. One minute we were driving along and the next he was gone."

"Just like that?"

Maddy sat on a kitchen chair and crossed her arms. "Not exactly."

"Then what exactly?" His voice was loud again.

"Everything was fine until he asked me to drop him off near some field outside Los Rios. I felt responsible for him since I'd brought him along. I couldn't just drop him off on the road. I told him to ride back here with me and once I got Zelda settled, I'd drive him home. That way I could talk with his aunt and uncle, too."

He frowned.

"Does that matter?"

J.D. walked over and dropped into a chair next to her. "No, not really. What matters right now is finding Zelda. Otherwise I can kiss this place good-bye."

"What does finding Zelda have to do with the ranch?"

"Two things. One, there's a stipulation in the will that requires me to keep Zelda safe and healthy. If anything happens to her before a one-year deadline, aside from an act of God, I forfeit the ranch and everything goes to Aunt Ethel's favorite animal shelter. And two, Zelda's residuals pay for this place. If she's gone, that money goes, too."

"Residuals?"

"Residuals from some television commercials she was in a while ago and a stint she did on one of those short-lived sitcoms." He gave a sarcastic laugh. "Zelda was Aunt Ethel's cash cow."

That explained Ethel Devereaux's reasons for

keeping Zelda when she hadn't kept any of her other animals. And without Zelda, J.D. was screwed.

A knot formed in Maddy's stomach. She felt sick. This was all her fault. She pushed forward on her chair, elbows on the table. "I can't imagine you'd lose the ranch if you explain that losing Zelda wasn't your fault."

He took a cigarette from his pocket and tamped it on the table. A few seconds later he flicked it into the trash. "No need to imagine anything. It's all laid out in the will. I guess dear Aunt Ethel thought that would guarantee her beloved Zelda would be cared for."

Tears welled behind Maddy's eyes. She couldn't let J.D. lose the Tripplehorne because of her. And poor little Zelda needed her medicine. She could get worse; she could starve to death or get hit by a car. She wasn't used to running wild. Maddy had to do something. "Can I borrow your truck?"

"What for?"

She bolted from her chair. "I'm going to look for Zelda."

His expression said he didn't believe it would do any good, or maybe he was just resigned to his fate. But after a moment, he sighed and stood up himself. "C'mon, we'll go together."

THREE HOURS LATER, they were back at the ranch—without Zelda. Maddy went to bed feeling as if the world had collapsed around her. What was she going to do? Maybe if she talked to Harold Martin he'd have an idea about what to do. Maybe that clause in the will only applied if J.D. was at fault.

He couldn't be held responsible for something *she'd* done, could he? But getting in touch with the attorney wasn't going to happen until Mr. Martin returned J.D.'s call.

Maybe Zelda would turn up—maybe even come home on her own. Maddy had read stories about dogs being lost hundreds of miles from their homes and somehow finding their way back. Apparently dogs had a keen sense of direction. Maybe they'd wake up in the morning and Zelda would be there.

Maybe Maddy would wake up and find this was all a dream.

More like a nightmare. Everything she'd accomplished could be wiped out in one fell swoop. Her stomach churned. She couldn't let that happen. She *wouldn't* let that happen.

Awakening at dawn with a renewed sense of determination, Maddy got up, walked to the French doors and opened the blinds. Varied tones of sky-blue and pink layered the horizon and in the center, a tiny crescent of gold slowly inched upward. Sunrises in the desert literally took her breath away, the combinations of colors like none she'd seen before.

She left the blinds open, showered and pulled on a pair of boxer shorts and one of the white sleeveless T-shirts, hurrying to leave before J.D. arose. Within fifteen minutes she was in his truck and on the road.

At the field where the dog had run off, she pulled to the side, parked next to the La Mancha sign and climbed down.

''Zelda,'' she called out. ''C'mon, girl, it's time to go home.'' She glanced at the tilled earth, hoping to see tracks she might be able to follow, but all she saw were the footprints she and J.D. had left the night before.

While the crops in this field weren't any higher than her thighs, they were tall enough to hide a small dog. She started her search systematically on her left near the spot where Zelda had disappeared. She would cover each and every row until she was certain poor Zelda wasn't lying limp in the field somewhere.

Her heart ached just thinking it. The dog had an infection, she needed the medicine the vet had given her. She could get worse if she wasn't taken care of properly. She needed water and food and loving care.

As Maddy searched, the sun rose higher and higher and sweat trickled down her face and neck. Her flip-flops kept coming off, her legs were itchy from brushing against the crops, and she was thirsty and tired and distraught. Despite her discomfort, all she could think of was poor Zelda out there somewhere, sick and alone and afraid.

And it was her fault. J.D. would, no doubt, fire her now, and with good cause.

Well, she didn't care about that anymore. What mattered was finding Zelda.

"Zelda, sweetheart, please come to Maddy." *Please, please, please.*

Two hours passed and still no Zelda. Maddy's throat was hoarse from calling, her legs were scratched and sore and her feet felt raw. She'd finally taken her flip-flops off. With every step she took, her spirits waned. She'd covered this field twice and Zelda was nowhere to be found.

It was past breakfast time at the ranch, and by

now, J.D. would know she was gone with his truck. She should go back, but she couldn't—not without Zelda.

The crossroad bisected four different fields, and so far she'd only covered one. What were the chances that Zelda had made her way to one of the other fields? She couldn't leave without checking them, too.

By the time she finished the second field, it was noon, and she felt something wet underfoot. She plodded on, and when the water covered her feet, she realized the irrigation had come on and all the spaces between the berms would fill completely.

Not that it mattered. She wasn't going to quit until she'd scoured every inch of every acre.

Mud squished between her toes, and the sun beat like fire on her head and bare arms. "Zelda, where are you? C'mon, it's time to go home."

Sometime around 2:00 p.m., with her shorts and shirt caked in mud and sweat, tears welled in Maddy's eyes. It was hopeless. Zelda was gone, and J.D. was going to lose the ranch. She didn't know which was worse.

She dropped onto the ground at the edge of the last field and let the tears run down her cheeks. She was an utter and total failure. No one should ever count on her for anything.

She'd wanted so much to take control of her life. She'd wanted people to have confidence in her, to believe in her, and she thought J.D. had begun to. But now he'd know his faith in her wasn't justified. Even if he didn't fire her, the ranch would be sold and there'd be no employees for her to teach, so what was the point?

No one to teach. By helping Carlos, Juana and Mariela's family learn English, she was giving them a skill that could better their lives. That was important—more important than her other goals, which suddenly seemed selfish and insignificant in contrast.

She wiped the back of her hand across her wet cheeks, brushing mud over her mouth in the process. She spat on the ground to get rid of the gritty taste, closed her eyes and took a long breath, and as she did, a deep, dark despair settled inside her.

She had to go back and tell J.D. that she'd failed to find Zelda.

As she sat there mustering the energy to get up, she felt something move next to her. She froze. Snakes and lizards and tarantulas were common here and everything she'd read about desert survival said to remain still. But she couldn't stay like that forever, and whatever it was, wasn't leaving. Slowly, she pried open one eye and then the other. Her heart rocketed to her throat.

A muddy, bedraggled Zelda snuggled closer and finally crawled onto Maddy's lap. "Oh, thank God! Thank God. It's you, Zelda. It's really you!" Even in her excitement, Maddy quickly felt around for Zelda's collar to make sure she had a secure hold on her. No way was she going to give the animal the opportunity to run off again.

She ruffled the dog's head, scratched behind her ears. "Zelda, Zelda, Zelda! I can't tell you how happy I am to see you. Are you okay, girl? You're not hurt or anything..." She quickly checked the dog, feeling for cuts and bumps. Nothing that she could tell.

Relief coursed through Maddy. Oh, God, she was happy! As happy as she could ever remember—and all because of Zelda.

A dog.

She smiled to herself as the irony sank in. If her mother could only see her now. She looked to the sky and laughed out loud. "Right!" she chortled, then cuddled the furry dirt ball in her lap.

"Zelda, Zelda, Zelda. I'm so happy to see you."

"DAMN WOMAN!" J.D. paced across the back deck, his gaze pinned on the road for any sign of her.

He'd gotten up at 5:00 a.m., and she was already gone—along with his truck. That was fourteen hours ago. Fourteen hours in which his emotions had run the gamut from anger over her stealing his ride, to worry about losing the ranch, and dammit, worry about Maddy herself. Where the hell was she? She couldn't still be looking for Zelda, could she? You'd think after six or seven hours, a person would give up.

Yeah, that would be a normal person. Madeline Inglewood was anything but normal. He'd never seen anyone so determined. She'd nagged him to death about helping. In the end, she'd gotten what she wanted. He had to admire her persistence.

But he didn't want to feel that way about her. He couldn't afford to feel anything for anyone, especially a woman who'd be gone within a couple of weeks. She'd made no bones about that. Adventure and excitement, that was what she was after. And she sure as hell wasn't going to get it at the Triplehorne.

The way it looked right now, there wasn't going to *be* a Tripplehorne much longer.

But none of that managed to keep him from thinking about her warm body next to his, and how she'd kissed him, long and deep and sensual. She hadn't held back at all.

God, he hoped nothing had happened to her. If only he hadn't told her he'd lose the ranch without Zelda, she'd be here right now. He should've been the one to go looking for the animal, not her. *He* knew the area. And he could defend himself if need be.

He whirled around, his mind spinning. She could've gone off the road, run out of gas or gotten lost somewhere in the desert. She could've stumbled on drug smugglers or coyotes...

He squeezed his eyes shut and stood with his hands flat on the porch railing. If something had happened to her... God. He couldn't even imagine...

But then, bad things always happened to the people J.D. cared about. The thought took him by surprise. He cared about her. Yes, he actually cared about her.

Damn!

Just then, he heard a sound, saw a cloud of dust spiraling up the road. Though he couldn't see the vehicle, it had to be his truck. He felt as if a huge weight had been lifted from his chest.

He paced some more, then stopped. He stuffed his hands into the pockets of his jeans and waited. When she pulled up and got out, his mouth fell open.

She had Zelda. She actually had the dog!

But that wasn't nearly as important as the fact that she was okay. Filled with relief, he walked over to her and said, "You stole my truck."

She hurried past him toward the kennel, pausing only long enough to say, "So call the police."

He did a double take. What the hell? Hey, *she'd* lost *his* dog and put the ranch in jeopardy. *She'd* stolen *his* truck and hadn't bothered to call or let him know what the hell was going on for fourteen hours. He had a right to be upset.

He followed Maddy to the kennel. "Where'd you find her?"

Opening Zelda's gate, Maddy looked up. Tear tracks stained her mud-smudged cheeks. Bloody scratches covered her arms and legs. Her clothes were wet and filthy and she was barefoot. He wanted to give her a hug.

"In the same place she ran away. It just took her a while to come back."

"Are you all right?"

"Do I look all right?" She tossed his own words back at him.

Okay, he deserved that. "No. You look terrible."

"So do you."

Sheesh! He pulled back. What had gotten into her? He was concerned, that was all.

She let Zelda down inside the kennel and closed the gate. "I'll clean her up in a minute."

"I'll do it. You go in and shower. I've got some first-aid stuff in the bathroom."

She crossed her arms over her chest. "No. It's my fault this happened, so I'd like to take care of it myself. Please let me do that."

That sense of responsibility again. And again, he

was impressed. She'd make a good wingman—or top gun. He reached out and brushed a smudge from her cheek with his thumb. "Okay. If you'd like."

"I'd like," she said more softly. "Thank you."

His gaze caught hers and held. A moment of understanding passed between them. A moment of truth. He wondered if she knew that he cared about her.

As if she'd read his mind and was a little embarrassed, she lowered her eycs.

The woman was an enigma. He hadn't thought so at first—he was certain he'd had her number. Rich daddy's girl, used to getting everything she wanted and content to let others wait on her.

Man, had he been wrong. Dead wrong.

YOU STOLE MY TRUCK! Was that all he was concerned about? The man was infuriating. Wasn't he glad to see that Zelda was home safe and sound? Couldn't he have managed one little thank-you?

Irritated, Maddy ripped off her clothes. She'd bathed Zelda, given her the medicine and made sure she was comfortable. Now it was her turn for a shower.

Not one little thank-you. Not one. He was the most unappreciative man she'd ever met.

Fine with her. She wasn't going to be around anyway, so what did it matter?

It didn't. But somehow it did. Maybe because she'd seen his soft side. The side that helped immigrants and little boys, and treasured the memories of his parents and grandparents. But could that side ever outweigh the other? The side that was dark.

Foreboding. Forbidding. The side that warned that one shouldn't get too close.

As Maddy got into the shower, the warm water stung the cuts on her legs and arms, but after a few seconds all she felt was the gentle pulse of water massaging her weary muscles. She wished it was J.D. massaging her instead.

Where did that thought come from? Who was she fooling? She thought about him all the time and found herself waiting anxiously to spend time with him. Even when she was working or teaching, she was wondering what he'd think or what his reaction might be.

She lathered up with her favorite mango-scented soap, and when she'd finished showering, she toweled off and smoothed soothing lotion over her skin, avoiding the cuts. Then she shrugged on her white terry robe and lay on the bed, debating whether to go out and talk to J.D. about dinner or simply take a nap.

"Maddy?" J.D.'s rich, deep voice came from outside her door.

"Maddy?" he repeated.

"Yes, c'mon in."

As the door swung open, J.D.'s body was silhouetted by the light behind him in the hallway. Just looking at him stirred her blood.

"I brought some first-aid cream." He came over and sat on the edge of the bed beside her.

She wrinkled her nose. "The stuff won't sting, will it?"

"Don't think so. Here, let's try some." He unscrewed the top and put a tiny dab on his fingertips.

Suddenly, he was smoothing the cream over a cut on her ankle.

"Mmm. You're right. It's soothing."

His eyes met hers. "Good. Now turn over, I saw some scratches on the back of your arms and legs."

"You checked me out?" she joked.

"From day one."

Desire fluttered in her stomach. She rolled over so he couldn't see her face. So she wouldn't give herself away. "If I remember correctly, on day one, you were desperately trying to get rid of me."

He chuckled. "And here I thought I was being smooth about it."

"Not."

He laughed again. "Doesn't mean I didn't check you out. And as I recall, you did the same."

Now *she* laughed. "You weren't exactly invisible standing in front of me half-dressed," she said softly, enjoying the rhythm of his hands massaging her legs.

"How does that feel?"

"Wonderful."

His words were like a soft hypnotic suggestion. His touch—now high on her leg—soothed and thrilled at the same time. "It doesn't sting at all," she added.

"Good. But I'd better quit. I'm beginning to enjoy this a little too much."

She rolled over onto her back. "I like it, too. You give good first aid."

He handed her the tube of cream. "Yeah, I'm a real Dr. Kildare."

For the longest time, they simply looked at each other, their eyes saying things that wouldn't be vocalized. Then J.D. said softly, ''Thank you for bringing Zelda home.''

A lump formed in her throat and suddenly tears welled up. ''I was so scared I wouldn't find her,'' she admitted, and the tears began to roll unchecked down her cheeks.

''Hey.'' He pulled her into his arms. ''But you did and everything's fine.''

Suddenly, as if she had no control, her tears evolved into great huge sobs that came from deep inside. She couldn't make them stop. ''Everything isn't fine,'' she cried, gulping air.

He held her closer, patting her back and stroking her hair, his moves tentative, as if he wasn't sure what to do. He was murmuring soothing words, but that just made her sob even harder.

She pulled away and sputtered, ''It's n-not fine, because I lost her. And you could've lost this place, and it would've been my fault.''

He held her at arm's length, incredulity in his eyes. ''But it didn't happen. You didn't lose her. And the reason you didn't was because you wouldn't quit. Look at you. You're all cuts and bruises and you still didn't quit. Not many people would've kept going like that. I wouldn't have. I wish I had half your determination.''

She rubbed her sleeve across her cheeks. ''You do?''

He nodded. ''I do. I admire that trait a lot.''

Tears started to run again. ''I feel like a broken faucet.'' She wiped her eyes again with her sleeve.

He admired her. He wished he had her determination. Her heart swelled.

''Maybe you should get a little rest,'' he said as

he reached behind her to plump up her pillow. She leaned back against it.

"Can you stay with me for a little while?"

"Sure." And he leaned back against the pillow beside her.

CHAPTER THIRTEEN

J.D. HAD LEFT her room somewhere in the wee hours of the morning. Now she stretched like a lazy cat, remembering how nice it had felt to fall asleep with him next to her.

Nice for her, anyway.

Lord. What must he think? She knew what he'd said, but did he mean it? Or was he just trying to calm her down, make her feel better?

Somewhere inside, she didn't believe that was the case. He'd seemed sincere, and he'd stayed there with her, cradling her in his arms until she fell asleep.

She wanted to feel good about that, but instead she felt needy and dependent. Maybe he thought she was pathetic. Here it was almost noon, and she was still in bed.

She got up, dressed and went to the kitchen.

J.D. had removed all the doors and hinges from the cabinets and had somehow gotten the supplies she'd had on her list. Stripper, rags, sandpaper, chisel, turpentine, and a small tool kit sat on the counter near another covered tray. A yellow sticky note was stuck on top and it had her name on it in J.D.'s bold handwriting. Smiling to herself, she lifted the cover. A cellophane-wrapped sandwich, a small bag of chips and a pickle.

Still smiling, Maddy poured herself a cup of coffee that smelled as if it had been brewing all morning and sat down to eat.

After that, she went to the kennel and gave Zelda her food and antibiotics, and then stayed to play with her for a while. Zelda seemed her old self and reveled in the company. Maddy had been right. Zelda was lonely.

The rest of the day flew by, and after dinner Maddy went to the old bunkhouse to set up shop for her new students. Filled with a mixture of excitement and trepidation, she took stock of her supplies. What else did she need? Tablets? Pens? She had all those. What was she missing?

Could she even do this? She'd been comfortable teaching Juana and Carlos, but how would she be with more people in the room? Some of Mariela's children might be too young to learn because they couldn't talk yet, but Maddy had told her to bring them along anyway. Mariela was a widow and had no one but Juana to help her. If she didn't have anyone to watch the children, she might not come.

Then there was Benito. Would he come?

He'd said he'd try it, but that was before he'd run off. And today, when she'd gone to talk with him, he'd disappeared, even though he'd been right there the minute before. J.D. had assured her he was okay and that he'd be in class tonight. She wasn't so sure.

"Need help?"

Maddy looked up. J.D. walked toward her, his long-legged strides purposeful, his thighs powerful. The man made her stomach flutter and her heart skip a beat. "No. I think I'm okay. I don't know how comfortable the benches will be for small children, though.''

His forehead furrowed. ''Small children?'' He glanced at the seating arrangement—two long picnic tables with attached benches that Carlos had brought in from the yard, and the extra chairs and table from before. ''Benito should be fine with what's there.''

''No, not Benito. I was talking about Mariela's children.''

Surprise registered in his eyes.

''Oh, dear. With so much going on, I guess I forgot to tell you that I invited Mariela and her children to attend the class.''

''Is there anything else that slipped your mind?''

''No.''

He was quiet for a moment, then said, ''Make sure you close everything up tight when you're done. And shut off the lights.''

Well, that threw her. She'd expected a protest. She was almost afraid to say anything. ''It's okay with you, then?''

He shrugged and turned to go. ''It's your class. I guess you know what you can handle and what you can't.''

She didn't. Not at all. Only he didn't need to know that. Hands clasped behind her, she rocked back on her heels. ''Right. It's going to be a lot of fun.''

Carlos entered the building; Juana and her sister and family not far behind. Maddy checked her watch. ''It's almost time.''

''Yeah, and I'm leaving.''

''You can stay, you know.''

"You think I need English lessons?"

"No," she said, smiling. "But you're still welcome to stay."

His gaze softened. "I've got other things to do. How about a rain check?"

She smiled. "Anytime."

As he walked away, he pointed a finger at her and clicked his tongue. "Later, kiddo."

Kiddo. She smiled. *Petunia.* He had lots of pet names for her, it seemed, and that made her feel...what? It made her feel good. Special. That was it. It made her feel that he liked her.

She gathered up papers and went to the table to sort out her work sheets. There were different ESL teaching methods, but since she wanted to do the most with the short time she had, she'd picked immersion with some support in their native language, hoping she'd teach them enough English to function in the U.S.

"Señorita Inglewood?"

Maddy swung around. "Yes, Carlos."

Carlos tipped his head toward the door. Benito was headed inside, and he was carrying some long cushions.

For the benches. So the children would be more comfortable. Special. Yes, she felt special indeed.

NO MATTER HOW APPEALING it might be to sit in on Maddy's class and watch her teach, J.D. had more important things to do.

He opened the glass door to the gun cabinet, lifted the 12-gauge from its slot and then went outside. He lodged the rifle in the back window of his truck and within five minutes he was driving down the bumpy, dusty back road to El Camino del Diablo, the route most used by illegals entering the country.

El Camino del Diablo. The Road of the Devil. Or the more popular term, the Devil's Highway—a hundred-and-thirty-mile stretch of the most desolate, inhospitable terrain in the nation. An arid dusky landscape where rugged, waterless mountain ranges blocked direct travel, where temperatures soared to a hundred and twenty degrees and dozens of stone crosses gave testament to those who'd paid the ultimate price in search of a better life.

Thirst and blast-furnace heat weren't the only enemies on El Camino. Windstorms, bandits and drug smugglers compounded the problems.

When he reached the furthermost point of the ranch, the sun had slipped below the distant mountains and the sky glowed pink on the horizon. He got out, pulled down the tailgate and made a ramp with a heavy board. Then he rolled one of the barrels from his truck.

He unhitched the chain securing the empty barrel to a concrete slab and secured the new one in its place. Then he rolled the empty one into his truck, wondering how long it had been empty. Maybe two weeks was too long between fillings. He climbed into the truck and he drove another ten miles and unloaded the second barrel and then another ten miles for the third. He left his truck lights on to see, and as he rolled down the last one, he noticed the keg he'd left before was missing.

Whoever had taken it had to have had a vehicle. He got his flashlight and looked for signs, tire tracks, brushed-over footprints, drag marks.

Just then, a low gravelly voice came from an arroyo behind him. "Well, well, fancy meeting you out here, Rivera. I should've guessed you'd be involved."

J.D. swung all the way around. Sheriff Collier was standing behind him with four men at his side. All four had clothes drenched with sweat, mouths caked with trail dust, lips cracked from dehydration. Some looked as if they could barely stand, yet they were handcuffed together like a chain gang. The sheriff must've lain in wait for the men to come for water.

"Involved in what?" J.D. shone his flashlight around and saw the sheriff's truck hidden in a wash behind a large paloverde tree. In the back was the missing barrel.

"You and your bleeding-heart groups can drop all the water you want, but it isn't going to change anything. We seized nearly two hundred thousand pounds of marijuana and eighteen hundred pounds of cocaine from smugglers last year. You're not helping anyone, Rivera. You're aiding and abetting."

"It'll help them." He nodded to the men. The "bleeding hearts" the sheriff had mentioned was Humane Borders, a Tucson-based group that had set up more than twenty water stations in the desert to reduce the number of deaths. But J.D.'s reason for doing this was personal. A little water would've saved his father's life.

"They'll get what they need when I bring them in."

"Doesn't look like they'll make it without water,

Sheriff.'' J.D. walked to the barrel, took the cup that was chained to it and filled it to the brim.

The sheriff didn't move, but one of the men lurched forward and the others stumbled along. He held the cup out and the first man grabbed it and drank in huge gulps. *''Gracias, señor,''* he said when he'd finished, a resigned acceptance in his eyes. J.D. had seen that look before—in his father's eyes right before he died. And in his dreams, J.D. saw it in his partner's eyes. He'd been responsible. Both times.

''De nada.'' He filled the cup again and gave it to the next man, and the next, and all the while, the sheriff stood there, his hands clenched at his sides and his body tense with rage.

When the last man finished, J.D. said, ''I'll be more than happy to help you take these guys in, Sheriff.''

The sheriff's mouth twisted. ''If you know what's good for you, you'll butt out and mind your own business.''

''Well, y'know, I've never really been good at judging what's good for me, so I think I'll follow you in, anyway. Just in case you need a little help with these guys.'' But more to make sure the men reached their destination in one piece.

Sometimes coyotes or other unscrupulous individuals paid a person's fee to cross over, and the ''clients'' were then placed into servitude until the debt was paid. Modern-day slavery. J.D. figured some big businesses in the area were involved, and he hoped to someday catch them in the act. But failing that, if he followed the sheriff to the border station, at least he'd know that all of these men would go back where they belonged.

"You interfering with my job?"

He shrugged. "Public road, Sheriff."

Cursing, Sheriff Collier herded the men into the back of his vehicle and took off, spitting sand and dust in J.D.'s face.

He followed the sheriff all the way to the border station at Lukeville, then circled around to go back home. As he peeled out, he gave the sheriff a two-finger salute and smiled. "Adios, amigo."

MADDY PUT the final touch on one of the kitchen cabinet doors, then dropped the brush into a can of turpentine. The whole job had only taken one week to finish. She felt good about that—and with the results. The stain on the cabinets was a rich warm oak, and the semigloss varnish gave it just the right patina. J.D. and Carlos had carried the doors to one of the outbuildings so that Maddy could work on them without disrupting Juana, who was now cooking full-time in the kitchen.

Between teaching and working on the kitchen project, she'd been busier than she'd ever envisioned—from the time she awakened till the time she went to bed, sometimes at midnight.

Her students were a delight, and with each passing day she became more excited about their progress. Benito had taken to the lessons like a scholar. He even came early, supposedly to prepare for class, but she knew it was so he could practice his English with her.

In one week's time, she and Ben, as he'd asked

to be called, had developed a friendship she wouldn't have imagined when she'd first met him.

But he still gave little information about his personal life, and for a while now she'd had more than a lingering suspicion he wasn't telling the truth. There was a reason he'd jumped from the truck—a reason he didn't want her to meet his aunt and uncle.

But until he was comfortable enough to talk with her about his family, she wasn't going to push it. She certainly didn't want him running away again.

Taking care of Zelda had become a pleasure instead of a dread-filled chore, and sometimes she even brought Zelda into class with her. Mariela's children loved having the dog there and Zelda seemed to like it just as much.

In two short weeks, she'd developed a deep commitment to the jobs she'd taken on at Tripplehorne and had come to feel an attachment to the ranch as well. She'd started out wanting to prove something to herself, but now she rarely thought about that. The ranch and the people she worked with had become important to her—almost as if they were family.

In the past week, she'd worked side by side with J.D. and found a quiet reassurance in doing so. He didn't compliment her at every turn—that wasn't his way. But his expectations for her were high—and to her, that was the best compliment he could give.

"Looks great."

Maddy turned and J.D. was standing there. He'd been working outside all day and he smelled like fresh air and sweat, and his hair looped over his forehead in the sexiest way. "Thank you. They came out even better than I expected."

"I knew when I saw your work plan that you'd do a great job."

"Really? What a nice thing to say."

"I'm not being nice, it's the truth."

"Humor me. I think it's nice. You're nice, too, though you do everything you can to give the opposite impression."

He cleared his throat. "Did you figure all that out on your own or did you read it in one of those self-help books of yours?" He wasn't being snide. It was just a question. He'd noticed the books when he was fixing the light in her room.

"I've learned a lot from books, but what I've learned about people has been on my own."

"What if you're wrong? What if I'm not nice," he teased.

"It doesn't matter. One of the things I did learn from those books is that, right or wrong, I'm entitled to my opinion—even when someone doesn't agree with it."

He crossed his arms over his chest and grinned. "Well, for future reference, keep those kinds of opinions to yourself."

She laughed. "Now you sound like my father. He could never understand that sometimes people don't want a response. Sometimes they just need to say what's on their minds."

He cracked a sexy smile. "It's a guy thing. And as long as we're giving out opinions here, I think you should take a break. You've been working harder than a stevedore."

"Oh, I will be taking a break, tomorrow in fact,

for the September Festival. I promised the ladies I'd help out."

"Okay."

"Have you thought any more about coming along? It'd be fun. You could work the booth with me."

"Uh...I don't think so."

"Why not? You need a day off more than I do."

"No, I don't."

"Well, I think you do. That's my opinion and I'm sticking to it."

She'd moved closer so she was standing right in front of him. He placed a hand on her upper arm, a glint of amusement in his eyes. "While your opinion is immensely important, it wouldn't be in your best interests for me to do that. I'd only spoil your fun."

"Why don't you let me be the judge of that."

"Besides, I've got a busy day. Lots of work to do." He started for the house.

She shrugged. "Have it your way."

Yeah, he would. Because he knew what being around her was doing to his libido. He knew that sooner or later his testosterone-induced fantasies were going to send him over the edge and he couldn't be responsible for what might happen. Being with her had changed him in many ways.

With each passing day, he found himself thinking more and more about Maddy and wondering what it would be like to have her there permanently. He thought about how happy his grandparents had been together and his mother and father.

Though his parents had only had six years together, the love between them was unshakable.

Why else would his mother go to Mexico with his father and never return—not even to see her own parents? Not until she was sick and dying.

What would it be like to have someone love you that much? He'd never even been close to that kind of relationship with anyone, not even with Jenna. When she broke off their engagement after the accident, it simply confirmed what he knew to be true—what had always been true for him.

People always left—one way or another.

But for some crazy reason, thinking about Maddy crossed every barrier he'd ever put up to protect himself. He wanted her. Wanted to spend the rest of his life with her.

If he had a life.

But he didn't, so he'd go about his business and wish her the best when she left. His stomach felt hollow every time he thought about what it would be like when she was gone—when he was alone again.

THE NEXT MORNING, J.D. awoke to the robust scent of coffee and voices and loud banging. He checked the clock. Man, he'd overslept. Still, it wasn't even six. He got up and peered out the window.

Carlos was outside with two other men J.D. didn't recognize. Maddy was out there, too, handing coffee cups to all of them. He brushed his teeth, took a quick shower and then, barely passing a towel across his body, put on a pair of jeans and went outside.

"Would someone mind telling me what's going on?"

Maddy's eyes lit up when she saw him and she

smiled. ‘‘Yes. I mean no, I wouldn’t mind telling you—as soon as I find out myself.’’

She spoke to Carlos in Spanish and he responded. Then she looked at the two men, smiled and nodded before turning back to J.D. ‘‘They both like their coffee black.’’

‘‘That’s what you asked? I want to know what they’re doing here.’’

‘‘They’re here to work for you.’’

‘‘I didn’t hire anyone.’’ But he did need help, and if these guys knew what they were doing… ‘‘What skills do they have?’’

Maddy spoke to Carlos again. ‘‘They’re carpenters. This is Jésus—’’ she motioned to the older man ‘‘—and this is his son, Daniel. Carlos told them you might be hiring and that they should come and talk to you.’’

J.D. shook hands with both men. ‘‘Does either one speak English?’’

She shook her head. ‘‘No.’’

‘‘I guess I’d need to see the quality of their work.’’

Just then a red pickup pulled into the driveway. Grady’s truck, but Annie was at the wheel.

‘‘Gotta go,’’ Maddy said, hustling over to the truck. She opened the door, stepped up on the lift and turned to J.D. ‘‘You oughta come. Even if it’s just for a little while.’’

She gave a wide white smile that showed her dimples, and right before she pulled the door shut, she added, ‘‘Unless you’re chicken.’’

CHAPTER FOURTEEN

STANDING ON THE CURB in front of the Sunflower Café, Maddy glanced up at the flapping red, white and blue banner spanning Los Rios's Main Street, announcing September Day, the annual arts and crafts festival. Booths filled with food and all manner of homemade items and trinkets made by the Los Rios Ladies' Club lined both sides of the street, which was still littered with the remains of the parade an hour before.

She checked the time. Five-thirty and still no J.D. She'd watched for him all day and now her hope was waning.

With his military background, he might've liked the parade. The high-school band had played snappy patriotic songs, the majorettes twirled their batons and the cheerleaders did zis-boom-bahs and dazzled the spectators by doing cartwheels down the entire two blocks that made up Main Street.

The only float in the parade was from Masterson's, a mock-up of the old brick building. The boy and girl sitting atop the float and waving like crazy wore banners proclaiming them Homecoming King and Queen of Los Rios High.

The little town was so like Epiphany, it made Maddy a bit homesick. She loved Epiphany and its people. She just didn't want to spend her whole life there.

She stepped off the curb and headed to a craft booth in the center of the block to relieve a woman named Gladys. Maddy had manned three booths already today, Mariela's, to get her started, the red-hot-chili booth and another that sold homemade pastries.

"Hi. I'm the relief squad," Maddy said on reaching the booth. The woman standing behind the counter stared blankly at her.

Maddy smiled and extended a hand. "I'm Madeline Inglewood. Annie sent me to spell you for a while."

Gladys, a woman in her mid-sixties or thereabouts, gave her a solid handshake. "So you're the one."

Maddy looked around. "The one?"

"The one staying out there at the Devereaux place."

"Oh. Yes. I was hired to teach the staff English."

The woman motioned for Maddy to go around the booth and come inside. "I'll show you what to do when someone wants to make a purchase," Gladys said as Maddy entered.

"Okay. That way I won't make any mistakes," Maddy said cheerily. The woman was trying to be helpful. No reason to tell her Maddy had done this before—in Epiphany more times than she cared to remember.

"He looks just like his father."

It took a few seconds before Maddy realized that Gladys was talking about J.D.

"Very much so, though I've only seen a photograph," Maddy replied.

"What a shame Raphael died so young and in such an awful way." The woman's voice held a note of both sadness and nostalgia.

"Awful? How did it happen?"

Ignoring the question, Gladys went on. "Powerful good-looking that man was. Powerful. All the women in town were after him."

"Really?" Intrigued, Maddy encouraged her. "Including you?"

Gladys, a solidly built woman with silver-streaked dark hair, laughed and clasped her hands behind her back.

"Yes, even me. That man had the ability to mesmerize everyone who met him—especially women. But some people in town didn't cotton to that."

"So did they heave a sigh of relief when he got married?"

The woman shook her head. "Not at all. That marriage had the old guard up in arms. They thought it a disgrace that a field hand would marry into one of the oldest families in town."

Just then, two teenage girls stepped up to the booth. One of them plucked up a hand-crocheted doily and plopped it on her head like a hat.

"Touch it for more than five seconds and you buy it!" Gladys said with the authority of a drill sergeant.

"Yes, ma'am, Ms. Hackert," the girl said, jumping back as if she'd been stung by a wasp and replacing the doily at the same time.

When the two girls left, Gladys said, "Well, dear. I think you can handle the booth now."

Maddy couldn't let her leave yet. She wanted to hear more about Raphael Rivera. "So, how did the story end?"

Gladys looked pensive, as if deciding whether to say more or not. Then she said, "Bad things can happen in the best of families. Envy. Jealousy. Some people never forget."

Maddy nodded, hoping Gladys would continue. "Do you mean the Devereaux family didn't want their daughter to marry a field worker?" she asked.

Gladys shook her head vehemently. "Robert and Mary Devereaux adored Raphael. He worked hard for them, and within a year, he went from *pizcador* to manager of the ranch. It was Ethel who was the jealous one—jealous of her younger sister from the day the girl was born. Some of us believed she was involved in the whole mess."

"The whole mess?"

"Hi." A deep, familiar voice came from the side.

Maddy swung around. Her heart skipped a beat. "J.D." She couldn't help the wide smile that formed. "You're here."

Then, remembering her manners and the woman at her side, Maddy motioned to Gladys. "J.D., this is Gladys Hackert."

He smiled. "Hello, Ms. Hackert. It's nice to see you again."

"Hello, James. I hope you've learned to control that temper of yours."

"Yes, ma'am. First thing I learned after leaving Los Rios. The military has a way of putting a guy in his place. Just like some sixth-grade teachers." He grinned.

Gladys smiled at J.D., and Maddy thought she

saw a warm gleam in the woman's eyes as she looked at him.

"Well," she said abruptly. "It's time for me to go." Gladys flung open the canvas in the back of the booth, and on her way out she said to Maddy, "Remember what I said, dear."

Gladys had said a lot of things and Maddy didn't know which of them she was referring to. But then the woman was gone and so was the opportunity to ask. Maddy gave J.D. a puzzled look and shrugged. "I should've known she was a teacher from the way she handled a couple of teenagers who came up to the booth. But I don't have a clue what she wants me to remember."

He winked. "It's probably better that way."

Her stomach fluttered. She felt like a teenager herself, all flustered and coy.

"I don't know about that." What Gladys had told her about J.D.'s father intrigued her and she wanted to know more. What had happened to J.D.'s parents? How had his father died and what was the "mess" that Gladys and others suspected Ethel Devereaux might've been involved in? But asking J.D. probably wouldn't win her any points tonight.

"So, now that I'm here, what would you like me to do?"

As he spoke, Maddy saw the heads of several passersby turn in their direction, and within seconds she felt as if all eyes were upon them. She was glad J.D. had his back to the street so he couldn't see them—he wouldn't like being the center of attention.

"I want you to have fun, of course. I'll be done

here in a half hour, so if you'd like, you can come in and keep me company."

He did a Groucho with his eyebrows. "Best invitation I've had all day."

He came around and inside. He smelled of sandalwood, a scent she hadn't noticed on him before, and suddenly the booth seemed smaller, the air thicker. Wearing a crisp white cotton shirt, open halfway down his chest, sleeves rolled to his forearms, faded jeans and boots, the man took her breath away.

J.D. THOUGHT HE SAW Maddy's face flush a little at his remark, but she didn't respond. Not wanting to be on display, he sat on a chair in the back corner of the booth. As he did, he saw a group of teenagers gawking as they went by. Just what he'd expected. God only knows why he'd showed up at all.

The festival hadn't changed a whole lot since he was a kid, either. Giant date palms lined both blocks on Main Street, four on each side, and all were lit up with tiny blinking holiday lights, which would be left on until after the new year. On the far end of the street was a raised plywood podium with Chinese lanterns lighting a stage where a mariachi band was already warming up. A wooden square on the ground in front of the band served as the dance floor and some little kids were already testing it.

With the music in the background, a festive energy filled the air. Small pockets of people chatted with each other, some were laughing and drinking beer, others eating Indian fry bread and the spicy hot chili he remembered well.

He watched Maddy, her bright smile engaging everyone who passed by. Her face seemed to glow with happiness and her ease with people surprised him. It shouldn't, he realized. She was used to this, she'd grown up in a small town and being friendly came naturally to her.

Even so, there was something different about her tonight. She was more exuberant. Her hair seemed blonder, her skin a little more golden. Wearing a purplish tank top, a matching skirt with a fringed scarf knotted at her hips, narrow black flip-flops that showed off pink-painted toenails, she was…beautiful. And sexy. Very sexy.

He felt a sudden pride and satisfaction that she was there with him. Hell, all those gawkers weren't interested in him, they were looking at *her*. He almost laughed.

The thought was liberating, and for the first time in two years, he was eager to enjoy the evening.

"Hey, beautiful," a male voice came from outside the booth. Sitting in the back, J.D. couldn't see who it was, but he recognized the voice. Grady sauntered over with Annie at his side. When he saw J.D., his eyes went wide. "Well, lookee who's here. Hey, buddy."

J.D. came forward. "Want to buy a doily?"

They all laughed at that, and then Annie said to Maddy, "Mariela's booth is lovely and her clothes are beautiful. I bought a skirt and scarf."

"Oh, let me see," Maddy said, and Annie pulled out a yellow gauzy piece of fabric from a brown paper bag.

"That was a great idea you had, getting her set up with a booth," Annie said. "She should've done it long ago. She's been here in Los Rios for three or four years and—''

''Hey,'' Grady interrupted. ''Enough yammering about clothes. Let's get to the important stuff. Food. I'm starving.''

Annie said to Maddy. ''How long are you chained to the booth?''

''Fifteen more minutes.''

''Well, why don't you two join us at the chili booth when you're finished.''

They all turned to look at J.D. He shrugged. ''Sure. Why not.'' When Grady and Annie left, he asked, ''So, what's the deal with Mariela?''

Maddy pursed her lips. ''It's nothing really.''

''It's something.''

''Well, Mariela makes these beautiful clothes—'' she pulled at her skirt ''—and I suggested she take a booth and sell them here at the fair. That's all.''

''That's all?''

Maddy rubbed her arms. ''Well, I helped her fill out the application, and Annie made a deal with the Ladies' Club to allow her to pay for the booth from her profits.''

''Nice of you, but you shouldn't have involved Annie.''

She seemed surprised at his comment. ''Why not? In fact, I was hoping to do more, maybe generate some interest within the ladies' group for a project to fix up the area where the migrant workers live, and maybe find some way to provide day care for the small children while their parents are at work. And from what I've heard, English lessons would be beneficial to most of them.''

"I don't think you'll find much interest—people in this town don't like change."

"Well, I believe you're mistaken. The ladies' club was more than happy to help Mariela."

"That was a one-shot deal. The other stuff you're talking about hits them in their pockets, and some people in this town don't take kindly to outsiders poking into their business."

"What do you mean? Are you saying something bad might happen?"

He shrugged. "It's happened before. But aside from that, think about what it'll be like when you leave in a few weeks. Everything will fall apart."

"Annie will be here. And if we get some support from the community—"

"Dammit, Maddy. It isn't as easy as all that. I know. I've seen what this town can do to people who…" His blood pressure rose like a rocket at the memories. He stopped to breathe. She'd never understand. She couldn't possibly. "I don't want to see you get hurt. And I don't want to see Annie and Grady have problems either."

"Why would they?"

"Trust me. If they support you on a project not sanctioned by the Big Three, they'd have problems."

"The Big Three?"

He signaled behind her to where the sheriff, Mayor Sikes and old man Masterson were holding court.

She glanced at the men. "I've met the sheriff, and I saw the mayor this morning when he gave a speech, but who's the other guy?"

"Charlie Masterson. He owns the town and has

since my grandparents moved here. He's got the others under his thumb. If any one of them has it in for you, you're dead meat.''

As if on cue, the three looked at J.D. and Maddy. Charlie Masterson scowled, then said something to Collier, who placed a hand on his gun. Then both the mayor and the sheriff nodded.

Maddy frowned, looking confused.

She didn't understand. She wouldn't unless she'd grown up here. Maybe he shouldn't have said anything, but he felt the need to warn her before she went off doing things she might regret. Or others might regret.

''So think about it. When you leave, Grady and Annie will still be here to take the flak.''

Maddy's expression softened. ''I wouldn't want that. But I don't understand why people wouldn't want to make the town better for all its citizens. If everyone did a little something, there wouldn't be a problem. Even you—you could help.''

A wry laugh escaped his lips. ''Hell, I can't even buy lumber from the people in this town. I can't even help myself.''

She frowned. ''Do you care what happens to the migrant workers?''

He closed his eyes and drew a long breath. Then as calmly and as evenly as he could manage, he said, ''Of course I do. But right now, all I have time to care about is the ranch. If I don't get the work done by the deadline, it won't matter what I feel about anything.''

Maddy shifted her weight to one side. He had a point. Who was she to think she could breeze into town and suggest major changes to people who'd lived here all their lives. But doing nothing didn't seem right, either. "I'd forgotten about the deadline, and I can see how that prevents you from doing much at this time. But maybe when the renovations are finished?"

"Maybe," he said. "But right now, I'd like to get out of this booth. I'm getting claustrophobic."

At that moment, a young woman who appeared to be in her twenties came over. "Hi. I'm Anita, your replacement." The girl was talking to Maddy, but her big brown eyes were fixed adoringly on J.D.

"Great," Maddy said, and feeling a sudden possessiveness, she took J.D.'s arm and led him out the back of the booth. "C'mon, I'm starving, too."

As they left Maddy heard a commotion down the block and when she glanced up, she saw the sheriff standing at Mariela's booth. And the poor woman looked scared to death! "Wait a second." She tugged on J.D.'s arm. "I need to see what's happening at Mariela's."

Maddy bolted down the street, and as she reached the booth the sheriff was fiddling with his handcuffs, as if ready to make an arrest.

"Qué pasa?" she asked Mariela quietly.

Mariela leaned toward Maddy. "He asked me what I was doing here. And when I told him, he asked to see my work permit and I can't find it. Now he says he's going to take me in, and what will I do about the children?" Panic shone in her eyes.

"Do you have a work permit?" Maddy asked. They spoke in Spanish, but Maddy was sure the sheriff understood.

Mariela nodded, frantically searching her bags.

"Well, I don't see it," the sheriff said, clicking his handcuffs together. "No work permit, no work."

"So, give her some time to go get it, Sheriff." J.D.'s voice came from behind.

"This doesn't concern you, Rivera. Or you either, Miss Inglewood."

"I know she has a permit," J.D. said. "She works for the La Mancha Ranch. She couldn't work there without a permit," he said pointedly. "Not unless someone was overlooking something."

The sheriff's eyes narrowed to slits. "People lie all the time. Work permits expire, and some people don't tell their employers. But I guess you know all about that."

The muscles on J.D.'s neck popped out, and his face got red. His hands were clenched at his sides, and Maddy was sure he was ready to punch the sheriff.

But just then, Mariela held out a piece of paper. "Here," she said. "Here it is."

"Great," Maddy said.

The sheriff barely glanced at it, gave a shrug and turned to J.D. "Keep your guard up, Rivera."

The tension between the two men was electric.

"No worry there, Sheriff. I'm real comfortable knowing you're here to keep the peace." J.D. took Maddy's arm. "C'mon. We've got some serious chili to eat."

Grady and Annie were waiting at one of the picnic tables near the chili stand and waved them over. J.D. acted as if nothing had happened, and they ordered bowls of chili and corn bread and a pitcher of beer. The four of them sat for over an hour—

eating, drinking and laughing. Maddy couldn't remember when last she'd had so much fun.

J.D. appeared to be enjoying the company as well, and several times she caught his gaze lingering on her. Tonight she felt closer to him than ever, as if they shared something special.

"C'mon, Mommy. Let's dance." Grady tapped Annie's hand, and they both got up.

When they were gone, Maddy looked at J.D. and on impulse placed her hand on his. "How about it, cowboy?"

His hand, callused from hard work, stiffened underneath hers. "I can't."

"You can't dance? Or…you don't want to? Two different things."

He averted his eyes, but after a moment his gaze came back to hers, and he said huskily, "Believe me, want has nothing to do with it. I just know better."

She frowned. "Why? Afraid you'll find me so irresistible you'll lose all control?"

He laughed. "Could happen. Then you'll be the one who's afraid." His hand went to his bad leg.

"It's a slow song. All you have to do is sway."

He shook his head. "I don't think so."

"Chicken."

His head came up, his eyes glinting. "I promise you'll be embarrassed."

"I'd love to dance with you."

He was silent. Finally, he sighed, got to his feet and extended a hand. "Don't say I didn't warn you."

Weaving their way through the crowd to get to the dance floor seemed to take forever. And once they were there, the song ended and the band geared up for another. She caught a glimpse of trepidation in J.D.'s eyes, but it dissipated as soon as the music started and it was another slow song.

Standing near the edge of the platform, he drew her close, snug against his chest. Her pulse quickened. He was warm, his muscles hard, and their bodies fit perfectly together. With her arms up over his shoulders and his hands clasped at her waist in the back, they swayed ever so slowly to the music, and the rest of the world suddenly fell away.

All she heard was the poignant Mexican love song and J.D.'s deep rhythmic breathing. All she felt was his warm body molded against hers—and his heart thumping against her cheek. It was as if they were two high-school students in love and oblivious to the world around them. And Maddy wanted to stay like that forever.

Too soon the song was over. They went back to the table and after more conversation and drinks with Grady and Annie and some other people who'd stopped by, it was time to go home.

J.D. had parked his truck in the school parking lot and they walked the two blocks slowly, quietly. The moon was full, the air balmy, warmer than usual for September she'd heard people say. She felt mellow and wonderful, exhilarated and happy.

She'd certainly never experienced anything like this living in Epiphany. But if J.D. had been there…maybe she'd have thought differently about her hometown? Maybe being with J.D. made the difference. The place, itself, didn't matter at all.

Her thoughts segued into a brief fantasy of what

it might be like living in Los Rios—at the Tripplehorne with J.D.

"Have you ever seen such a fat old moon?" J.D. asked, making her pay attention.

"I never imagined the desert was so beautiful."

They neared the entrance to the parking lot. "That it is," he said. "But it can also be a desolate, unforgiving place."

Almost before he finished the sentence, they heard a loud bang and a crashing sound. "What was that?" Maddy grabbed J.D.'s arm, her old fears suddenly resurfacing. They stopped to listen.

There was another crash and another and then a gunning noise, like a race car without a muffler, a screech of tires burning rubber, and finally, a big black motorcycle roared into view. It exited the lot, spun around in a circle and blasted off in the other direction. The rider was clad in black from head to toe.

Maddy gave a sigh of relief as they watched the bike disappear into the night, but she didn't let go of J.D.'s arm as they walked cautiously to where he'd parked.

When she saw J.D.'s truck, Maddy's hands flew to her mouth. "Ohmygod!"

"Dammit all to hell!" J.D. spat out.

The front windshield was completely bashed in, and the other windows looked like spiderwebs. The tires had been slashed and something was leaking onto the asphalt from under the engine.

J.D. pivoted, his eyes scanning the area. "Son of a bitch."

"Look," she said. A baseball bat lay on the ground near the front fender.

J.D. picked it up, his knuckles turning white as he gripped the handle.

"I can't imagine who would do something like this."

Lips thin, J.D. passed the bat from one hand to the other, his rage barely contained. "I can."

"You think it was vandals? Teenagers out for some reckless fun? I know some kids who did something similar in Epiphany once. They broke into a gas station and trashed the place for no reason at all."

His eyes were as dark and hard as onyx. "Take a look around."

She searched the parking lot. "I don't see anything. Just other cars."

"Exactly. All in perfect condition."

Maddy caught her breath and J.D.'s arm at the same time. "You think someone deliberately singled out your truck?"

She felt his muscles tense.

"I know so."

"But why?"

He closed his eyes for a second, as if calming himself. Then he said, "Don't worry about it. It doesn't concern you."

But it did. If it affected him, it affected her. He didn't know that, though. And now was not the time to tell him. "We should probably call the sheriff."

J.D. snorted. "Yeah, let's call the sheriff. Maybe he can give us a ride home." His words were bitter and dripped with sarcasm.

Then he took out his cell phone and walked away to make a call. Obviously he didn't want her to hear who he was talking to or what he was saying. She was disappointed. He didn't trust her enough to hear his end of the conversation.

When he'd finished, he came back and stood next to her. "Grady will be here in a few minutes. He'll pull the truck to his station and give us a lift home."

"Did you call the sheriff? Won't he have to fill out a report or something?"

"No point to it."

Why? Did he think he knew who'd destroyed his truck and was he planning to take care of the matter himself? She didn't like that idea at all. "I don't understand. Wouldn't the sheriff—"

"You don't need to understand. You're not involved. It doesn't concern you, so just drop it, okay?"

Annoyed, she felt her nose twitch. She didn't like the way he said that, either—like an order, and she was through taking orders from anyone. "Excuse me? I'm standing here in the middle the night, in a parking lot miles from home with no way to get back there, and you're telling me I should just drop it?"

"I told you, Grady's coming—he'll take us home."

Just then, Grady's red truck rumbled into the lot. Okay, she'd drop the subject for now—but not for good.

She was concerned—and she was involved.

Whether he liked it or not.

"DAMMIT ALL TO HELL," J.D. muttered aloud as he sat alone on the front steps at 2:00 a.m. tossing rocks into the dirt. He had no vehicle, no money, and now he was going to waste at least another whole day getting the truck fixed. Maybe two days.

Maddy had gone to bed right after Grady had brought them home. It'd been close to midnight and she'd been working at the festival since early morning. She hadn't said a word the whole way back—not since he'd told her to mind her own business. He hated being such a jerk, but he couldn't let her get involved in something she might regret.

She was leaving in a few weeks, anyway. The thought made him even more depressed. Having her here had changed his life. He'd gone from not caring about anything to caring more about someone than he'd ever believed possible. And because of her, he found himself thinking about a lot of other things. Like family and friends. Like permanence and having a place to call home. *Like love.*

He heard the creak of the front door, the clink of ice in a glass. "Are you okay? Did something else happen?" Maddy asked, coming to stand on his left, her mouth tight with concern.

He nodded. "No. Nothing else has happened."

She frowned. "Are you sure? You're not just telling me that because you don't want me involved, are you? Because I'm going to find out anyway, and if you think you can keep me from being concerned or involv—"

"Shh." He pulled her down beside him. "Trust me. Nothing's wrong that wasn't wrong before."

The tightness in her face eased. "Would you like some iced tea?" she asked, handing him her glass.

Wearing an oversize pink T-shirt that she'd apparently slept in, she looked so innocent. So trusting. So different from him.

"Sure. Thanks." As he took the glass, their fingers touched, driving a hot jolt of desire through him. Their eyes caught and held, and she leaned closer, her shoulder against his arm.

He took a sip, but his gaze never wavered from hers. There was something in the air tonight, something that was making him crazy. He wanted her more than he could stand, even though he knew there was no future for them. They both knew that. But tonight...was tonight.

He set the glass down, reached up and laid his fingertips against her cheek. "Madeline," he whispered. "Sweet, beautiful Madeline."

She wanted this man. Oh, how she wanted him. And seeing the hunger in his eyes, feeling the controlled gentleness of his touch told her how much he wanted her, too. And this time, she wasn't going to let him stop.

When his fingers trailed slowly from her cheek to her neck and ever so slowly down to her breast, Maddy knew he wasn't going to.

With a shiver, she took his hand and kissed his scarred knuckles, and with the desire growing more intense inside her, she slipped his finger into her mouth.

He drew a quick breath.

She tasted one finger and then another, liking the salty, sweaty flavor of him. She smelled soap and shampoo and sandalwood mixed with the heat of the day and that of his body. She inhaled deeply, loving his scent. At that moment, she couldn't think of anything except making love with him.

As if he'd read her mind, he said, "Let's go inside."

CHAPTER FIFTEEN

WHEN MADDY TOUCHED HIM, the whole world seemed to wash away. It was easy to forget all the reasons he shouldn't make love to her, why he shouldn't *love* her.

With her, it was easy to forget that he was scarred and flawed and undeserving. It was easy to feel whole again, and right now, he needed that. Needed it desperately. Even if it was just for a little while.

He stood up, took her hand and led her inside and toward her bedroom, but she urged him in the other direction toward his. "You sure? It's a mess."

"I've never been more sure of anything."

Once inside, he sat on the bed and she sat next to him, curling her smooth legs and slim bare feet underneath her. As if it was the most natural thing to do, she leaned in and kissed the side of his neck. Man, she was perfect, so desirable and sexy, she took his breath away. It astounded him that she wanted him as much as he wanted her.

But would she still feel that way when he took off his pants? Would she still feel that way if she knew everything about him? He should warn her. He had to warn her. Because he couldn't stand it if she looked at him with disgust—the way Jenna had.

But she was kissing his neck and breathing in his ear and his heart raced. He closed his eyes as her fingers trailed across his chest and she gently pushed him back to lie on the bed. "Maddy."

"Shh." She came closer, her chest against his.

"Maddy," he said again, his voice strained. It was all he could do to stay focused. He *had* to tell her. Warn her. "Maddy. My leg."

"Oh." she pulled back and sat up. "I'm sorry. Did I hurt you?"

"No, no." He shook his head.

"It's just that..." He sucked in some air. "It's really ugly."

"Does it prevent you from having sex?"

He almost laughed. "No. Not much interferes with that."

She kissed him then, soft and intoxicatingly slow. He felt as if he was drowning in the sweet softness of her lips and the warmth of her body. He wanted to lose himself in the silkiness inside her and forget who he was. Forget what he'd done.

With her, he could forget. If just for tonight.

He started to lift her T-shirt up from the back, but she sat up again and took it off herself. She wore no bra and only the skimpiest pair of white bikini panties. Her skin glowed in the dim light, and he reached to touch the delicate underside of one breast. She gave a sudden inhalation of pleasure and after gently touching his face, her hand moved down his chest until she came to the waistband on his sweatpants.

For one brief moment, he wanted to stop her. He didn't want her to see him as he was. Didn't want her to regret her decision. But her fingers were fast, tugging his waistband farther and farther down on his hips, and then she leaned forward again and her mouth covered his in a breathtaking kiss that melted all his resolve.

He helped her then. Kicking off his pants and rolling over her, he slipped her panties down, too. Her spiky blond hair stood out in contrast with the dark navy of his sheets, and her pale blue eyes gazed up at him with all the trust in the world. Her lips parted and the heat in her eyes said yes. Definitely yes. Now.

He kissed one pink nipple and then the other. He caressed her face with his fingertips and then brought his hands down between her thighs. He wanted to be gentle and not rush her, but he wasn't sure how much he could handle himself.

Maddy shifted her hips underneath him, pressing against his arousal. She liked being in his bed, and lying on sheets that still held his scent. Being here, in his sanctuary, she felt closer to him than ever.

She opened her body to him with reckless abandon, surprising even herself. For once in her life she wasn't going to hold back, wasn't going to deprive either of them the pleasure they both wanted. But there was more than that. He'd given up no small amount of pride in mentioning his leg, and to do that, she knew he had to feel something for her. It wasn't just sex. It couldn't be just sex.

If it was, he wouldn't have warned her, wouldn't have tried to take it slow and gentle. No, J. D. Rivera was as involved as she was, whether he wanted to admit it or not.

"Touch me, Maddy," he said, his voice low and husky.

She brought her hand to him. "Like that?"

''Mmm. Exactly like that.'' His breath came hard and ragged and then, as if he'd just thought of something, he pulled back, a slight panic in his eyes. ''You're not a...''

She laughed and kept caressing him, all the while kissing him on the chest and neck, working her way upward to his mouth, and when her lips were almost against his, she whispered, ''No. But I'm not very experienced at some things, either. And I want to do it right. Which reminds me, do you have...uh—''

''Protection?'' He nodded, then fumbled inside a drawer on the nightstand. Then she felt him relax under her, and in that moment it occurred to her just how much they didn't know about each other. But she knew the important things. He was honest and kind and loyal and he was true to himself. His integrity was above reproach.

Though he'd said differently, she believed he was capable of great love, too. He just had to believe in it himself. Yes, she knew the important things.

How all those feelings fit with her plans to go to New York didn't matter right now, either. All that mattered was this moment with J.D.—and she was going to enjoy every single second.

As she stroked him, he gave a low moan of pleasure. ''That's probably enough for now,'' he said, his voice raspy. He lifted her hand to his lips. ''If you keep doing that it'll all be over in a flash.''

She laughed. ''I'm glad I affect you that way.''

''You affect me all right,'' he said, nestling himself between her legs. ''In far too many ways.''

Hearing that, all her feelings coalesced into one all-encompassing emotion—love.

She helped him with the condom and then he was inside her. She felt as if she was going to burst with happiness.

Their bodies found the same rhythm, slow at first and then faster and faster until their skin was slick with sweat and tingling with pleasure and suddenly the world rose up and exploded around her. ''Ohhhh,'' she called out in exquisite pleasure, and seconds later she felt his muscles tighten. He thrust hard into her and she responded again and again until he called out and his body stiffened and released.

Out of breath and feeling warm and loved, she held him in her arms, tightly, securely. She wanted to stay like this forever.

The thought was like a brilliant white light, a realization that she didn't care about going to New York, she didn't care about the new job or her family in Epiphany—all she cared about was J.D.

Sleepy and sated and very content, she snuggled closer, her head on his shoulder and her hand on his heart. She loved him.

J.D. AWOKE WITH A WOMAN in his bed. That hadn't happened for nearly two years. The fact that it was Maddy made it even more ironic. She was the last person he'd have pictured himself with, and yet, here they were.

He looked down at her, angelic in sleep. He'd meant it when he told her she affected him in many ways. She'd had a monumental effect on him—on his emotions—and he didn't know what to do about it. But then, maybe he didn't have to do anything. She was the one who was leaving. She was the one off to the big city for adventure and excitement.

Her head rested against his shoulder as when they'd fallen asleep. He'd slept better in the last few hours with her in his arms than he had in years. He'd had no dreams. No nightmares. Just sweet blissful sleep, and something to remember when she was gone.

He glanced at his watch. Grady would be there in ten minutes. He slipped out of bed, taking care to draw the sheet up over Maddy as he did.

Quickly, he showered, shaved and made a pot of coffee. It was Sunday and his crew—Carlos, the two carpenters and three other men he'd hired—wouldn't be coming today. When they worked on the weekends, he paid them overtime and right now, with the truck to fix, he didn't know whether he could afford to pay them extra. A portion of the trust money was supposed to come through this week sometime, but J.D. wouldn't count on it until he had it in the bank.

He took his coffee outside to the deck to wait for Grady. They'd have to order glass for the windows on the truck, and that would take a while, but as long as he could get the tires and make sure it was safe to drive, he'd have wheels.

Grady careened around the corner, then came to a stop. He got out, a manila envelope in his hands.

"What's that?"

"It's for Maddy from Annie. Some Internet research stuff they're doing."

"For what?"

Grady shrugged. ''I didn't ask. Something for the ladies' group, I imagine. Open it and see.''

J.D. shook his head. ''No. If she'd wanted me to know she'd have told me.''

Grady nodded. ''Well, if you don't mind driving without glass in the windows, I think we can have the truck up and running in a few hours.''

''Great. Just let me know how much I owe you, okay?''

''Sure.''

J.D. brought the envelope into the kitchen and placed it on the table for Maddy, poured some more coffee and headed out with Grady.

BLISS. The last week had been absolute bliss, Maddy decided while riding with Annie back to the ranch after their meeting with the Los Rios Ladies late Saturday afternoon.

Her days had been filled with work and the nights with lovemaking. Neither she nor J.D. talked about her leaving. It was as if they had an unspoken agreement to enjoy what time they had together and not spoil it with talk of the future.

Her class had expanded even more after J.D. told his new hires that part of the deal was that they took Maddy's English classes.

During the week, she'd finished cleaning the fireplace in the kitchen and had only a few stones to replace and a few more to recement. J.D. had given her permission to contract people to finish the work, replace the old flooring, paint and paper the walls.

The truck had been fixed and they'd both talked to Harold Martin. Maddy learned that he *had* sent her a letter about her employer's death, explaining that it didn't change anything, the contract was still in effect and she still had the job. She'd never received the letter, though he said he'd sent it certified to her parents' home. She was glad. If she'd received it early on, she might not have come.

J.D. had also learned from Mr. Martin that the trust money was in place and he could go ahead with the major reconstruction. And apparently, his aunt had left him a letter—to be opened once he'd fulfilled the stipulations in the will.

During the week, Maddy and Annie had also gotten information from the Internet regarding laws that regulate migrant workers' pay and housing, and Maddy discovered that the town could apply for a grant to hire someone to teach the workers English on a permanent basis. Maddy and Annie were excited and had brought the information to the Los Rios Ladies' meeting that morning hoping to convince them to take on the project to help the people of the *colonias.*

Most of the members knew about the housing conditions, but not the fact that medical assistance wasn't being provided.

They'd assumed the corporation that ran most of the local ranches and hired the workers took care of all that for the employees. But according to Maddy and Annie's research, the La Mancha Corporation had no benefits plan.

Maddy arrived home at dinnertime, energized and ready to work. When they drove up, J.D. was sitting on the steps taking a break. Maddy waved goodbye to Annie, walked over to J.D. and sat down beside him.

"Where is everyone?"

"They just left."

"So, how's everything coming?"

"Good." He nodded. "I'm actually starting to believe we might finish in time." His excitement shone in his eyes.

"Wow, that's great." She felt excited herself, happy to be part of it. "I have some good news, too."

He turned to her, his expression suddenly somber. He cleared his throat. "You hear about the new job?"

"No, silly." She tapped his arm. "Annie and I presented our project to the women's group today, and it looks really positive. I think they're interested, but we won't know until after the board meeting next week."

He looked relieved. "So, what's the project? Another festival?"

She shook her head. "It's what we talked about before—the project to force those who hire immigrants to comply with the laws regarding migrant pay and housing. We also asked the ladies' group to talk to the city planners about hiring a permanent teacher to help the workers learn English and finding a place to hold the classes."

As she was talking, his eyes got dark, stress lines formed around his mouth. She stopped. "What's wrong?"

He raked a hand through his hair. "Do you have any idea what you're doing?"

She pulled back. "Of course. I'm trying to help people. You said earlier that no one would be interested, but they are. I thought you'd be happy to hear that."

"Never mind that you're going to leave in a few weeks."

"The other people will still be here. If this gets off the ground, it'll be wonderful for all the workers. The project might even revitalize the town."

He blinked, shaking his head as if it was pointless to say any more.

"The migrant labor force is vitally important to the town's commerce and should be treated as an asset. What would happen if they all packed up and left?"

"More would come."

"But you can't just ignore the situation."

"I'm not. But I know the people who run this town don't take kindly to others horning in. You should know that after last weekend."

"You mean the incident with the sheriff and Mariela?"

He nodded. "That's part of it."

"What else? The only other thing that happened was the tru—"

He nodded again.

"I can't imagine they'd be involved in something like that. It's absurd."

"Is it? You think it's just a coincidence that the Big Three were having a discussion right before the sheriff decided to check out Mariela's work permit?"

"I thought it was just a formality. And she got upset about it and that's what caused a ruckus."

"Nothing is a matter of formality in Los Rios. This town runs on Charlie Masterson's nickel, including the La Mancha Corporation that owns the land. And I can tell you right now, Charlie isn't going to like anyone even suggesting changes for his employees.''

She swallowed. ''But someone has to do something.''

''Maybe there are people doing things you're not aware of.''

''Like who? Name someone. *You* could do something, but all you care about is your ranch.''

''That's all I can afford to care about right now.''

''I'm sorry. That wasn't fair. But I don't think you should put down those who want to do what they can.''

His hands suddenly curled into fists and he launched to his feet. ''Dammit, Maddy. I'm not putting anyone down. But I learned a long time ago that what a person wants and what he gets are two different things. In your cozy little cocoon of a world people might get everything they want, but real life isn't like that. And it isn't fair for you to build up others' hopes and dreams, because when you leave everything will fall apart.''

''Others will carry on.''

''Are you sure? This isn't their project, it's yours, and do you think anyone else is going to oppose the powers that be, after you're gone? Don't forget, they still have to live here. Despite good intentions, people fall short of their promises.''

''So we should all sit back and watch those who need assistance sink or swim?''

''Some people work in their own quiet way to make changes. And sometimes that's a more permanent solution.''

Reeling from everything he'd said, Maddy felt as

if she'd been punched. "I'm going in now." She got up and went to her room.

Was he right? She *had* been sheltered, and she had been given everything she wanted. She'd had two bad experiences and had let those two things color her whole life. She'd gone into hiding because of them—and stayed there for four years. Survivor's guilt and post-traumatic stress disorder, her doctors had said.

But she'd never experienced anything like what the migrant workers lived with every day. When she'd left Epiphany, her main goal had been to find a fulfilling career and add some excitement to her life.

Selfish. Truly selfish.

Depressed, she felt even worse when her mother called to say she needed Maddy. The family needed her. Maddy felt ungrateful and even more selfish. She sighed and flopped across the bed.

Maybe she would be better off just going back to Epiphany.

J.D. SHOVED BACK the chair after eating dinner alone while Maddy sulked in her room. Her usual MO, he guessed. Well, it might work on her family but it wouldn't work on him.

He was right in what he'd told her. She didn't know what she was up against, and if she kept pushing the issue, she could get hurt. He wasn't going to let that happen. He cared about her too much.

Still, he felt like a creep. She'd been so excited, her heart in the right place, and he'd squelched all that. When he saw her shoulders sag and the light fade from her eyes, all his protective instincts had surged to the fore. But he knew that what he'd told her was true.

She'd leave and nothing would change. Charlie Masterson would see to that. No one was going to cut into his business, The La Mancha Ranches were the biggest and most profitable in the area. If he had to start paying minimum wage and hospitalization, he'd lose money. But even more important, old Charlie had to be in control.

He gave a sigh and looked at the time. Seven. Sundown, and it was time to make a run.

Outside, he backed the truck to the storage shed where he kept the supplies, got out, opened the door and began to load up.

"Can I help, please?" a small voice said from somewhere around his waist.

"Ben. What are you doing here? I thought you rode home with Carlos. It's late. Do your aunt and uncle know where you are?" J.D.'s feeling for quite some time was that Ben hadn't been truthful about his living situation. He'd suspected that the boy wasn't staying with anyone, that he might be homeless. And if that was the case, he was probably undocumented, too. Why else would he have bolted from the truck when Maddy mentioned talking with his family.

Orphans, homeless kids, sometimes crossed the border alone, but most came with others. Either way, the trip was brutal. "Or did they go to Mexico again?"

Ben nodded. "Can I stay?"

The boy's English had improved dramatically in

the past two weeks and he was becoming more conversational. ‘‘How long will they be gone?’’

He shrugged. ‘‘A long time, I think.’’

‘‘Okay. You can sleep in the same room as before.’’

‘‘And can I help?’’

‘‘Sure thing. You can keep me company, too.’’ He ruffled the boy’s hair. ‘‘Here…’’ He tossed a sack of grain to Ben to load into the truck, his mind flashing back to his own ill-fated trek across El Camino del Diablo with his father. A nightmare.

They continued loading, and when they’d finished, got into the truck and took off.

MADDY AWOKE EARLY SUNDAY morning with a headache. The night before, she’d watched from her window as J.D. had loaded the truck with supplies. Benito had been helping him. She didn’t know why the child was there so late and she was puzzled about what they were doing. She’d wanted to find out but wasn’t sure what kind of reception she’d get after their discussion. And just when she’d decided to do it anyway, J.D. and Ben climbed into the vehicle and took off down the road.

She’d lain awake for hours waiting for J.D.’s return—tossing and turning as their earlier conversation played over and over in her head. Was she really that wrong in wanting to help? Couldn’t something be done? Was it hopeless to think she could facilitate change? Exhausted, she’d finally fallen asleep.

Now she needed an aspirin and maybe some coffee. She went to the kitchen in her nightshirt and on the way, smelled the aroma of coffee already brewing. She heard hammering outside.

The man was relentless. Working sixteen or more hours a day, he was going to go up in flames if he didn't slow down and get some rest. She poured a cup of coffee and walked to the kitchen door to see where he was.

He was doing something at the gate to Zelda's run. She watched his biceps flex and release as he worked. Handsome. Sexy. She liked to watch him work. Holding the hinge with one hand, he lifted the hammer and brought it down hard. He jumped back, yelled and bent over, clutching his hand. Maddy dropped her cup on the counter and ran out to him.

"Let me see," she said, falling to her knees as she reached him.

His face was etched with pain. "I'm okay. It's nothing."

"Let me see."

He held out his hand and blood squirted from a deep gash on the top side. He put his other hand over it to stop the flow. "Don't move. Just hold it like that to stop the bleeding. I'll get my first-aid kit."

Through his pain, he said, "You carry a first-aid kit?"

"Yes, I do. And right now, that should make you happy." She scrambled to her feet, hurried into the house to her room, got the kit and dashed outside again.

He was sitting on the ground, his back against the gate. She knelt down beside him. "Have you had a recent tetanus shot?"

"Yeah. I scraped my other arm on a rusty nail the first week I was here and had one then."

"Good," she said, checking to see if the bleeding had stopped. Though it hadn't completely, she cleaned the wound with antiseptic.

"Ouch. That stings. You should use the stuff I used before."

"This is better."

"What? If it hurts, it's better?"

"No. It has more potent ingredients. Now be quiet and let me bandage you up. You might need stitches."

"I'll be fine. Put the bandage on so I can finish the gate before Zelda decides to make another run for it."

Maddy hurried, and when she was done, J.D. went back to the gate to finish. "You're going to do that with one hand?"

"Yes, unless you want to come over here and help."

"Okay. But you have to promise not to pound on me, though you might feel like doing that right about now."

His gaze caught hers. "I feel like doing a lot of things to you, but that's not one of them."

Her face flushed. Silly. They'd had sex. Plenty of it. She'd been naked and totally without modesty, and done things she'd never imagined herself doing. And now she was blushing? It didn't make sense.

They finished the gate, and Maddy asked, "Would you like some coffee?"

"Sure. I need a break." He sat down on the back steps.

Maddy poured him a cup and brought it outside with hers. She sat next to him. It was still early and the air was crisp and fresh and smelled almost sweet. "Mmm. That's good," she said after a long sip. "Did you learn to make coffee in the military?"

"No, I actually learned watching my grandmother." He got a nostalgic look in his eyes.

"I bet it was a lot of fun living on the ranch back then."

He nodded. "Yeah, I have a tendency to forget the good times, but there were lots. It all ended when they died, though, and dear Aunt Ethel shipped me off to military school in Maryland."

"Why didn't she just stay here with you?"

He gave her a sidelong look. "She hated the ranch. She hated me. Just like she hated my father."

"But why?"

Drawing a breath, he said, "Well, there are two stories. The one I pieced together from listening to my grandparents was that Ethel was in love with my father and became hateful when he married my mother, her younger sister. After that, Ethel moved in with Sheriff Collier and a while later, moved to New York. She wasn't around when I came back here to live after my parents died. But when my grandparents passed away, Ethel inherited the ranch and became my guardian. I guess her hatred for my father carried over to me, so she sent me off to military school."

"That's so sad. And what's the other version."

"Aunt Ethel's version—that my father loved her and when she rejected him, he married my mother so he could take over the ranch. Ethel discovered he'd been misrepresenting profits on cattle sales he made to Charlie Masterson's son, C.J., and had been pocketing the money. Supposedly, after Ethel called him on it, he killed C.J. to keep him from talking, and then started a fire to cover it up. That's the story the newspaper carried—the one most people around here believe.''

That fit with what Gladys Hackert had told her. ''What happened then?''

''He was arrested, thrown in jail, but somehow managed to escape, and we went to Mexico to live. We were very poor because my father couldn't find much work, but we were happy together. Then, when I was four, my mother got real sick and my father sent her back here to the ranch to get medical care.''

Maddy waited for him to go on.

He took a sip of coffee and leaned forward, elbows on his knees, cradling the cup in both hands.

''But my mother didn't recover and when my dad got word that she was dying, he couldn't stay away. Since he was wanted by the law, he couldn't just go visit, so he had someone drive him to the border and crossed over undetected. I was supposed to stay behind, but I hid in the back of the truck and rode along. By the time he found me, it was too late to send me back.''

Pain etched his face. ''We didn't make it,'' he said almost inaudibly. ''I learned later that my mother died while we were en route.'' He took a breath, cleared his throat and went on, almost as if he couldn't stop. ''I watched my father die in the desert,'' he said, his voice cracking. ''I realized later that he'd given me all the water and hadn't taken any for himself."

Oh, God. He felt responsible. He not only felt guilty for his partner's death, but also his father's.

"When they found us, I was sent back to Mexico to an orphanage until my grandmother got word and sent for me."

Maddy's head spun. Stories like that only happened in the movies, not to people she knew. But then, she'd never have believed some of the other things she'd seen and heard recently, either. J.D. was right when he said she'd lived in a cocoon.

"My father always insisted he was framed, but there was no way to prove it."

Maddy managed to pull herself together enough to ask, "But who would frame him—and why?"

"I don't know. My father thought it was Ethel."

"Do you think she had something to do with the fire?"

He shrugged and gave a weary sigh, as if all his energy had been depleted. "I don't know. One of the men who died was Charlie Masterson's son. I asked some questions about the fire when I first came back, but no one wanted to talk about it. All I found out was that Ethel and Charlie Jr. had been good friends.

Gladys had said that some people believed Ethel was involved in the mess. Maybe that was what she'd wanted Maddy to remember. "Y'know, J.D. you should talk with Gladys Hackert. She seemed to know a lot about the past, and she mentioned your father. Maybe she has some information that would help clear things up."

"Really," he said with a flicker of interest. But

a second later, his eyes darkened. "Everyone's dead now, anyway, so what's the point."

Hearing his words, she felt as if a lightbulb had gone off in her head. No wonder he was reluctant to get close to anyone. Everyone he'd ever cared about had died.

"Maybe if you had some answers, you could find some peace. Maybe you could stop punishing yourself for things that you had no control over."

He looked her in the eyes. "More of your pop psychology?"

"Yeah, I guess. Sorry." She took a sip of coffee, and then rolled her cup between her palms. She glanced at J.D. and saw the pain in his heart reflected in his eyes. His burden of guilt was so heavy it would destroy him if he couldn't let it go.

She understood. She'd never told anyone about Georgetown, and had let the guilt fester within her until it had almost destroyed her life. Maybe if she told him…maybe it would help in some small way.

Nerves taut, she inhaled deeply, "When I was in school at Georgetown, I shared an apartment with another girl. Someone broke in one night when we were sleeping." She swallowed, wondering if she could get it all out. But it seemed important to tell him right now.

"He broke into my room through the window. I tried to fight him off, but he had a gun and threatened to kill me if I made a sound. He tied me up and gagged me. Then it was my roommate's turn. He brought her into my room, tied her up and then went through the place, taking our money and jewelry and…before he left, he…" Her throat closed. "He raped her. We learned later it was someone I knew from a class. He'd thought that I liked him—had encouraged him. When he found out differently…''

Oh, God. Tears brimmed in her eyes but she bit them back. ''I couldn't stop thinking that somehow the whole thing was my fault. I felt so horribly guilty. That it was me he'd come looking for.''

J.D. reached out to touch her, but she waved him away. She needed to finish. ''After that, I felt a sense of helplessness—that I had no control over the things that could happen in my life, and that horrible feeling grew and grew. Eventually, I pulled inside myself, so much so that my life literally stopped. I moved in with my parents for four years because of it.''

She let her head fall back and closed her eyes for a second before continuing. ''Eventually, I went into therapy. I realized then that while I'd never forget what had happened, and would probably always wonder if I could've done something, I had to let the memory go if I wanted to have a life.''

She turned to him and smiled. ''Now I enjoy one day at a time. No more, no less. I hope someday you'll be able to do that, too.''

MADDY PREPARED for class on Monday evening, her spirits elevated because J.D. had confided in her. After listening to his story, she was even more aware of how little she knew about real hardship. Yes, she'd been attacked by a dog, and she'd been the victim of a brutal assault and had suffered emotionally as a result.

But she'd been a child of privilege and even when things were bad, she'd had a support system.

J.D. had no one at all. She admired his strength. And she was humbled by the people she worked with every day, amazed by their generosity of spirit and never-ending determination to make better lives for themselves.

Michael Bruchetti could take lessons from some of them.

Despite what J.D. had said about people in town not being willing to follow through with the project, she wasn't convinced. The positive response was encouraging. In fact, she was going to find out tomorrow about the grant for a full-time teacher. If the town council approved nothing else, helping workers learn the language would give them the tools to get better jobs and earn more money.

Her students were in rare form tonight, eager to learn and enjoying some of the new exercises she'd shown them. Tonight she'd started by having Carlos hum a few lines of a song he liked and then the others had to identify it in English. They'd all laughed at how Carlos couldn't carry a tune. In another exercise, she'd taken a page from one of Benito's comic books, blanked out the dialogue, made copies for each student when she'd been in town with Annie, and then had them fill in what they thought the characters should say. They were laughing and having a great time when loud voices sounded outside.

The doors suddenly crashed open on both sides of the building and someone shouted, "*La migra. La migra.*" A half-dozen men wearing dark blue uniforms converged on them like an army invading a hostile country. Mariela's children began to cry and they all backed away. Carlos and the rest of

J.D.'s workers stood in front of the women and children as if guarding them.

La migra. Immigration authorities. Maddy whirled around, dashed over to stand beside her students. Sheriff Collier was with the uniformed men, so she addressed him. "What's going on? You can't just barge in here and—"

"*Muéstreme sus papeles,*" one of the men said.

They wanted to see papers.

"*Cualquiera sin papeles viene con mí.* Anyone without papers comes with us," the sheriff said.

Benito's eyes went wide. He bolted for the door, but one of the men grabbed him by the arm and jerked him back. Benito struggled to get free, his skinny arms and legs flailing like a marionette, but the official held him.

Sheriff Collier sauntered over. "Well, well. Who do we have here?"

CHAPTER SIXTEEN

"YOU CAN'T PUT a little boy in jail!" Maddy followed the sheriff out the door, her mind spinning, frantic, wondering what to do. "Please don't take him. Let me contact his aunt and uncle. They'll have his papers."

"We'll take care of it, Miss Inglewood," the sheriff said. "If he's documented, there won't be a problem. You just tell your boss he needs to do a better job checking papers when he's hiring. There's a hefty fine for people who continue to break the law. Tell him I'll overlook it once, but not twice."

Maddy could only sputter as she watched the officers take Benito and the other workers J.D. had hired away. When it was all over, Juana and Carlos and Mariela and her children were the only ones left. Devastated, Maddy was beside herself and pacing in circles. J.D. was gone, she didn't know where, and everyone else seemed to accept this *roundup* as a matter of course.

The whole thing was beyond belief. J.D. would be furious. His carpenters were gone. He wouldn't be able to get the work done. Benito was gone, too. But he was only ten, the authorities certainly couldn't keep a little boy in jail, could they?

"*Señorita,*" Carlos said.

"I'm sorry. Did you say something, Carlos?"

"Benito has no papers."

Maddy glanced from Carlos to Juana.

Juana nodded. "He has no family here."

She'd been afraid of that. Worse yet, she'd ignored her instincts. But he had to have someone. "Where does he go every night then? Does he stay with friends?"

Juana shook her head. "When Mr. Rivera found out, he gave him a place to sleep and food."

"What about his family in Mexico?"

"He has no one."

Maddy slumped into a chair. The boy was homeless. How had he managed living on his own at age ten. "I don't understand any of this. And why would the authorities come here looking for papers? Who would even know there was anyone here."

It hit her. Oh, God. Everyone knew.

She'd told all the women at the club that she was teaching J.D.'s workers and there was no reason for them to keep the information quiet. Was this her fault? Was this what J.D. meant when he'd said she didn't know what she was getting into? Had someone who didn't like what she was doing notified the authorities?

She closed her eyes. "Does anyone know where Mr. Rivera is and when he'll be back?"

"It will be late," Juana said. "He's making deliveries."

"Deliveries?"

"Food and water. The food to the *colonias*. The water barrels into the desert."

She knew about the water, but not the rest. And she'd accused him of doing nothing. She ran a hand through her hair. She was hot and sweaty and her study papers were all over the place. She couldn't just leave her remaining students standing here, but she didn't have the energy to finish. She wanted to go off in a corner and hide. God, she was stupid.

Then Carlos started picking up papers and soon the women and children were helping, and when they'd finished, they all sat in their seats again, ready to continue—as if nothing had happened.

"Okay." She gave a shaky smile, took a huge gulp of air, stood up and walked to the table. Her hands were trembling when she picked up the dry-erase pen. "Where were we?"

IT WAS MIDNIGHT when J.D. pulled in. The lights were on in the house, and he hoped Maddy was still up. He'd had a lot of time to think about their conversation. A lot of time to reflect on what she'd said. Was he using his guilt as a crutch? Was it an excuse to drop out? A reason to feel sorry for himself because his life and everything he'd planned had gone down the tubes.

He knew that technically Eric's death wasn't his fault, but if he hadn't convinced his friend to do the show, Eric would be alive today. And if he hadn't tagged along with his father, Raphael might be alive, too.

He didn't know if he'd ever get over that guilt. But Maddy had made him take a good look at his situation; he'd never allowed himself to do that before. Maybe he would never completely get over the losses—and he knew he'd never forget—but if he found something—or someone—to fill the void, life might be worth living again. He certainly felt that way when she was there.

He'd meant it when he'd said she was an amazing woman. Stronger than she knew. God, he wanted her to stay. But he'd accepted the fact that she was going to leave, and no matter how he felt about her, he'd closed off a small part of himself because of it.

Enjoy each day for what it is, she'd said. He smiled to himself. Yeah. He could do that—for whatever time was left.

As he rounded the corner, he saw Maddy bent over at the kitchen table, her arms out and her head resting on top. Damn. She'd worked so hard she couldn't make it to bed. He stole into the kitchen, but his boot hit a chair leg on the way. She jerked her head up.

He sat beside her, resting his hand on her shoulder. "Sorry, I didn't mean to startle you."

When she turned to look at him, her eyes were red and puffy and she looked as if she'd been crying for hours. Was she upset about their conversation? Had what she'd told him brought up too many bad memories? Or maybe she'd heard about the job she wanted—bad news. "What's wrong?"

Her lips quivered. "You were right. I've screwed things up to hell and back and I'll leave here right now, tonight, if you want me to."

"That's ridiculous."

"No, it's not."

"Whatever it is can't possibly be that bad." He smoothed the hair from her eyes.

Tears welled, but she took a deep breath and staved them off. She sat up straight. "The immigration authorities came into my classroom tonight and rounded up everyone without papers.''

He stared, not wanting to believe what he'd just heard.

''I told you it was bad.''

Clearing his throat, he pulled his chair closer. ''What immigration authorities?''

''Sheriff Collier and a bunch of men. They came and hauled off everyone who couldn't show papers, including Benito. Juana and Carlos and Mariela and her children were the only ones left.''

He banged a fist on the table so hard it vibrated, then launched to his feet, his chair clattering to the floor. ''When?''

''About seven-thirty. They just burst right in and ruined the doors Carlos built. How can they do that? Don't they have to have a search warrant or something?''

He shook his head. ''I'm sure they had whatever they needed. They're within their rights. I should've checked papers when I hired the men.'' Which would've put him back even farther on the renovations.

''What about Benito? Can we talk to the sheriff? They can't keep a small child in jail, can they?''

''Yes. Or they'll take them all directly to the border station.''

''What about a temporary permit or visa or something?''

''Right now, there's not much we can do except get some sleep.''

''It's my fault, isn't it? You warned me there might be repercussions and I didn't listen. I just kept on thinking I knew everything, and now you have no men to finish the work and it's my fault. Not to mention that Jésus and Daniel and the others will be deported because of me.''

He gave a long sigh and sat down beside her again. ''Those men should've had papers. It's not your fault. I didn't check. That's *my* fault.''

''But you help them, Juana told me. With food and water.''

''I don't want to see anyone die in the desert regardless of their citizenship. But the authorities still have to do their job. As far as food, I know the field workers don't get paid much and need all the help they can get. But they have to have papers. That's the law.''

''And what about Benito. He's just a little boy. A homeless little boy.''

''Yeah. I know,'' he said softly, his voice cracking. In his mind's eye, he saw himself sitting alone at the immigration station—with Sheriff Collier rocking back on his heels next to him—his father dead and no knowledge of his mother's condition. Later he'd learned she'd died that same night. ''I'll see what we can do in the morning.''

ONE OF THE LONGEST NIGHTS of her life. Maddy kicked off the sheets. J.D. hadn't blamed her, and that made her feel even worse. The next morning, she showered mechanically and got dressed. J.D. had said he'd see what they could do for Benito.

''Hey,'' he greeted her, when she came into the kitchen. She could tell he felt as bad as she did. Probably worse.

''Morning.''

''You didn't sleep much.'' It wasn't a question.

"Not much."

"Me neither." They sat together at the table. "There was a message on the machine for you. I guess it came last night when you were outside. It was Annie."

Maddy's shoulders sagged. "Yeah. I wonder what trouble I've gotten her into."

"Nothing that she wasn't aware of before."

Maddy angled her head to look at him. "I thought you were against my involving Annie in anything."

"I was. I am. But beyond that, Annie's lived here a long time. She knows what she's getting into and that's her choice. She just might be the person who'll carry the project forward when you're gone."

Another reference to her leaving. He seemed to do that a lot lately. And even though she'd caused him one problem after another, the tone of his voice and the softness in his eyes gave her the impression he regretted it a little.

"Well, I'm not going anywhere for a while. I haven't heard about the other job and I can't even think about that when I'm so worried about Ben. What can we do?"

"I've got a few ideas. But I'll have to keep them to myself for a while. I'm going into town in a few minutes, but I'll call and let you know what's happening."

"I'm coming along."

"It's better if you don't."

She didn't like the sound of that, but from his tone she could tell he wouldn't change his mind.

So she didn't push. She'd call Annie and tell her what had happened. Maybe she'd have some ideas.

After J.D. left, Maddy busied herself with Zelda, and brought the dog inside to keep her company while she worked in the kitchen. A few hours later, she heard a car outside and rushed to the door, hoping J.D. was home with good news.

He wasn't there, not in back where he usually parked. Then she heard a knock at the front. Hurrying, she picked up Zelda and went to answer. At the door, through the glass, she saw a woman's familiar form. She grabbed the knob and yanked open the door.

"Maddy, sweetheart."

"Hello, Mother."

"Ohhhh." Her mother screamed and jumped back. "What are you doing with that...that animal?"

Maddy smiled. At last she could prove something to her mother. "This is Zelda." Maddy ruffled the dog's hair and scratched behind one ear. "Here..." Maddy held Zelda out. "Would you like to hold her?"

Rachel Inglewood fanned herself with one hand, her lips pursed and her head pulled back. "I don't like dogs. You know that. Not after...well, you know."

"I know. But *I'm* the one who was traumatized, and if I can get over it, so can you."

Rachel sputtered a few times, obviously taken aback. "Madeline. Is that any way to talk to your mother, someone who's had only your best interests at heart for your whole life?"

Guilt. And her mother was right. No one cared

about Maddy the way her family did. It was just that standing here holding Zelda, she suddenly felt liberated. "I know that, Mother. I just wanted to show you how good it's been for me to be here. I've gotten over my cynophobia. Well, at least with Zelda."

"That's wonderful, dear. Now can I please come inside?"

"I'm sorry. I guess the informality of the ranch has caused me to forget my manners."

Rachel sniffed. "That will never happen, sweetheart. You're an Inglewood."

That she was. And her mother would always remind her of it. "C'mon in and I'll pour you some coffee."

Her mother followed her into the kitchen. "Does the animal have to stay here? I feel a little queasy."

"No, she has her own place. Come and see." She led her mother to the back. Rachel walked outside, hiking her purse under her arm as she did. Maddy felt a rush of affection for the woman who looked so out of place, with her cream-colored silk pantsuit, pearl earrings and blond hair always worn in a classic, elegant bob. At sixty, her mother was still an attractive woman.

"That's Zelda's house." Maddy pointed to the White House and went down the steps to let Zelda into her run.

"Oh, my goodness," Rachel said. "You know, I saw a house just like that on one of those news programs a couple years back. It was built for the dog in a television series. I can't remember the name."

Maddy didn't think Zelda's past was any big secret, but she should check with J.D. before revealing anything he'd told her. "I'll have to ask Mr. Rivera about that. Maybe Zelda is a celebrity."

Back inside, facing her mother, Maddy asked, "So what brings you here this time?"

THAT MORNING, the first person J.D. went to see was Gladys Hackert. Remembering what Maddy had said, he realized that Gladys might have some information that he could use as leverage to strike a deal with Charlie Masterson. Because making a deal with Charlie was J.D.'s only option. If anyone had any influence with the authorities, it was Charlie.

Sitting in the living room of his old teacher's home, he listened as Gladys told him the same thing she'd told Maddy—that many people believed Ethel was involved with the fire. Nothing there to help him.

"Okay. I guess that's what I wanted to know." J.D. stood up to leave.

"You might also want to ask Charlie what his son was doing in the barn when it caught on fire," Gladys said with a glint in her eyes.

"And ask the sheriff how your father escaped that night."

Very interesting. All questions he'd asked himself at one time or another, but which hadn't seemed to go anywhere in clearing his father's name. He thanked Gladys, then headed for Collier's office to see if Benito was there.

"Sheriff?" J.D. knocked on the back door of the jail. No answer. Damn. They'd probably gone directly to the border station last night, and the sheriff was no doubt sleeping late after putting more notches in his roundup belt.

Since Benito was already gone, the only thing left to do was to go see old Charlie. Within ten minutes J.D. was at the gates of the Masterson estate. Another car, a sedan, was parked on the circular driveway in front.

J.D. drove in and pulled up behind the other vehicle, a Lexus, he noticed when he got closer. Charlie kept all his vehicles, including his vintage collection, in the twelve-car garage in back, so J.D. knew Charlie had a visitor. He got out and climbed the steps, lifted the heavy door knocker and brought it down three times.

Waiting, he noticed the paint on the place was a little chipped, and the yard wasn't as immaculate as before.

No answer. He knocked again, then craned his neck to look in the window. He saw nothing. Maybe Charlie was out back with his vehicles. He stepped down and walked across the grass and around the perimeter of the house, avoiding the thorny bougainvillea that surrounded the place. A sweet floral scent gave the warm morning a sultry southern feel.

As he came to the corner he heard voices raised in anger. He stopped. Maybe Charlie was chewing out the help. Then the voices rose a little more. One of them sounded familiar. He peered around the corner and saw two men facing off in the yard—the sheriff and old Charlie. He inched closer, hidden by the plants now.

"You botched that one," Charlie said.

"I did my job. That's what you wanted, wasn't

it? Rivera can't finish the place without workers to help him.''

J.D.'s muscles tensed, his hands curled into fists. If they believed that delaying him would make him leave, they didn't know him at all.

''The longer he stays, the bigger the risk. And now that woman is making things worse for my farms.''

''Screw your farms. Ethel is gone. That leaves only you and me who knows what really happened. It was thirty-five years ago, for crying out loud. Even if Rivera sticks around, he isn't going to find out the truth, and if by some chance he does, no one in town will believe anything he says, anyway. He's a Rivera. And as far as that teacher goes, she's leaving soon. I'll just make sure she doesn't upset anything before then. After that it's business as usual.''

Interesting. From their conversation, it was obvious that Ethel *had* known something about the fire, and they were worried about it getting out. He might be able to use that to his advantage, and—a surge of excitement ran through him—he might even be able to clear his father's name.

He stepped out. ''Howdy, gentlemen.''

Both men jerked around. ''You're trespassin', Rivera,'' the sheriff said.

''Yeah? Well, I was thinking you might want to invite me in for a chat.''

The two men eyed each other. ''We've got nothing to talk about.'' Charlie spat a line of chewing tobacco into the grass.

''Oh? But we do. Specifically, the letter my aunt Ethel left for me,'' J.D. bluffed.

A flicker of panic flashed in the sheriff's eyes. "She's a lying bitch, and I told her that when I kicked her out of my place." His face was red and he was having trouble breathing.

"Shut up, you idiot!" Charlie rounded on him, his mouth twisted in disgust. "You don't even know what he's talking about." He swung around to face J.D. "She died suddenly. She didn't have time to write any letters."

"The letter was written well before she died. I guess she couldn't keep all those secrets to herself anymore. You can call her attorney and verify the letter." J.D. pulled out his cell phone and flipped it open.

When nobody moved, he tucked the phone back in his pocket and continued. "I know my father was framed, and I have a letter to prove it." He walked closer, staring them down, Charlie first and then the sheriff. He was taller than Charlie by almost a foot and he stood eye to eye with Collier.

"But there's something I want and I'm willing to deal."

The sheriff darted an anxious glance at Charlie, whose face was locked in a grimace, his eyes as cold and flat as ice. J.D. didn't wait for a response. "I want supplies made available to me while I'm renovating the ranch. If I need carpenters or other craftsmen, I expect them to be available, too."

"That's it?" the sheriff said, his expression puzzled.

"No. I want the boy, Benito Perez, brought back to Los Rios with a visa or whatever it takes to keep him here."

The sheriff shrugged and looked at Charlie. "I—I don't have that kind of influence."

"No, but Charlie knows how to make things happen." He started walking away. "Oh, and one more thing. The La Mancha Ranches need to start providing some employee benefits and paying minimum wage with time and a half for anything over forty hours. Let me know before noon if we've got a deal."

"That's blackmail. I could have the sheriff haul your ass in right now."

J.D. shrugged and held out his wrists to the sheriff. "While he's doing it, maybe he'd like to explain how my father escaped." He glared at the sheriff. "Or would you like me to do it. I'd like nothing more than to call a press conference right this minute. I might even want to talk about what Charlie Jr. was doing in the barn that night."

Silence hung in the air for the longest time. And then Charlie slowly lifted his chin. He brought himself up as straight as he could and cleared his throat. "If a guy were disposed to try and help you out with those things, just because he's a nice guy, what guarantee would he have that you can be trusted?"

"You have my word." It was all he had. It was all his father had had. "Take it or leave it."

"WE NEED YOU AT HOME, Maddy. Your father is lost without you, and Randy, no matter how hard he tries, can't seem to do the job like you did." They were on their way down the hallway to Maddy's room so her mother could wash up.

Maddy stopped cold. "Well, maybe Daddy can

hire someone else then,'' she said, a familiar feeling of guilt coming over her.

''We tried. It's not the same. Your father doesn't like other people knowing all our business.''

The same old argument. ''Even if I came back now, which won't happen, I'll be leaving for New York in a few weeks. You're going to have to get used to the idea sooner or later.''

''We could buy you a house—your own house. You wouldn't have to stay with us, if that's what's bothering you.''

Maddy sighed heavily. ''That's really nice, Mother. But that's exactly the kind of thing I don't want to do. I don't want to be dependent on you and Dad—or anyone else. I want to make my way in life by myself.''

Rachel wiped her forehead and then fanned her face with one hand. ''I haven't been feeling at all well lately, and worrying about you all the time just seems to make me feel worse.''

Guilt, guilt, guilt. ''Why didn't you forward the letter from Mr. Martin to me?''

''The letter?''

''The one Mr. Martin told me he sent certified to your house. Someone signed for it.''

''Oh, that. Well, I didn't think you'd need it since you'd already left for Arizona.'' She shrugged in dismissal. ''I'm so worried about you, dear. Look at you—look at this place. And remember what happened when you were away at school... Just thinking about that makes me sick with worry, so much that I fear I'm going to have a heart attack. I think of that and all the other things that caused you distress and how fragile you are, and I can hardly get through the day. You need us, Madeline. You need people who are there for you—who can pick you up when you fall.''

As her mother rattled on, everything suddenly became clear. Her mother's problem was that—with Maddy gone—she had no one to worry about. Rachel Inglewood took care of her family; that was what she did. And if her family didn't need her anymore, she felt worthless.

Maddy took a breath. *Focus on the goal.* Her mother would be fine. She'd find a charity to get involved in.

''Mom—'' she took her mother's hand ''—I appreciate everything you and Daddy have done for me. I truly do. God knows, I couldn't have made it through some tough times without your support. But I'm stronger now. And that's good. And I hope it's what you always wanted for me. I need to be in charge of my own life. I've worked hard to make my dreams come true, and it would be nice to know that you and Daddy were happy for me.''

''What if you fail? Then all your hard work will be for nothing.''

''There's no failure in trying. The failure is in *not* trying. And I know all about that. I've done it for years.'' Admitting that, saying those words, boosted her self-confidence another notch—and it gave her a strange sense of power. ''If I fail, I'll have the satisfaction of knowing I tried my best. That's all anyone can do.''

''But—''

''I'm going to New York, Mother.''

A noise sounded behind Maddy. She swung

around to see J.D. standing in the archway. ''Oh, J.D., I didn't hear you come in.''

IF HE'D EVER BELIEVED there might be a future for him and Maddy, he couldn't have been more wrong. The woman knew what she wanted, and what she wanted *wasn't* in Los Rios or at the Tripplehorne Ranch.

The point had never been made more clear.

After greeting Rachel, J.D. went into his bedroom and shut the door. It hurt to hear how much Maddy wanted to leave, but he silently cheered her on for standing firm with her mother.

God, his head ached. He reached into the shower, turned on the water full blast and stripped off his clothes. What he'd accomplished today was good. He could only hope that Charlie would follow through. But even if he didn't, J.D. felt a sense of relief.

He had confirmation that his father had been framed, and now both Charlie and the sheriff were aware that he knew about the lie they'd sold to the town for so many years. That alone gave him an enormous amount of satisfaction.

He'd probably never know what had really happened. Did it even matter anymore? He couldn't bring his parents back and he couldn't change the past. All he could do was move forward and, as Maddy had said, make each day count. Maybe someday the truth would come out, but not now—not if he wanted to see some changes in Los Rios.

''Hey, cowboy. You in there?''

Maddy's voice.

''Yeah, c'mon in. I'll be right out.''

He rinsed off the soap and wrapped a white towel around his midsection. She was sitting on the edge of the bed when he came out of the bathroom.

"Mother's gone." Maddy said. "I hope I didn't hurt her feelings."

"She'll survive."

"Yes," she said wistfully. "I suppose she will." A look of concern crossed her face. "Were you able to do anything about Benito?"

Standing in front of her, he ran a hand through his wet hair and slicked it back. "Yeah. I think so. But it's going to take a little time."

"Will he be able to come back?"

"It's not a done deal, but yes, I think it'll happen. There are lots of things to sort through, including finding out if he has any family in Mexico. I'll be working with some social workers and other officials on it. Charlie Masterson has agreed to help, and if anyone can set things in motion, he can."

Her eyes lit up. "How on earth did you manage that?"

"Charm and savoir faire." He grinned. Damn, it made him feel good to see her so happy. "Masterson's also going to see what he can do about getting me supplies and ensuring the migrant workers receive health benefits and minimum wage plus time and a half for work over forty hours."

She jumped up and hugged him. Kissed him. "And the other men?"

He shrugged. "I don't know. But my gut feeling is that they'll be back sooner or later."

CHAPTER SEVENTEEN

"DID YOU KNOW that Charlie Masterson *and* Mayor Sikes are partners in the corporation that owns La Mancha Ranches?" Maddy asked J.D. after her class that same evening. She gathered up some papers.

"Yes, but how do you know that?"

"Annie got the information from public records. And if that's true, I can't imagine Masterson agreeing to go along with everything you asked for since it will affect him financially."

"We'll see. We made a deal."

"That sounds ominous. If he's the kind of man you said he is, what would make him do it?"

"He thinks I have some information about my father's death and he wants me to keep it quiet."

"And do you know something?"

His eyes sparkled. "No. But as long as he believes I do, it doesn't matter."

It was a side of him she hadn't seen. She laughed. "I didn't know you had a devious side." She pulled up a chair and sat at the table.

J.D. sat in the chair next to her, his expression suddenly turning somber. "This came in the mail for you today." He handed her a letter.

The postmark was New York, the return address... "Ohmygod. This is it." Her breath left her lungs. She looked up at J.D. "What if they don't want me? What if—"

"Just open the damn thing."

Her hands shook as she ripped one corner, trying not to disturb anything inside or even the official-looking stamp. As she slowly, carefully, drew out the letter, she felt beads of perspiration trickle down her face. She lifted the paper to read.

"Oh!" she called out. "Oh, oh, oh. I got it." Tears brimmed in her eyes. "They want me."

"Great." J.D. didn't look at her. "When?"

Her eyes went to the letter again. "Three weeks. Ohmygod. Three weeks." Her hands flew to her face and suddenly, in that single moment, she realized what that meant. It meant saying goodbye to J.D.

"So let's celebrate. I've got champagne." He took her hand and led her back to the house.

Somewhere she found a smile. This was the moment she'd been waiting for, her dream come true. A fantastic job, great pay, adventure and excitement. She was the luckiest woman in the world. She was happy, excited, delirious…wasn't she?

He brought her to his room, and asked her to wait while he went to the closet and pulled out a bag from which he took a bottle of champagne and two glasses. "You always keep champagne in your room?"

"No. I bought it for this very occasion." He took her hand and led her down the hall again. "Let's go to your room, it's more comfortable."

She followed along, happy to be with him, but not as happy as she thought she'd be at hearing the good news. Because the good news also meant she'd be leaving Tripplehorne Ranch. Not only wouldn't she see J.D. again, she wouldn't see Zelda or Juana or Carlos. She wouldn't see Benito. Her heart ached at the thought. They'd truly become her family.

Inside her room, J.D. set down the glasses, popped the cork and poured the champagne. "Hope you don't mind that it's a bit warm."

Her heart bumped. His sweet, sweet attempt to celebrate this moment—her moment—touched her very soul. She moistened her lips and her voice shook a little when she said softly, "Not at all. I like it better that way."

He held up his glass. "To New York. To your new job and an exciting future... To the most amazing woman I know."

Tears welled, tears of happiness, she guessed. What else could they be? Lifting her glass to his, she said, "To what we've accomplished in the past few weeks. *That's* amazing."

Their eyes met and they sipped their drinks, and when they'd finished, she set her glass on the dresser next to the bed and held her hand out to him. "As much as I like champagne, I know of a better way to celebrate."

MADDY PULLED INTO the driveway at Annie and Grady's place, her emotions in flux. The past three days had been hell and she'd never felt more confused. Annie greeted her from the door where she was waiting.

"Hi, sweetie," Annie said, giving Maddy a hug after she came in.

Annie's house was like Annie herself. The soft,

warm colors and sink-into-me furniture reflected her warmth and kindness.

They settled in the family room where Annie had set out some iced tea and cookies.

"Okay. I have the information you wanted," Annie said without preamble. "Through Housing and Urban Development and some other agencies like the Comité de Bienestar, federal funding for sewer, water and wastewater in the *colonias* may be available." She tapped a ream of papers and a large manila envelope on the coffee table. "And the information you requested from the University of Arizona on the ESL teaching programs also came."

"Great." Maddy managed a weak smile.

"Okay—" Annie crossed her arms and leaned back against the puffy couch pillows. "What's wrong?"

In the short time Maddy had been in Los Rios, she and Annie had bonded like sisters. Annie had been the first to agree that something needed to be done in the *colonias* and she'd supported Maddy all the way.

Maddy poured them both a glass of tea. "I don't know. I just feel so lacking in energy. I don't know what's the matter with me."

Her friend's eyebrows scooted up. "You're not—"

"No! Of course not." Not that the thought hadn't entered her head when she'd fantasized about spending the rest of her life on the ranch with J.D.

"Are you depressed?"

She shook her head. "I don't think so. Though it depresses me to think about leaving here when there's so much to do."

"It'll get done. I'll make sure of it."

"I know you will. It's not that...it's just that I won't be a part of it."

"But you'll always be a part of it. If it weren't for you, none of this would be happening. And now, you'll be part of something else, something very important with all those diplomats and heads of state in New York."

"I'll have to prove myself first. Probably start by working with students or something."

"Well, you gotta begin somewhere. It's going to be so exciting!"

"I'll miss you."

Annie leaned over and gave Maddy a squeeze. "I'll miss you, too." She sighed. "You can't imagine how much." Then Annie pressed her lips together. "There's always vacation time. You can stay here. And we can visit you. I'd love to see New York."

"I feel like I need to be here to finish what I began. I *want* to be here."

"Even more than fulfilling your lifelong dream?"

She shrugged. "I don't know." Somehow the dream didn't seem so important anymore.

"You're in love with J.D., aren't you?"

Maddy's eyes filled with tears. She nodded. "Uh-huh."

"Is it mutual?"

She shook her head. "No."

JUANA AND CARLOS had been given the weekend off, and J.D. spent most of it pounding nails. He was a man possessed, Maddy thought. Which didn't make sense, since he'd found a crew to start working for him the middle of next week. In the past few days, he'd barely talked to her and she desperately missed the closeness they'd developed.

But she knew why. *People leave.*

The craftsmen he'd contracted came on Saturday to put the finishing touches on the kitchen, and on Sunday, she decided to spend some time by herself. In the morning, she took a long walk in the desert, took a leisurely bath and then stayed in her room to read some of the books she'd brought with her. As she was reading, it occurred to her that her goal in taking this job had been fulfilled. She'd gotten her life back. She had control. She was in charge. Suddenly she was acutely aware of what she needed to do. *Focus on the goal.* A new goal. No risk, no reward.

On Monday morning, she returned from jogging, energized and ready to get things done. With the letter from the personnel director in hand, Maddy went into the kitchen and picked up the new phone they'd installed. Nervous, she punched in the number.

Glancing around as she waited for someone to answer, she felt enormous pride at how wonderfully the kitchen had turned out. It looked just the way it did in the photograph she'd seen of J.D.'s grandmother cooking for guests when the ranch had been at its peak. The room felt warm and inviting with its rich woods and warm adobe floor. She'd chosen golds and creams and rust for the tablecloth, the cushions on the chairs and the curtains. She could imagine J.D. as a boy playing at his grandmother's feet, watching her make coffee.

It took a while to get through to the director who'd signed the letter. She introduced herself and explained why she was calling.

J.D. came into the room just as she was finishing. He seemed uncomfortable and went to the refrigerator to get out a bottle of orange juice. Silently, he gestured to ask if she wanted some. She nodded, then continued her conversation.

"Yes. I know. I'm sorry the job took so long to come through. I had to take another position and I'm now unable to take the position you offered."

She'd barely hung up the phone when J.D. slammed the juice bottle on the counter and swung around, fire in his eyes. "I hope to hell that wasn't what it sounded like."

"It is," she said simply. "I decided not to take the job. I'm staying in Los Rios."

"That's plain ridiculous! It's what you've worked for, what you dreamed about, everything you ever wanted. Are you crazy?"

"I've never been more lucid." She walked to the cabinet, got down a glass to pour herself some juice and then went out to the veranda.

He followed on her heels, the door banging shut behind him. "I don't believe it. How can you do this?"

They stood at the railing. Why was he so angry? Was the thought of her staying in Los Rios so abhorrent? "I'll finish my contract here, and then I'll move out. I'm checking on a small apartment in town and I've secured information to get a grant to set up classes to teach survival English to the migrant workers. My hope is that a few of them will want to learn how to teach as well."

Shock. That was the look on his face. "I don't understand," he muttered. "You told your mother. You told me. You told everyone how much that job meant to you—and now you're tossing it all away to stay in a one-horse town in the middle of nowhere?"

He swung around. Raked a hand through his fresh-from-the-shower hair. "You can't give up something you've wanted for so long, something you've worked so hard for—you'll regret it. Believe me, I know what it's like to give up a dream."

"I do, too. I'm giving up on one right now." The dream that somehow he might love her as much as she loved him. "But it's my choice."

"You can't do this."

"Yes, I can. Because for the first time in my life, I know what I really want. I like it here and I enjoy feeling…needed. That sounds a little pathetic, I know, but it's true. After my mother came here the last time, I finally realized why she was so desperate to have me come home. It wasn't because she was worried about me, it was because she needed someone to care for. She wanted me there for *her*. I can understand that now because I've discovered I'm not all that different from her. It gives me great pleasure to help others. The difference is that before, I was doing things because other people wanted me to. Now I'm doing them because *I* want to. Big difference."

His arms fell to his sides, and when he spoke, his voice was quieter. "What about your education, your language skills? What about travel, adventure and excitement?"

"I'll be using my skills, at least some part of

them, and I'll be learning even more with the classes I'm going to take. Living here, I'll be experiencing a life far different than I would in Iowa or New York, and that sounds like a pretty great adventure to me.'' She placed a hand on his arm.

He stiffened. ''You'll regret it.''

''No, I won't.'' Because she'd never been so sure of anything. She wanted to do this, with or without him in her life. She only had one regret. Somewhere along the line, she'd hoped he'd learned that he needed love in his life, that he deserved it as much as anyone. But apparently not.

Should she tell him how she felt about him? Would he feel any differently if he knew someone loved him? No risk, no reward. Yes, she had to say it. ''I love it here,'' she said. ''And I love you.''

He blinked, his expression blank. Then— ''You don't know what you're saying.''

She stepped back. ''Excuse me. I know exactly what I'm saying. That's how I feel.'' She couldn't keep a tiny smile from emerging. It felt good to tell him she loved him. Even if he didn't love her back. ''But in case you're wondering, my staying in Los Rios has nothing to do with how I feel about you. That's a separate issue altogether.''

J.D. stifled his own smile. She loved him. Was she serious? *She* loved *him.* Obviously she didn't know what she was saying.

''Do you love me?'' she asked bluntly.

Yes. That was the problem. She was wonderful and kind and wholesome and beautiful and he wasn't worthy of her. ''I believe we've developed a close relationship.''

She stepped forward, her face nearly touching his

chest, her bottom lip quivering. ''That's it? That's all you feel for me?''

The hurt in her eyes almost broke his heart. A lump formed in his throat. He wanted to take her in his arms and kiss her silly. He wanted to tell her that he'd like nothing more than to wake up every morning for the rest of his life with her at his side, that he wanted babies with her and to love her as she'd never been loved before. He wanted to give her everything.

But he couldn't. He couldn't because he didn't have anything to give. His own future was as uncertain as rain in the desert, and anything, any small glitch could screw things up. Charlie might not come through. He might not finish the renovations before the deadline, something could happen to Zelda. He had no guarantees. But it tore his heart out that she believed he didn't care. ''No,'' he said. ''That's not all.''

''Then what? What do you feel?''

Why did she keep pushing? ''I can't give you what you need. What you deserve.''

''That wasn't my question.''

Maddy watched a puzzled frown form on J.D.'s face, as if she'd asked him about the theory of quantum physics. ''The original question was, what do you feel for me?'' She had to know and she had to hear it from him. Good, bad or indifferent, she needed him to tell her.

She waited, tapping her fingers nervously at her sides, and when he didn't say anything, her heart felt as if it had split in two. Tears welled behind her eyes, and before she made a weeping fool of herself again, she threw up her hands in resignation and started to go into the house.

But before she did, she turned to him and, in a fragile, shaky voice, said, "You must be the loneliest man in the world. I pray that someday you'll be able to open your heart to someone, because if you can't, you'll always be alone. Love isn't about how long the people we love are with us, it's about how much we love them when they are."

She turned and went inside. And standing in the beautiful kitchen, she let the tears stream down her cheeks, not just for herself and her breaking heart, but also for him.

She heard the door, and seconds later felt warm hands on her shoulders. He eased her around to face him.

His eyes were filled with gentleness and deep longing, and he started to say something but couldn't seem to get it out. When he did, his voice was husky and rough with emotion. "I love you. That's how I feel."

Through her tears, a big wide smile emerged. He'd said it.

"But you deserve better."

"I think I should be the judge of that." And she all but leaped into his arms and kissed him. He kissed her back, deeply, crushing her in a long hard embrace.

"I can't promise you anything," he said when they came up for air.

"Did I ask for promises?"

"I don't know what next year will bring."

"Neither do I. But if you did? If you knew everything was going to be perfect—"

He closed his eyes, as if what he was about to say was the most difficult thing in the world. "I'd ask you to marry me."

"So ask me anyway."

He searched her eyes, as if maybe he could find an answer there.

She whispered, "Chicken. No risk, no reward."

A long moment passed, and then he smiled lovingly. "Will you marry me, Maddy?"

One word and only one word formed on Maddy's lips.

"Yes." And he swung her around like a little kid and in the distance, she heard Zelda bark as if she knew exactly what was going on.

"Yes, yes, yes," she repeated as a great warm flood of love flowed through her.

And this was only the beginning.

EPILOGUE

Six months later

"HOW DOES THIS LOOK?" J.D. said, putting the finishing touches on the fat yellow ribbon that they were going to cut in honor of the grand reopening of the Tripplehorne Guest Ranch. "Maybe we should christen the place with a bottle of champagne instead? Like a boat."

He grinned at her, his smile radiating a happiness she never dreamed she'd see on his face.

"We have only five hours to get this place in shape before people start to arrive," she said. "We can't start changing plans now."

"We have just enough time to read this." J.D. held up a plump manila envelope that was lying on the chair next to him.

"What is it?"

"The letter from my aunt."

Harold Martin had been to the ranch the week before and he'd brought Kayla, who was staying till after the wedding. Maddy couldn't have a wedding without her best friend. Kayla was now inside taking care of last-minute preparations with Juana and Maddy's mother in the kitchen. Everyone would be there, her whole family, Annie and Grady and their new baby, Stella, all Maddy's students and most of the town.

And Benito. Her heart swelled at the thought. When the adoption papers were completed, he'd be living with them for good.

They'd planned the wedding and the grand opening for the same day. Kayla had thought it strange that Maddy wanted to share her wedding day with the opening, but Maddy knew that if it weren't for the ranch, she wouldn't be here today, marrying the man she loved.

"C'mon, sit down and we'll read it together."

"Are you sure? It's probably personal."

"So? Sharing the rest of our lives is pretty personal. We ought to be able to share whatever is in this envelope."

"Okay."

He opened the packet. Inside were several pages and some photos.

J.D. opened the letter.

Dear James,

If you're reading this, then you've succeeded in completing the ranch. Congratulations. I didn't know if that would happen, which is why I made most of the stipulations in the will. You can't blame me, considering the condition you were in for quite some time after your accident. I was afraid if I gave you the ranch without a commitment on your part, the property would be in someone else's hands by now and the money gone. I was sorry to hear about the accident, but I hope you've overcome your problems.

We all have things we regret, but if there's

one thing I've learned in life it's that we just have to go on.

Unfortunately, as I'm writing this, I know my life isn't going to go on. I have metastatic cancer and it's only a matter of time. We don't all get to know when we'll die and I guess I should be grateful that I do, because it gives me time to take care of my personal business, and maybe even find a little peace within myself.

Which brings me to this letter. This is not an apology as such, but more of an explanation. I wasn't much of an aunt or guardian. I have no excuse for that except to tell you that I was very self-centered as a girl and, indeed, for most of my adult life. In fact, this letter is probably my way of trying to atone and assuage my guilt over some of the things I've done. I've hurt other people, in particular, you, your mother and your father.

I don't expect your forgiveness. I simply need to get this off my chest before I die. Your mother was a beautiful woman and a wonderful sister. I destroyed whatever relationship we had. Your father was an intelligent, hardworking man, and of course, he was extremely handsome. I was in love with him, and as the whole town knows, he chose to marry my sister. I was a vindictive girl and tried to change that.

The fire wasn't your father's fault. It was mine. In my jealousy, I imagined that if your father had to leave the ranch in disgrace, Rebecca wouldn't go with him and that would leave the field open for me. C.J., Charlie Jr., and I had been very close since we were kids, and he agreed to help me spread a story about your father siphoning Tripplehorne funds, and the fire was supposed to be his cover-up. Unfortunately, the fire got out of hand, and C.J. and a hired hand who was sleeping in the barn, died as a result. I never intended for anyone to die. I regret that more than anyone can know.

When your father was arrested, I went to Charlie Masterson and told him what C.J. and I had done, but he wasn't about to have the Masterson name dragged through the mud. He also accused me of lying because I was in love with Raphael. Your father had been beaten badly for resisting arrest and was thrown in jail. At that point, I did the only thing I could. I knew Tom Collier was sweet on me, so I told him I'd move in with him if he allowed your father to escape.

But after a while, I couldn't live in Los Rios anymore. I couldn't face any of it. And when I inherited the ranch, I couldn't face you.

So, there you have my pitiful story. Nothing can absolve me of my guilt, nothing will bring back your parents or give you the childhood you would've had if they hadn't died. But maybe you will get some peace of mind knowing your father had nothing to do with the fire.

By the time you read this, I will have been gone for quite some time. Only Harold Martin knows the story of my "accident" and after you read this, I'm sure he'll tell you all about it if you really want to know. I'm not very proud of it, but then I'm not proud of much of my life. Bottom line is that I'm not brave enough to wait around for a horrible painful death to take me, either.

I hope you'll find it in your heart to continue to take care of my Zelda, even after the year designated in the will. Though I can't blame you if you don't. That will be up to you. There are no more stipulations, but my hope is that you'll keep the ranch in the family and pass it down to your own children.

My parents—your grandparents—would want it that way.

I've enclosed the photos and a few small memories I had of your mother and father and hope they'll mean as much to you as they did to me.

Maddy dabbed at a tear in her eye. "That confession must have been very hard for her to write."

J.D. slid the letter back into the envelope and picked up the photos, most of which were of his mother and father and him as a baby. "I don't have a single picture of us together." His hands shook as he lifted the next item. It was a folded hankie with his mother's name embroidered on it, and inside, her wedding ring.

"Oh, God," he said, burying his face in Maddy's hair. One low wrenching sob escaped and he crushed her in a bear hug.

She held him and after a moment, she said softly, "Maybe we should cancel the plans for today."

He lifted his head in surprise. "Not a chance."

Then he took her hand in his and placed the ring on her finger. "I believe this goes with the dress you're going to wear."

Now it was her turn for tears—tears of happiness.

Your opinion is important to us! Please take a few moments to share your thoughts with us about your experiences with Harlequin and Silhouette books. Your comments will be very useful in ensuring that we deliver books you love to read.

Please take a few minutes to complete the questionnaire, then send it to us at the address below.

Send your completed questionnaires to:
Harlequin/Silhouette Reader Survey, P.O. Box 9046, Buffalo, NY 14269-9046

1. As you may know, there are many different lines under the Harlequin and Silhouette brands. Each of the lines is listed below. Please check the box that most represents your reading habit for each line.

Line	Currently read this line	Do not read this line	Not sure if I read this line
Harlequin American Romance	❑	❑	❑
Harlequin Duets	❑	❑	❑
Harlequin Romance	❑	❑	❑
Harlequin Historicals	❑	❑	❑
Harlequin Superromance	❑	❑	❑
Harlequin Intrigue	❑	❑	❑
Harlequin Presents	❑	❑	❑
Harlequin Temptation	❑	❑	❑
Harlequin Blaze	❑	❑	❑
Silhouette Special Edition	❑	❑	❑
Silhouette Romance	❑	❑	❑
Silhouette Intimate Moments	❑	❑	❑
Silhouette Desire	❑	❑	❑

2. Which of the following best describes why you bought *this book?* One answer only, please.

the picture on the cover	❑	the title	❑
the author	❑	the line is one I read often	❑
part of a miniseries	❑	saw an ad in another book	❑
saw an ad in a magazine/newsletter	❑	a friend told me about it	❑
I borrowed/was given this book	❑	other: ______________	❑

3. Where did you buy *this book?* One answer only, please.

at Barnes & Noble	❑	at a grocery store	❑
at Waldenbooks	❑	at a drugstore	❑
at Borders	❑	on eHarlequin.com Web site	❑
at another bookstore	❑	from another Web site	❑
at Wal-Mart	❑	Harlequin/Silhouette Reader Service/through the mail	❑
at Target	❑	used books from anywhere	❑
at Kmart	❑	I borrowed/was given this book	❑
at another department store or mass merchandiser	❑		

4. On average, how many Harlequin and Silhouette books do you buy at one time?

I buy ______ books at one time ❑
I rarely buy a book ❑

MRQ403HSR-1A

5. How many times per month do you shop for any *Harlequin and/or Silhouette* books? One answer only, please.

1 or more times a week	❑	a few times per year	❑
1 to 3 times per month	❑	less often than once a year	❑
1 to 2 times every 3 months	❑	never	❑

6. When you think of your ideal heroine, which *one* statement describes her the best? One answer only, please.

She's a woman who is strong-willed	❑	She's a desirable woman	❑
She's a woman who is needed by others	❑	She's a powerful woman	❑
She's a woman who is taken care of	❑	She's a passionate woman	❑
She's an adventurous woman	❑	She's a sensitive woman	❑

7. The following statements describe types or genres of books that you may be interested in reading. Pick *up to 2 types* of books that you are most interested in.

I like to read about truly romantic relationships ❑
I like to read stories that are sexy romances ❑
I like to read romantic comedies ❑
I like to read a romantic mystery/suspense ❑
I like to read about romantic adventures ❑
I like to read romance stories that involve family ❑
I like to read about a romance in times or places that I have never seen ❑
Other: ______________________________ ❑

The following questions help us to group your answers with those readers who are similar to you. Your answers will remain confidential.

8. Please record your year of birth below.

19 ____

9. What is your marital status?

single ❑ married ❑ common-law ❑ widowed ❑
divorced/separated ❑

10. Do you have children 18 years of age or younger currently living at home?

yes ❑ no ❑

11. Which of the following best describes your employment status?

employed full-time or part-time ❑ homemaker ❑ student ❑
retired ❑ unemployed ❑

12. Do you have access to the Internet from either home or work?

yes ❑ no ❑

13. Have you ever visited eHarlequin.com?
yes ❑ no ❑

14. What state do you live in?

____

15. Are you a member of Harlequin/Silhouette Reader Service?

yes ❑ Account # ____________ no ❑ MRQ403HSR-1B